JILLIAN HUNTER

A Duke's Temptation

The Bridal Pleasures Series

A SIGNET SELECT BOOK

SIGNET SELECT
Published by New American Library, a division of
Penguin Group (USA) Inc., 375 Hudson Street,
New York, New York 10014, USA
Penguin Group (Canada), 90 Eglinton Avenue East, Suite 700, Toronto,
Ontario M4P 2Y3, Canada (a division of Pearson Penguin Canada Inc.)
Penguin Books Ltd., 80 Strand, London WC2R 0RL, England
Penguin Ireland, 25 St. Stephen's Green, Dublin 2,
Ireland (a division of Penguin Books Ltd.)
Penguin Group (Australia), 250 Camberwell Road, Camberwell, Victoria 3124,
Australia (a division of Pearson Australia Group Pty. Ltd.)
Penguin Books India Pvt. Ltd., 11 Community Centre, Panchsheel Park,
New Delhi - 110 017, India
Penguin Group (NZ), 67 Apollo Drive, Rosedale, Auckland 0632,
New Zealand (a division of Pearson New Zealand Ltd.)
Penguin Books (South Africa) (Pty.) Ltd., 24 Sturdee Avenue,
Rosebank, Johannesburg 2196, South Africa

Penguin Books Ltd., Registered Offices:
80 Strand, London WC2R 0RL, England

First published by Signet Select, an imprint of New American Library,
a division of Penguin Group (USA) Inc.

First Printing, November 2010
First Printing (Read Pink Edition), October 2011
10 9 8 7 6 5 4 3 2 1

To Mel Berger
Perfect agent.
Perfect gentleman.
You're an incredible person and I don't know what I'd do
without you.

Thank you.

Acknowledgments

Special thanks to Graham Jaenicke at William Morris Endeavor for all your finesse and behind-the-scenes work. You brought the year to a great end.

Prologue

Lord Anonymous had seduced more women in Europe than a man of discretion would willingly admit. Although he had forgotten the dates of these affairs, he had fondly recorded his lovers' names in a red morocco leather notebook that he kept under lock and key. He had done his best to leave each of his ladies with a happy ending.

But sometimes a man had to let go and conquer other challenges.

He had stolen the virtue of a French *comtesse* on her wedding day and helped her escape her cruel bridegroom an hour before she was to take her vows. He had made love to a German princess in the Black Forest and guarded her in a hut until the traitors who wanted her lovely head could be caught. There were trolls involved, as he recalled. He had killed every last one.

Still, depending on his mood, he might be considered not only an epic hero but a classic villain. Among his less gallant acts, he had once abducted an innocent lady and imprisoned her in his castle for seven months. He had set out to despoil her, and he had.

It was further recorded, in his own hand, that the lady had refused to be rescued when her brothers stormed the bailey.

She had been ruined for life, she proclaimed from the tower where this depravity had taken place. So enslaved was she by her unprincipled abductor that she ordered him to murder her siblings if they dared intervene again. She had no desire to be redeemed, and she would stab even her own brothers in the heart before she would give up the dark nobleman who had disgraced her.

Lord Anonymous could turn from valiant deed to bloodthirsty revenge in a heartbeat.

It was no wonder he had been accused of corrupting the populace.

Chapter 1

London, 1818
Lord Philbert's Literary Masquerade Ball

*I*t was common knowledge in the beautiful world that Samuel Aubrey St. Aldwyn of Dartmoor, the fourth Duke of Gravenhurst, and ninth Baronet, was a radical young rake and champion of unpopular causes. Samuel realized that society considered him to be one of its most charismatic and controversial figures. He did his best to oblige. He was one of the first guests invited to an event. He was also usually the first asked to leave by nature of his declaring himself bored to death.

His appearance tonight at Lord Philbert's masquerade party guaranteed that the other guests would go home well amused.

On this point both his friends and rivals agreed—the duke was a most entertaining man.

One could even say that he *lived* to entertain.

He spoke infrequently, and then only to a select few, but he always spoke his mind and cared little whether he shocked anyone.

Because he was young, dangerously beautiful, and as elusive as a dark angel, the duke got away with offenses that would have cast out another man. Still, society knew only the half of who Samuel was when he wasn't in London. He hoped to keep it that way. He valued his private life, spending most of the year on his secluded Dartmoor estate, with people he completely trusted.

His impertinence infuriated certain members of the aristocracy and invigorated others who welcomed a breath of fresh air. But tonight, at least, he was among his own, other patrons of the arts and the artists grateful for their generosity.

The thought crossed his mind that he might find an intelligent mistress at an affair like this. He and his last lover had parted several months ago. The closest she had come to showing any interest in literature was to hurl a volume of Milton at the door when he announced he was leaving her.

It was exhausting trying to live up to his reputation. Excess drained the energy he could put to better use.

Dressed as his favorite literary character, Don Quixote, Samuel shrugged off the stares of recognition that followed his entrance. He paused only once in the hall, dented helmet, shield, and lance in hand, to bow before acknowledging any single person with his attention. Let the world think he was aloof. His breastplate was killing him. Cutting into his ribs like a butcher's knife.

"Decent work this morning, Your Grace," someone said, reminding him of the mock duel he had fought at dawn.

"Good show, Gravenhurst."

Show. He smiled to himself. It was all show. To further his secret career. And to keep a promise to his host and partner in literary crimes, the London publisher Lord Aramis Philbert.

"You deserved to win," a gentleman at the end of the line declared above the others. "How dare anyone challenge your decadence so early in the morning?"

"I'll challenge it later tonight if His Grace is inclined," a sultry voice said from the crowd.

His gaze cut through the glittering maze of guests to a lady languidly waving a fan hand-painted with a variety of improbable sexual poses.

"Madam," he said, "I am an aristocrat, not an acrobat."

At her startled laugh, he presented his usual devil-may-care grin to the crowd, retreating to the antechamber that Lord Philbert reserved for Samuel's private use. In the past he might have engaged the lady in a tryst. But she didn't seem worth the trouble of taking off his armor. He would never get it back on again for the rest of the party. Why did the literati perpetuate the myth that lust made fools of only the lower classes?

"Honest to God," he muttered to the towering valet who handed him a bracing glass of burgundy the moment Samuel dropped into a chair. "One would think I had cured the world of cholera instead of challenging a friend to a drunken duel. It's embarrassing, Wadsworth. Are you not embarrassed on my account? Loosen this body armor. I'm turning into a damned tortoise."

The valet ventured a smile. "Sit forward, Your Grace, while I bend the wrench under your breastplate again. The only thing you have in common with a tortoise is your fondness for lettuce. There we go. Don Quixote can tilt again. The world does love a hero."

Samuel snorted. "Even when that hero isn't real? How many of the dearly deluded are here tonight?"

"Bickerstaff guessed at over three hundred, Your Grace." Bickerstaff was Samuel's butler. "Tickets were still being auctioned off at clubs around the city this afternoon."

"I assume we bought a good share."

"One hundred twenty at last count."

Grinning, Samuel rubbed his cheekbone. "As long as it goes to a good cause. What *is* our current cause?"

"Legal counsel against the war loan hucksters, Your Grace. Would you like to read what the papers are saying about you now?"

"Why bother? I probably wrote it."

The duke downed his wine, put his glass on the table, and stood. He took the battered shield that Wadsworth whisked from the corner and scowled at the reflection in the dented metal. "Whose idea was it for me to dress as Don Quixote for this affair?"

The valet polished the right corner of the shield with his coat sleeve. "I believe it was Marie-Elaine who suggested it, knowing how you enjoy playing the knight-errant."

"Remind me in future that I am not to take a house-maid's advice. And . . ." Samuel looked under his chair. "I don't suppose you know where I left my lance?"

"Perhaps the majordomo took it into safekeeping. Ah, no, my mistake. You put it in the potted fern on your way in."

Samuel tucked the useless weapon under his left arm. "If Don Quixote looked mad, I'm sure I won't make a different impression. Please instruct Emmett to have the coach ready in an hour. I doubt I can keep myself under control any longer than that."

Chapter 2

*I*t was a night designed for making dreams come true.

By its end, Miss Lily Boscastle of Tissington, Derbyshire, would be able to share the secret she had been keeping as tightly laced as her great-aunt's corset since the beginning of the year. Her days of pretending to husband-hunt and playing wallflower at country assemblies would be forgotten. At the breakfast that followed the all-night literary party, Lily and her dear friend Captain Jonathan Grace would quietly announce their intention to wed and allow their families to collapse in relief before setting the wedding date in stone. After all, an engagement, even one as sensible as Jonathan and Lily's, could not be taken for granted.

Not even Nostradamus, however, would have predicted a dire outcome for the appealing young couple. Lily had been born a cheerful flirt who had accepted all the blessings that effortlessly came her way. Captain Grace had come through the wars much as he'd gone in: easily influenced, but as gentle-natured and as dedicated to Lily as from the first day she had knocked him down in the nursery and bitten his ear. He still defended Lily whenever a family member brought up the story at the Tissington assembly.

"She's a solid girl, my Lily," he would say, "even if she's a little exuberant at times. I knew that when she bit me she meant it as a token of affection. Thankfully she has learned other means of showing her esteem over the years."

Another gentleman would have been embarrassed to recount the story of her toddler savagery to friends and family. Jonathan made it sound like one of his fondest memories. She wondered if they had become too comfortable with each other after all these years. In fact, Lily wondered at times whether her affection for him would deepen into anything that resembled romantic passion.

Dear friends. Wasn't that enough? She trusted Jonathan.

Besides, he'd never given her reason to suspect he had passionate feelings for anyone else. And neither did she. Unless one counted the fictional characters in the books she devoured, which every dedicated female reader understood did not count at all. Fantasies spawned from romantic works became private intellectual property.

The literary masquerade party tonight was already

a dream come true. Lily had attended a play, the museum, and Astley's Royal Amphitheatre in the last month. She had enjoyed these diversions well enough, but *this* was a once-in-a-lifetime affair. The night had not opened with a traditional ball, with debutantes and bachelors preparing for mortal battle.

Instead, the guests were invited to attend one of three violin concertos given throughout the evening, nibble on imported delicacies in open supper rooms, or linger in one of the first-floor salons, where conversation emulated the intellectual Parisian soirées that had enlivened the previous century.

Lily was utterly in her element, rubbing gloved elbows with guests masquerading as characters from literary works, and with a few of the writers who had created them. Not that she would recognize any of her favorite authors behind their intriguing disguises. Society had sent Lord Byron into exile. Percy Shelley was in Italy, too. It was a heady experience for a young lady from the country whose obsession with reading worried her family out of their wits.

Her parents insisted that nothing good came from a girl who read. It wasn't natural. Staying up half the night to finish a romantic story would unbalance her mind. How could she ever hope to advance socially when she immersed herself in the ideas of utter strangers?

She could never make them understand that she had few social aspirations. Or that sometimes she didn't want to be advanced as much as entertained, swept into a different world.

And suddenly, tonight, she had been swept away, except that this world was real. She had eavesdropped on so many titillating conversations that she lost track of whether a certain writer was said to be sleeping with his wife's sister or his own, and whether Lily had exceeded her capacity for champagne for the evening or for the entire year. Even though wickedness went on in Tissington, it went on at a trudging pace. Here Lily found herself consumed with curiosity and overwhelmed, in a pleasant way.

Still, the best was yet to come. At midnight the guests would unmask. Contest winners would be announced. Everyone in costume had been promised a prize for taking part. Lily didn't give a fig about the contest, or the original play that would be previewed afterward in the ballroom before it opened on Drury Lane. She wanted to cut through all the buildup to the climax—the predawn tour of Lord Philbert's literary gardens.

Everything that preceded this event served as mere stage-setting in her imagination.

None of the guests had been permitted outside to sneak a look. Still, it wasn't a secret that an army of master gardeners and engineers had conspired for months to design a paradise of private arbors representing scenes from fictional works. The northwest parterre had been turned into an Italian courtyard to re-create *Romeo and Juliet*. The wedding scene from *The Tempest* was depicted inside a gazebo nearby. To the east the guests could enter Dante's Gates of Hell, wafts of sulfur and an occasional burst of artificial thunder in the background enhancing the production. There was even said to be a glade landscaped from *Gulliver's Travels* that featured the giantess Glumdalclitch.

But it was what waited at the garden's end that Lily would barter her soul to reach. According to her cousin and chaperone, Chloe, Viscountess Stratfield, a fabulous grotto had been built to honor popular fiction's latest darling, the author known only as Lord Anonymous. He had written several volumes of dark-hearted fairy tales and a half dozen or so novels about strapping warriors set in medieval Scotland.

Lily had devoured every word. She could recite certain pages by heart. But it wasn't until he published the first book in the series entitled *The Wickbury Tales* that he was denounced as immoral and became an immediate bestseller.

His stories seethed with swashbuckling adventures that drew the breathless reader to the last page—once in a runaway carriage, another time to a cliff edge on a galloping steed. The series always followed the same basic plot—the hero, a Cavalier earl in exile, battled an evil wizard, who also happened to be the hero's half brother. They fought not only for opposing politics, but for the same lady's heart.

What intrigued Lily the most, though, was that after

six books, the lady still couldn't make up her mind whether to choose the noble Lord Wickbury or the thoroughly wicked Sir Renwick Hexworthy. Heated arguments broke out in circulating libraries to debate the issue upon publication of each new edition.

Gentlemen tended to favor the exiled earl because he fought fairly and represented the right order of things. Sir Renwick was a villain through and through, an unpredictable malefactor, in their view, who would stop at nothing to win his beloved lady. In Lily's opinion, she was an unworthy, lukewarm wench who did not deserve either man.

Unfortunately, Lily wasn't the only lady at the party enamored of Lord Anonymous. Footmen stood guard at the French doors to the garden to keep the curious from spoiling Lord Philbert's surprise. Lily contemplated resorting to shameless flirtation to be one of the first to view the gardens. If there was any chance at all to meet the author . . . Oh, she *was* a goose.

She wasn't even sure she wanted to know what he looked like. Or discover whether the author was a male at all. She would probably be disappointed if she met him. She'd be crushed to find he was a conceited popinjay.

Nothing could ruin tonight for her.

A respectable captain intended to marry her. She had never made an enemy or taken a misstep in her whole life. True, she was spoiled rotten, and sometimes she took advantage of her position. Not to do anything unlawful or spiteful. She simply liked to have her way. But what of it? It wasn't her fault she had been born to privilege. Or that the worst decision she had ever made was to disguise herself as the Brothers Grimm's Goose-Girl. It had seemed like a tantalizing idea three weeks ago when Chloe had thought of it.

Tonight Lily regretted the choice. How was anyone to know that she was wearing a shimmering gold silk gown underneath her unattractive plumage? She felt nothing like a fairy-tale character at all. In fact, it would take a genius to realize that she was meant to be a princess before she shed her disguise.

And that genius, unfortunately, was not her soon-to-be betrothed, Captain Jonathan Grace, polite escort that he had always been. He did not seem to appreciate her costume. She caught sight of him shouldering a path to reach the line into which she had drifted. She guessed that it led into one of the supper rooms. At the front of the queue she spotted her cousin Chloe, who motioned distractedly at her to come forward while she carried on an animated conversation with her friends.

Jonathan, tall and shaggy haired, battled for a place beside her. "Why are you standing here by yourself?"

"Because I'm unable to move. I've been bumped enough for one night. My feathers are bent and falling off like leaves. And I can't keep up with Chloe. She disappears every time I turn around."

"She's a dreadful chaperone," Jonathan said, planting his legs apart in such a way as to shield her.

Still, for all his bluff, he was mild by temperament and had never sought a single confrontation since Lily had known him. If anything, he allowed others to order him about. It upset Lily when he hesitated to stand his ground.

"Chloe has been charming to me," she said.

"Charm runs in your family," he added with a reluctant smile. "I'd prefer it, though, if you don't take any lessons from your cousin. I have a hard enough time refusing you as it is."

"That," Lily said, "is because you are a gentleman. Even if some of your friends in town are not."

"They're not all that bad. Life is different in London."

"I've noticed." She brushed a crumb from his sleeve, tsking to herself. "What have you been eating?"

"One of the maids slipped me a bun. I'm fair starving. Should I ask her to pinch you a bite?"

"Certainly not."

"Well, I think you should eat before you get weak."

"I am not sneaking a bun in line. It would look uncouth."

"Nothing you do could look uncouth," he said.

The line into the brightly candlelit buffet crawled a few steps forward. Lily heard the couple behind them mention *The Wickbury Tales*, and her heart lost a beat. She knew she ought to mind her own business and pretend she wasn't listening, but when the lady whispered, "And Philbert said Lord Anonymous might make an appearance to acknowledge the tribute to him tonight," Lily could not restrain her curiosity.

She leaned around Jonathan, ignoring the tug he gave at her sleeve that the line was moving again. "Please excuse me for interrupting, but I can't resist. Is Lord Anonymous really going to be here?"

The lady sighed. "He might have already come and gone."

Come and gone? Lily's heart sank.

Could she have missed him that easily?

Had she brushed against his arm without realizing it?

"Did anyone say what he looked like?"

"Nobody—"

"Perhaps he's anonymous for a reason," Jonathan said loudly, nudging Lily back in place. "Perhaps he's hiding something."

"Such as?" she asked.

He frowned. "I don't know and I don't care. But *I* have a confession to make before I go upstairs to play cards."

"I'd know him if I met him," she said absently. "Which is unlikely, standing in this awful line."

"How the devil would you know him if no one else does?" he asked teasingly.

"I could tell by the way he spoke." She gestured

with her hand. "His words. He'd say something and I'd recognize him right away."

"Silly Lily," he said, making a face. "I'd be jealous if he were anything but a writer." He bent his head to hers. "Don't you want to hear my confession?"

He looked so earnest and endearing with his papier-mâché King Lear crown tucked under his arm that she felt wicked for wanting to laugh. As close as they had become over the years, she doubted whatever he wanted to confess would be as intriguing as meeting a mysterious celebrated author. Besides, she and Jonathan would have the rest of their lives for confessions.

"Come clean," she whispered. "What have you done? Knocked over a vase?"

He hesitated. "I never finished reading *King Lear*. In fact, I couldn't make it through the first act. People keep throwing quotes at me about ungrateful children, and I've no clue what they mean. I had to take off my crown so that I wouldn't be recognized."

"Oh, Jonathan. What am I to do with you?"

He gave her a helpless grin. "Answer for me the next time anyone asks about the plot. I keep acting as if I can't hear properly."

She reminded herself of all his good qualities. He didn't drink. He thought she was the most beautiful woman in the world, and at times she believed him. He always behaved like a gentleman in her presence, and, obviously, he needed her.

"You should have told me this before," she whispered. "It's too late to worry about it now. And it isn't as if Shakespeare will appear to ask your opinion."

He looked completely unconcerned. "I wouldn't have even come here tonight if I didn't know how much you loved your books. Have your evening, Lily. But know that I'm counting the hours until we share a bed. Give me a kiss for luck before I go."

"Where are you going?" she asked in vexation.

"I just told you. Kirkham and I have been invited upstairs for cards."

She lifted her face covertly, then pulled away, aware of an attractive gentleman lounging against the wall. He was dressed as a knight, and although he was too far away to hear what she and Jonathan were discussing, his insolent stare indicated that he found their encounter amusing.

How long had he been watching them?

A strange prickle of warmth stole down her neck into her white-plumed bodice. She forced her attention back to Jonathan's reassuring face. "Don't be late for the unmasking. Put the crown on before you come back."

He nodded. "Stay where Chloe can keep an eye on you until then. I promise I won't be long. And, Lily—don't let any rakes steal you while I'm gone."

Chapter 3

$\mathcal{L}$ily smiled ruefully at Jonathan's parting remark. He could be overly protective at times and utterly oblivious at others. As if she would let a rake ruin her evening. In the first place, the only gentlemen she had met at the party had expressed more interest in the fine arts than the amorous ones. Which was what one would expect at a literary affair.

Furthermore, it would take an unprincipled scoundrel to pursue a lady in such elite company. If the unthinkable happened and she found herself accosted by a rogue, her cousin would come to her rescue.

The viscountess had been Lily's official chaperone in London over the past two months and had confided openly in Lily about her past experiences with the opposite sex. A dedicated wife and mother now, Chloe freely admitted that she had not only caused but courted a few scandals in her day. She seemed to regard it as her penance to guard a country relation like Lily from succumbing to the same temptations.

What those temptations had been Lily could only guess. She suspected the greatest of them had been Dominic Breckland, Chloe's brooding viscount.

Lily spotted Chloe talking to yet another pair of gentlemen, neither of whom was her husband, who had refused to wear a costume. "Lily!" she called gaily. "Don't stand there all alone like a little lost duckling! Come and meet two of my dearest friends."

Lily shrugged helplessly. Guests hemmed her in at every angle. She straightened to squeeze toward an opening to escape, only to be bumped forward into the next person in line. Lily was not a petite person. She played a strong game of bowls and ate generous meals. She could have given the rude guest a return shove with her rear end that would have knocked him back a few yards. Instead, she craned her neck and attempted to catch Chloe's attention to signal her inability to move.

"Would somebody be so kind as to—"

She broke off. No one was paying any notice except the insouciant scoundrel leaning against the wall, who appeared to be enjoying her dilemma. She glanced up at him amid the tricornered hats and frilly caps and bewigged heads that bobbed back and forth before her.

Some sort of spear stood at his side. If he was supposed to be a knight, he struck Lily as more wicked than chivalrous. His lithe figure conveyed a leashed energy that she could feel across the room. He kept nodding at whatever was being said to him.

But his eyes glittered at Lily from the slits of his black silk mask. A lady's hand reached through the crowd to caress his shoulder. To Lily's amazement, he showed no reaction to this impropriety. It did not appear to provoke him in the least. Nor did he seem pleased by it. But then Lily had let Jonathan kiss her on the cheek, and she had pretended not to notice in the hope no one else would either.

Don't let any rakes steal you while I'm gone.

Who would want to steal her?

She wasn't the sort to excite that much passion, even in a rake.

Lily blinked. What had come over her? She would not drink another glass of champagne. At least not until after she ate. And she would not sneak another glance at the man whose stare had practically singed her skin.

She lifted her gaze. Her last look, she promised herself. It wouldn't hurt. No one else would ever know. One. Final. Look.

Relieved and a little disappointed, she realized that he was no longer looking at her. She assured herself it was for the best. Heartbreak might as well have been emblazoned on his forehead. She wasn't surprised that females made up the innermost group of guests that he'd attracted.

Still, how he managed to appear lost and affected

with lethal boredom was a skill that Lily could only admire from a guarded distance. His negligent elegance announced to the room that he accepted his influence and felt no guilt in wielding this gift as he desired.

Lily might not have recognized such inborn arrogance if she had not possessed some weaponry of her own. Nothing of his magnitude. But she adored the thrill of secret flirtations. And—

She wasn't merely looking at him now. She was studying him like a masterpiece in a museum. How on earth did he manage it? He gave the impression of a masked god who had dropped in on the party only to let the world of mortals worship in his shadow.

Was that air of dark indolence part of his disguise? Perhaps he was an actor and that was why he had an audience that basked in his presence. She liked that notion. The longer she appraised him, the more she wondered whether he was holding court as part of a well-rehearsed performance.

Demon, actor, or social darling, she found him captivating, too, judging by her furtive analysis of his person. And then it dawned on her that the weapon at his side was a rusty lance, and he wasn't an ordinary knight-errant. He was Don Quixote de la Mancha, mad and self-appointed protector of the helpless.

"Lily!"

She turned reluctantly toward the sound of Chloe's voice, her musings interrupted. Then it happened again. Unexpected, breath-catching. Like watching a star tumble from the midnight sky.

He lifted his head and stared at her, as if he'd been waiting to catch her off guard again. What impeccable timing. His lean form straightened. His hard-lipped mouth curled at one corner.

A farewell to their brief flirtation or an invitation to something far more dangerous? Lily couldn't decide.

She started to look away. She knew better than to encourage this sort of nonsense. A man who stared at a lady like that and didn't mind who noticed only offered trouble. But all of a sudden her own instinct for mischief took over. Lily could flirt, too, and the fact that she was wearing a costume gave her a false sense of anonymity.

Just for tonight she wasn't the unsophisticated Miss Lily Boscastle of Tissington, who in a month would become a bride and settle down to a respectable life as Captain Grace's wife.

She would never see this knight-errant again. The unabashed attention he paid her begged for an answer. But what kind? An alluring smile to admit that she was intrigued? A firm shake of her head that meant a definite no? Or perhaps a little shrug to indicate that while he flattered her, she wasn't willing to reciprocate with anything riskier?

Would that be too wicked of her? It wasn't as if he could leap into the air and snatch her up in full view of innumerable witnesses.

She smiled back at him, a playful coquette's smile, over the shoulder, straight in the direction of his handsome face.

There.

Take that.

And he did, inclining his head in open approval, the devil acknowledging his due. What had she done? She took a breath, transfixed, as he raised his helmet in a tribute that tempted and immobilized her in the same delirious moment.

Several members of his group turned their heads to identify her. He hadn't been subtle at all. She barely felt the person behind her give her another shove. This time she was too distracted to take offense.

In fact, she was so unbalanced that she allowed herself to be propelled directly into an opening in the line, into temptation's path, and heaven only knew how far the shameless man would have carried this scandalous exchange had a firm hand not caught hers and an urgent voice not whispered in her ear, "*Lily.*"

She tumbled back to earth, recognizing the raven-haired enchantress who was rightfully attempting to restore her common sense. "What has come over you?" Chloe demanded under her breath. "What are you doing?"

"I'm not doing anything." Not that she would readily admit.

"I am going to give you a belated warning," Chloe

went on in such a breathless voice that Lily was forced to listen. "I assumed that because you flirted so well, you fully understood what a dangerous game it can be."

Lily bit her lip. From the corner of her eye she observed an older, distinguished-looking gentleman entering the room to a chorus of warm cheers. "I've no idea what you're talking about," she lied. "But perhaps you ought to lecture me later. Isn't that our host, Lord Philbert, just making an appearance?"

Chloe was clearly not to be deterred. She pointedly stared at the gorgeous creature standing up against the wall. Lily wasn't positive, but she thought Lord Philbert had broken through the ranks that surrounded the charismatic one, which indicated that while the other man might be a rake, he was, as she suspected, an important one.

At least Lily hadn't smiled at a nobody. There was some consolation in that.

Chloe released her grip on Lily's hand. "Do you have the vaguest idea who that gentleman is?"

"Which gentleman? The room is full of them."

"I saw you smile at only one."

Lily realized it was self-defeating to deceive a lady as observant as her cousin. "I couldn't help it, Chloe. I mean, I couldn't help noticing him. It was wrong."

"Everyone notices him," Chloe continued in a forgiving voice. "There is nothing to be done for that. But the problem is that *he* is making a point to notice you. And that is why it is crucial that I warn you. He is the Duke of Gravenhurst."

Lily knew this announcement should have given her a scare.

"Does the title signify some inherent evil?" she asked cautiously.

Chloe straightened the gold circlet that pressed her fringe of black curls to her forehead. "I don't know all that much about him myself. He is said to have inherited it after some family tragedy when he was a boy. As the story goes, he went a little wild as he reached his maturity. His supporters attribute his rebellious nature to the responsibilities he took on at a young age."

"Supporters?" Lily said, lifting her brow.

"In the House of Lords. He gives persuasive speeches for causes that other people pretend don't exist." Chloe studied her in concern. "He's *very* persuasive, from what I've gathered."

"That isn't a crime, is it?"

"It depends on whom you ask. The opposite party thinks so. As do several parents whose daughters have formed a society to follow him around the capital with telescopes when he visits. His foes consider him a traitor to the peerage."

"Well, I don't plan on joining any admiration societies in the near future, and it's doubtful Jonathan will ever land in the House of Lords. Especially since he cannot even be bothered to finish a book, and his brother is going to inherit the family title."

Chloe calmed down a bit. "At least your captain is a decent person."

"And the duke is not?" Lily asked before she could censor the question.

"A man that handsome, who has only to smile to mesmerize, cannot be unaware of his charm."

"Is it his fault that he is beautiful?"

"He is rumored to run through women like . . . racehorses."

Lily reared back at this appalling image. "That is disgusting. And not beautiful in the least."

Chloe drew a breath, clearly mollified by Lily's reaction. "*If* it is true," she added in an apparent bid to be fair. "I can't honestly say that I've had personal experience with the man. But I seem to recall a bit of gossip—Oh, dear."

" 'Oh dear,' what?"

"I think I read that he wakes up at midnight with one woman and blazes through the streets until dawn in his cabriolet with another. And that he has appeared at three routs in a single hour."

"No wonder he's lean."

"Lily, *listen*. When other gentlemen come home to change into their evening clothes, he is removing his. Do you realize what that means?"

It could mean anything, Lily thought. He could be nocturnal by nature. He could be allergic to daylight or city fog. It could mean he preferred the intimacy of the night. Perhaps he was simply one of those men who came alive when the sun went down. Lily knew only that his presence irradiated the room, and that it could be morning or midnight right now and she would not have noticed the difference.

But a man who dressed as Don Quixote at a masquerade *must* harbor a keen sense of humor. A disguise like that mocked beauty rather than enhanced it. Unless, like Lily, he was only wearing the costume that a sharper wit had suggested.

She was afraid that her runaway imagination had gotten the better of her again. It was entirely possible that the duke was no more a misguided knight than Jonathan was a tragic king.

Chapter 4

*S*amuel straightened as he recognized the white-bearded, heavily built gentleman who had just barreled through the group. Most of the ton knew that Samuel and Lord Philbert were friends and political allies. Few guessed, however, that there was a stronger bond between them. Lord Philbert published Samuel's books, and Samuel held a share of the business. He gratefully allowed Philbert to draw him apart from the gathering.

"Your Grace," he announced in his blustery, authoritarian voice, "I have a distinguished personage in the private gallery who would like to make your acquaintance. If your audience would excuse us for a few moments . . ."

Samuel smiled faintly, blew a kiss to the ensemble in general, and followed the larger man toward the door. "Wait a minute. Is this a rescue or is there really someone I ought to meet? I'm not a blasted marionette, after all."

"You looked cornered, Gravenhurst, and rather dangerous with that lance at your side. I thought you would appreciate a few minutes of solitude to soothe your nerves."

"There is nothing wrong with my nerves."

"I think there is. Your book was due last Monday, and you manage to change the subject every time I mention it. I am tearing out my hair by the tuft."

Samuel pivoted, refusing to take another step toward the door. "I see someone in this room whose acquaintance I *would* like to make."

"There you go again, changing—"

"In private. I would like to meet this lady in private. But I'm aware that such an arrangement would be considered bad manners, so I'll settle for a correct introduction."

"I worry about you, Samuel. What is wrong with the novel? Do not try to deceive me. I recognize the signs. You haven't written a word, have you? I knew it would happen one day. I—"

"I am unhappy with the last chapter. I need an extension."

Philbert looked as if he would collapse with relief. "Fine, but let me read it and be the judge. I have told you that I can write the ending myself."

Samuel gave a snort. "I told you that we should have bought the copyright of the *Encyclopædia Britan-*

nica when it was offered. We could have both retired on the revenues."

"That is a sore point," Philbert admitted. "The Scots won the day, no doubt. It is that James and John Harper in New York I'd like to buy. You cannot trust the colonials."

Samuel smiled. "Knowing their origins, I'm inclined to agree."

Philbert let a moment pass. "We should be editing your next book."

"Remember how I feel about discussing an unfinished work."

"I shouldn't tell you this—God forbid it go to your head—but I've just had a request from Ennis Desmond to write the new stage version of the series."

Samuel turned to look at him. "Absolutely not. Desmond has a hand like a mallet."

"*Your* version only ran for a week."

"Nine performances."

"At least he understands stage direction."

Samuel stared back into the crush of costumed guests. He had momentarily lost sight of his pretty flirt when Philbert had arrived. But he quickly found her curvaceous form, sheathed from creamy shoulder to high-slippered heel in soft white plumes. A cluster of coppery brown curls fell demurely down her back against an intricate ladder of golden laces. His throat went dry. She struck him as unbearably vulnerable in that dress.

"She's just asking to be plucked," he said without thinking.

Philbert lifted his head in alarm. "I beg your pardon?"

"Is your wine deceptively strong or is that young lady in white impossibly lovely?"

Lord Philbert finally relented and traced the direction of the duke's intense scrutiny. He heaved a sigh. "Offhand, I'd say both."

"That's what I thought." Samuel handed Philbert his helmet and readjusted his mask. "This room is overcrowded. Where did all these people come from, anyway?"

"Someone told me that tickets were being passed out free in Piccadilly," was the droll reply. "You would not believe the riffraff we've had to turn away."

Samuel blinked in convincing innocence. "But aren't the riffraff encouraged to read?"

"Don't bring politics to my party, Gravenhurst. If you are that devoted to your readers, I suggest you give them the next book in the series. When," he demanded, "are you going to finish the bloody thing?"

"Three weeks."

"Damnation, man—"

"Two days if you introduce me to her before she loses any more of those feathers."

Lord Philbert shook his head. "I don't even know who she is myself."

"Someone must."

"Perhaps she's one of the random shopgirls you so liberally invited out of the goodness of my pocketbook."

"If that's true," Samuel said, never perturbed by the mention of money, "then it's fate that I meet her. And if she is as intriguing as she looks, I'll be indebted to you for a long time."

"You are indebted to me now, you rascal. I will not advance you another shilling until I have the next *Wickbury* in my possession."

"I'm only asking for an introduction," Samuel said, staring straight past Philbert with a determined smile. "I wouldn't have come to London if I hadn't almost finished the book. I'd have been hiding somewhere you'd never find me."

"Your readers are not the only ones left hanging in your imagination. Let me make this clear, Samuel. Book Seven is overdue."

"I have rewritten the ending almost fifty times."

"Good heavens, what is the matter?"

"My characters are pitching a rebellion against my plot. I feel they are trying to tell me something, and I don't know what."

"Perhaps they are telling you to give them one of your rousing endings. And soon."

Samuel reluctantly turned to meet the older man's concerned stare. "This party was *your* idea. The garden tour, the erudite and the shallow minded, where the beau monde meets the world of books, and so forth. I don't think either of us is here for our health."

"Speaking of which—"

"Let's not," Samuel said. "Did you notice her smiling at me?"

The veins that crisscrossed Lord Philbert's cheeks met in several vivid crimson splotches. "I can't say that I did."

"At *me*, Philbert, of all the wrong gentlemen at the party. White feathers of purity with a blush of wickedness waiting to be revealed."

"Dear God. Not another one."

"Someone has to protect her from scoundrels like me."

"I've lost count. You mustn't do this again. How many of them can be trusted with your secret?"

"Calm down, Philbert, before you give one of us a fit of apoplexy. You needn't make me sound like—"

"A deluded knight? You and your dangerous ideas of chivalry."

Samuel paused as his beleaguered publisher and friend raised his quizzing glass to examine the lady who had sparked this clash.

"Oh, for pity's sake. How can you find her intriguing when all one can see of her is feathers? Nicely adorned, I'll agree. A lovely face. But not the sort of blatant temptress you typically choose. She looks more like a baby owl than a mistress in the making."

Samuel laughed in delight. "Sometimes I think you believe the lies we perpetuate. But it doesn't matter. She's the Goose-Girl, by the way. And underneath that disguise, I'll wager there is a golden princess waiting for the right man to see her worth."

"Another fairy tale," Lord Philbert said with a deep sigh of resignation. "I should have guessed. Your dreams will be the death of us yet."

Chapter 5

"You aren't going to ruin this party for me," Lily stated with conviction. "Nothing is."

"It's your ruination that is at stake," Chloe said crossly. "Flirting with a man of Gravenhurst's repute. You, who look so demure and who—"

They glanced at each other, both attempting not to smile. ". . . shall be the envy of London tomorrow," Chloe concluded grudgingly. "We'll clip out all the articles about you in the papers and put them away for your old age."

"It's a good thing Jonathan doesn't read."

"It's a good thing he wasn't here to witness your friendly exchange with Gravenhurst. There would be breakfast for one tomorrow instead of for this entire assembly."

"What else has the duke done that is so forbidding?" Lily asked in a low voice. "Quickly, quickly.

He's looking this way again. I think he might be reading my lips."

Chloe snorted lightly. "If the duke is staring at your mouth, I doubt that reading has anything to do with it."

"But what has he done?" Lily persisted.

"Everything."

"What?"

"I don't know, Lily. Nothing. Everything. It depends on what you believe. It's probably all baseless rumors. The Boscastle family has been accused of every manner of misdeed. You should have heard the things said of me."

Lily held back a laugh. "Then why let the rumors of his reputation influence your opinions?"

Chloe cast her a woeful look. "A few of the things said of me were true. And do not ask me which. I don't feel compelled to confess every single one of my sins. It wouldn't discourage you as much as it would give you ideas. And— Dear heaven, he's coming over here. Hide behind me. No. Don't move. Don't breathe. Don't even blink."

Lily hazarded a glance in the duke's direction. It was true. He seemed to be blazing a trail straight toward her. And *blazing* was not an exaggeration. The air smoldered as he strolled across the room. She couldn't bring herself to stare into his face again, but the nearer he drew, the harder her heart seemed to race with hideous excitement. "He's coming to meet you, Chloe," she said with absolute certainty.

"Nobody knows whether the stories about him are true," Chloe murmured.

"Then there isn't any harm in meeting him."

"Nobody knows that they *aren't* true," Chloe countered. A frown creased her forehead. "But there was something else I heard. Something dark and . . . I wish I could remember it."

"Whatever he has done cannot be as bad as the acts of depravity I'm beginning to imagine."

"You are a country mouse," Chloe said after a rueful silence. "You understand only enough to land yourself in trouble. I daresay the duke would lead you there without a second thought."

"But your bouts of mischief ended well, didn't they?"

Chloe gave a half smile. "If you are referring to my husband, mischief is a nightly affair."

"Go on."

"I will not."

"You are cruel, cousin," Lily whispered, "to speak of your many delicious misdeeds and deprive me of a single one."

"Better to deprive you now than to sanction a life of . . . depravity."

"You sound like a fusty old governess."

Chloe bit her lip. "I know. Who would have dreamt it? The young lady who was exiled to a duck pond for letting herself be kissed by a stranger in the park."

"A stranger?"

"He had a name," Chloe said, laughter welling in her voice. "I just neglected to ask it before I let him kiss me."

"Hypocrite," Lily said more loudly than she intended.

"Innocent," Chloe replied, as if daring Lily to cross an invisible line.

"You are worse than wicked," Lily said. "You have become . . . uninspired."

Chloe raised her hand to her breast. "I have not."

"I have been told," Lily said in an undertone, "that you hid Dominic in your dressing closet before you were married."

A dead silence enshrouded them.

Chloe looked at Lily without expression.

"I'm sorry," Lily said in a heart-stricken voice. "I should never have repeated such a hideous piece of gossip."

"Why not?" Chloe broke into a pleasant grin. "It is the wonderful truth."

The two of them dipped together in a curtsy, the duke so close that Lily suddenly found herself swallowed up in his shadow. Chloe captured Lily's hand again as they rose gracefully together, composed enough to whisper one remark in her charge's ear, "By the look of him, your mischief is about to begin."

Chapter 6

*S*amuel resisted looking directly at her. For one thing her companion had already sent him a lethal stare. For another, he had revealed enough of his intentions for a first impression. A mask could disguise a man's outward appearance. It tended, however, to accentuate his true nature. And Samuel was struggling to keep his instincts under control. He bowed, his downcast gaze covertly studying the lady dressed in white.

He managed to affect his usual detached but courteous manner as Philbert mumbled through the introductions, presenting Samuel to the dark-haired woman first. Viscountess Stratfield. The title stirred a memory Samuel could not grasp until she, and not Philbert, revealed the other young lady's identity.

Boscastle. That was a surname he recognized. *Miss* Lily Boscastle, cousin of the former Chloe Boscastle. He began to understand.

No wonder the viscountess viewed him with overt suspicion. It took a sinner to recognize one. Lady Stratfield's family escapades rivaled his. But then, he was only one, and the Boscastles formed an entire clan. Still, it wasn't Lady Stratfield who attracted him. It was the younger lady beside her, in her white-feathered mask and matching cloak. The lady who had given him a beguiling smile.

Lily. The name suited her, evoking a purity that implored protection. He wondered if she was of the imported belladonna variety or the blood hybrid that had withered in his hothouse. Would she flare like a torch lily with a bolder touch?

"His Grace," Philbert intoned, looking foolish with Samuel's helmet in his hand. "The fourth Duke of Gravenhurst, the ninth Baronet—"

"You don't need to go through the whole list," Samuel said, bowing again to Chloe and then, at last, looking up, with a stare perfected for maximum impact, into a pair of bewitching blue eyes that drew the breath from his body. Fortunately, he was adept enough at deception to hide his intense pleasure.

"I am Don Quixote de la Mancha," he said smoothly, handing a disgruntled Philbert his shield and lance. "Knight-errant," he added, "who seeks adventure."

"Knight-errant, indeed," the viscountess retorted, giving him a frank look. "What was your latest act of chivalry, or shouldn't I ask?"

Samuel caught the smile that lurked on Lily Boscastle's full lips. "I fought a duel this morning in Hyde Park."

Lord Philbert regarded him in dismay. "Isn't that a provocative conversation piece? What does it have to do with honorable acts?"

He and Samuel had played the roles of incautious rogue and discreet adviser for so many years that they had not only perfected them; they earnestly lived them. "Honor had nothing to do with it. My opponent is a close friend."

"What did you duel over?" Chloe inquired after a short hesitation.

"He dared me to shoot his boot off his head," Samuel replied. "And then he took a shot at me. It was a prank. I didn't invite the press to attend." But he had sent them an unsigned letter, stating that the duel would take place. He had also published an editorial on London's sewer system that same day, and his notoriety would help draw attention to those who might otherwise not read the piece.

Lord Philbert flushed as if he were coming to a boil. "If you're going to tell the story, you might as well finish it. Both men missed."

"At least a lady's honor was not involved," Chloe said with a meaningful glance at Lily.

Samuel smiled. He was doing his damnedest not to stare at her again himself. Why had he felt compelled to explain that the duel was a boyish caper? His reputation was at risk. He'd never admitted an innocuous motive to explain his antics before. But he had never tried to impress a lady in such a short time, either. What chance did he have of seeing her again if her guardian declared him an enemy of virtue?

And that guardian, in her vivid beauty, gave him the impression that she had dealt with a rake or two in her own past. Chloe. Chloe Boscastle. He frowned then, looking at her with renewed respect. "Lady Stratfield, I *do* know of you."

"Oh, my," Chloe said with an uncertain smile. "Not in front of my cousin, please."

"I've never had the pleasure of an introduction," he went on, his admiration genuine. "But I am aware of your work in the female penitentiary."

Chloe appeared taken aback. But then her eyes glistened in delight. She released Lily's hand from her defensive clasp. Samuel observed the significant gesture in relief. Common ground. His instincts had proven true again.

"That was some time ago," Chloe confessed. "What a memory Your Grace must have. Nobody cares about that segment of society."

"Don't we?" he asked in a dangerously intimate voice. "I admire your bravery."

"Do you?" she asked, cynicism slipping back into her tone. "You're brave yourself."

He scented victory and felt not the slightest guilt in forging onward. A knight-errant was forced to do what he must do to win his lady fair. He waited for the next opening. It came as Lord Philbert's senior footman approached the quartet and said sotto voce to his master, "Pardon me, milord. But there is a lady frolicking in the main fountain."

"Then get her out," Philbert muttered, withdrawing a handkerchief from his vest pocket, Samuel's knightly accoutrements banging awkwardly in his grasp. "She'll catch her death at this time of night."

The footman bowed, his words practically inaudible. "Especially as she is in the raw and shouting for the Duke of la Mancha to save her."

Lily lifted her gaze.

Her blue eyes kept returning to his, even though she must know better. Her mouth was tempting as a plum. He had to have her. He shrugged. "I have nothing to do with this."

Lord Philbert turned toward the retreating footman. "You will have to excuse me for a few moments, ladies. Gravenhurst, I trust you will keep our lovely guests *politely* entertained."

"I have a brilliant idea," Samuel said, his gaze locked with Lily's. "Why don't I escort the ladies on a private tour of the gardens? The formal affair will be a crush."

Lord Philbert shook his head. "It hasn't been properly lit up yet. You won't be able to see much in the dark."

"All the better," Samuel said with a deep chuckle, "if we have a naked noblewoman in our midst."

*   *   *

"That is a wonderful idea," Chloe said after Philbert trudged off to take care of his frolicking guest. "Lily and I would love a peek at the gardens. I would also love another glass of champagne."

"Allow me," Samuel said, gesturing to a pair of footmen stationed in a candlelit alcove.

At his subtle movement one footman braved the crowd to make way for the other to balance a tray that held three glasses of champagne. Lily could not believe it. Had the duke brought his own staff to the party, or had Lord Philbert assigned individual servants to attend him? Either way, she was growing more impressed with him by the moment.

Across a room he had drawn her notice by appearing to be an insouciant rogue. Up close he countered the image with a geniality that neither she nor Chloe seemed able to resist. Handsomeness was one thing. Personal magnetism was another. Look how easily he had persuaded them to go out into the gardens. Indeed, it was hard for Lily to hold any sensible thoughts in her head when she was caught up in his charm. And he *was* beautifully formed, his frame agile and almost slender. She would have felt ungainly if he hadn't topped her by several inches.

His face, or what she could make out of it beneath his half mask, fascinated her. His brown eyes brewed with unfathomable emotions above hollow cheeks that gave his face its chiseled symmetry. His strong chin balanced what at first glance seemed to be a seraphic appeal, marking him as pure, dangerous male. She reassured herself again that he posed little danger to her at a party.

Still, she wanted to pull off his mask and put the rest of his features in perspective. The parts of his face she could not see might explain what it was about him that mystified her. That seemed missing. He was definitely *not* an uncomplicated man.

"Come, Lily. Your Grace," Chloe said. "We cannot stand here staring at one another forever. Let's view the gardens that London is raving about. Don Quixote, would you be so kind as to lead the way?"

He straightened, grinning at the loud creak his breastplate made. "With pleasure. Please excuse any rude noises coming from my costume."

Lily stifled a laugh as he gave her another engaging grin. He was going out of his way to amuse her. Should she be flattered or raise her guard?

"There is a private anteroom in the main hall that leads through the dining room," he explained, bending his head between the two women. Lily caught a whiff of his lime cologne. Divine.

"From there," he continued, "the last door to the right takes you into a private gallery overlooking the garden."

Chloe gave one of her low, uninhibited laughs. "Your Grace is an architect, too?"

He smiled artlessly. "Madam?"

"How else do you know the secret exits so well?"

"I've been forced once or twice to make an escape."

"By yourself?"

"Her Ladyship is naughty to ask."

Chloe inclined her head in acknowledgment. "Your Grace is naughty not to answer. Understand that my cousin is my concern."

"Rightly so," the duke agreed. "It would be remiss of you to entrust her to a . . . scamp."

Lily listened to their exchange in envy. Her cousin could tease to her heart's content as a viscountess and reformed sinner. What a shame Lily had never come to London for lessons in the wicked graces. They seemed delightful. But who was charming whom here? She couldn't decide whether Chloe or the duke had won the match. Was it possible that *she*, an unknown girl from the country, was the prize?

Undoubtedly not. Gentlemen like Gravenhurst viewed young ladies as—she glanced down at her dress—feathers to put in their caps. Still, she was enjoying his attention. His playful energy attracted her more than all of London's other entertainments combined.

"To the gardens," Chloe said with a spirited laugh.

And the evening might have ended innocently, the three of them absconding together, had another band of the viscountess's past admirers not intercepted them as they approached the gilt candelabra in the corner.

"Chloe, Chloe, *Chloe!*" a chorus of beguiling voices

called. "Don't run away yet—we haven't seen you in ages!"

Chloe halted, unable to resist glancing back, beau-monde butterfly that she was. Overall, in Lily's opinion of her, which grew warmer by the minute, Chloe resisted little when it came to indulging convivial pleasures.

"I'll only be a moment, I promise." Chloe bit the edge of her lip in clear hesitation. "Dash it all. Go on without me. I'll be right there. And I mean it."

Lily took a breath. "But I—"

Chloe gave her a light hug. "Don't do anything I wouldn't do," she whispered. "And that goes double for you, Your Grace. We Boscastles have spies everywhere."

Lily heard the duke's voice beckoning her. She looked up slowly. "You will be perfectly safe," he said. "Lady Stratfield knows where to find us. Our challenge will be making sure that the rest of the party doesn't catch on."

He opened a door behind him that she had not even noticed. But then, how would she have been aware of an exit when she had been staring at the winsome Gravenhurst all night?

Chapter 7

They stole through the interconnecting corridors like a pair of thieves. Samuel took light hold of Lily's elbow. Now that he'd gained the opportunity he'd wanted, he wasn't about to let her slip away. The viscountess knew a thing or two about trysts. She wasn't liable to abandon Lily for any length of time to a man of his repute. Still, for now they were alone. Sufficient unto this moment was the temptation thereof.

"Oh." Lily caught her breath.

Samuel had slowed to unlatch the French doors of a private courtyard, where a three-tiered fountain glistened beneath the moonlight. She was standing too close to him for propriety's sake. But then, as if she realized that pleasant fact, she took a discreet step back.

"That isn't *the* fountain, is it?" she asked over the duke's shoulder.

"No." He drew her outside with one hand and

closed the doors with the other. "Not a naked lady to be seen."

"Thank goodness," she said with feeling.

He grinned. "Come on."

"Where are we going first?"

"Do you have a preference?" It was amazing how she had turned an event he dreaded into a novel experience. And because he couldn't help himself, he asked, "Do you have a favorite author whose work is being displayed tonight?"

"I . . . Yes." She pulled herself free and gathered her feathered cloak around her arms. "No one knows his true name. Or whether he is one person or many." Her voice dropped. "Whoever he is, he writes with a passion that—" She fell silent, clearly trying to curb her enthusiasm.

"Do continue," he said gravely. "This passion . . ."

"His writing sweeps me off the ground," she whispered.

"In any particular direction?" he asked slowly.

"Yes." She raised her voice back to its ladylike tone. "Toward the gardens. Where my cousin is joining us, perhaps even with her husband. That would be Viscount Stratfield. Perhaps you've heard of him. He doesn't live in London, but he's got a name, I understand, and something of a temper."

Samuel reached back instinctively for her hand, half listening, aware of wasting time. He had seen the gardens only once or twice in various stages of construction and felt more uncomfortable than anything about viewing a tribute to his books. It wasn't that he didn't appreciate Philbert's efforts to immortalize *Wickbury* in boxwood. But he was presently more interested in fleshy things than in foliage or public accolade.

"Viscount Stratfield, did you say?" *Good God*. Now that he put his mind to it, Samuel *did* remember an intriguing rumor he had read a few years ago, when he was ruining his own image in the press. "The viscount who came back from the dead?"

He didn't add that Lord Stratfield's resurrection had allegedly occurred in his wife's dressing closet, specifically in a trunk of Chloe's undergarments, where Stratfield was said to have been hiding. That scandal had so delighted the ton that it hadn't mattered whether it was true or not. Having just met Stratfield's wife, Samuel tended to believe it was. What a story that must have been.

Lily's grin suggested that the scandal had not been a fabrication. "I refuse to deny or confirm any gossip about my relatives."

"Good for you. I admire a lady who isn't influenced by low talk. And I admire . . ." His gaze traveled over her, his meaning explicit.

Her mouth tightened in reprimand.

". . . your costume," he said, guiding her around the fountain to a flagstone path. "It's very original. I don't believe I've seen another Goose-Girl at a masquerade before. I realized who you were the instant I looked at you."

"You were looking at me rather a lot."

He looked at her now with unabashed candor. "You didn't mind, did you?"

"Shame on you," she said mildly, pulling her hand from his. "Are you sure you know where we're going?"

"Not really. But there are footmen standing guard in case we get lost. Be careful here where you step— the stone is slippery. You looked at me a lot, too. And I didn't mind at all. Do you enjoy reading fairy tales?"

She glanced back at the brightly lit house. He wondered for a moment if she would run away. But then she turned back and said, "Yes. I especially love the Brothers Grimm."

"You read German?" he asked her in surprise.

"My great-aunt does." She gave him a guarded smile. One of her pale feathers fluttered to the ground. "I think," she said, staring down with a frown, "that their stories are sheer genius."

Competition. He released a disgruntled sigh. It followed him everywhere. He led her a few steps deeper into the garden before he replied, "I'll admit the two of them have a certain flair for the fable, but then, how many of their stories were taken from other unsung authors through the ages?"

She broke into laughter. It was an infectious if unexpected reaction, and he found himself grinning at her.

"What is so amusing?" he asked as they slowed at the entrance to a parterre.

"You are," she said. "You may never have met another Goose-Girl, but I've never met a gentleman who confessed he reads fairy tales, let alone has given their origins serious thought."

"This is a literary masquerade."

"But not all the guests are literate." She looked a little guilty. "I shouldn't have said that. It sounds mean."

His chest felt suddenly constricted. Either he needed to undo his breastplate, or Lily's sultry laughter had stolen his breath.

"I'd no idea the Grimm brothers were literary thieves," she said wistfully.

Now *he* felt guilty, not only for disillusioning her, but for maligning the young writers whose work he envied. "I didn't mean they stole ideas. I think the brothers are brilliant."

" 'The Pink' is the best."

"Some ladies do not approve of fairy tales at all. The violence offends them. But I thought that your favorite author was this mysterious fellow Lord Anonymous."

Another of her feathers drifted from her dress onto his padded sleeve as she smoothed the seams of her off-white gloves. She moistened her lower lip. Samuel watched her in absorption. A suit of genuine armor and a shield would not be enough to protect either of them from the instincts that Lily had incited. She had to know she was desirable. He plucked the loose feather from his sleeve, capturing it between his fingers.

"I was hoping that Lord Anonymous would make an appearance," she admitted, edging around him to stare into the garden. "Do you think that there's any chance?"

He grimaced. "Positively not."

She swung around, her eyes wide with astonishment. "Don't tell me the two of you are personally acquainted."

"All right. I won't."

She took a breath that lifted her lush décolletage. For a moment Samuel could not have repeated his own name, let alone the pseudonym that always made him cringe when he heard it. His ducal title did not appear to impress her. His secret identity as Lord Anonymous did. Was he reckless enough to betray himself for a wicked kiss in the dark?

He feared he might be.

He bent his head. "You are the loveliest woman I have met in . . . in forever."

"How nice of you to say." She paused. "Tell me what you know about Anonymous."

Samuel blinked. "I meant what I just said."

"Yes," she murmured. She gave him a measuring look. He wasn't sure whether to be amused or offended. Judging by how quickly she had dismissed his compliment, she was either accustomed to flattery, or she thought he was a complete scoundrel who could not be trusted.

She tilted her face up to his. "I would be ever so grateful if you whispered his real name. I promise I'll keep it a secret. On my honor as a Boscastle. I'll carry your confidence to the grave. Please, Your Grace. Please."

If ever Samuel had been tempted to confess that he and Anonymous were one and the same, this was the time. Or at least, she was the temptress. "I wish I could," he said in genuine regret. "Assuming I knew— and I'm not admitting I do—I would not be at liberty to say."

She stepped a little closer to him. "You don't know anything, do you? He has never been caught out in public."

He examined the brown-speckled feather she had shed on his sleeve. "This belonged to a hawk."

"Possibly. It wasn't easy finding enough pure white feathers to cover a costume, so a few other birds sneaked in."

"A hawk is a bird of prey," he said reflectively. "This changes my perception of you."

"I think you know more than you are telling me about the author of *Wickbury*."

"Tell me your theory about him."

"You give me your word you won't laugh?" she asked with a wicked smile that made him want to kiss her.

"My word."

"But I'm not sure I can trust you."

"Why not?" he said in surprise. "I've been on my best behavior."

"Maybe it's because you have a dangerous air that's supposed to warn young ladies like me to be on guard."

"You have a wicked air yourself," he countered.

"Well, I don't consider myself dangerous." She hesitated. "Do you?"

"Very much so."

She stared up at him for a long time. He thought she liked the idea of being a femme fatale. But she must have been regarded as one before. "I'll tell you my theory about Lord Anonymous, but only if you promise not to make fun of me."

"I wouldn't dream of it. And I have to say, Anonymous aside, you have a way of heightening a suspenseful moment yourself."

She lowered her gaze.

"A genuine page-turner," he added. "I am hanging on your every word."

She looked up. "My theory is that the writer is a woman."

"He's a *what*?"

"A woman," she said again, with a certainty that hinted she knew something about him that he didn't.

Lord Anonymous had been accused of many things, primarily that he had corrupted the morals of his readers with his dark plot twists and protagonists that acted beyond the pale. And, like any other author, he often inserted part of himself into his characters without realizing it. "Why a woman?"

"I explained it before. It's the passion."

He had to reflect on this. He had to prove to her that he was, well, not a woman of his word.

"No one has ever suggested such an outlandish idea before. It's preposterous. Talk about a fairy tale."

She gasped. "You said you wouldn't make fun of me. And you are wrong. There was a critic in the *Quarterly Review* who suggested that Anonymous might be a retired French courtesan."

He cleared his throat. He had missed that review. It wasn't one of the slanders he'd invented on his own. Or perhaps Philbert had kept it hidden from him. He refused to let Samuel read any critiques while he was in the early stages of a book. Samuel would have to investigate this slur at another time.

Two minutes later he and Lily stood before a Gothic-design black wrought-iron gate built into a brick archway. He took a golden key from his vest pocket and opened the padlock. The rush of a waterfall rang in the garden stillness. Lily gazed through the gate. Her enraptured smile made sneaking from the party worthwhile.

"Welcome to *Wickbury*." He guided her through a woodbine-smothered archway. "I hope you won't be disappointed."

Chapter 8

$\mathcal{H}$e led her deeper and deeper into a maze of clipped box hedges. The music of water pipes drifted across the topiary walk. Despite all the anticipation surrounding the event, she doubted anything could match the magic of *Wickbury*. Or the pleasure of a private tour given by the duke. Yes, she was skeptical of his motives.

To be fair, he might have instigated their flirtation, but she had flirted back, thinking she could tease him with impunity. He'd promised to behave, even if his eyes suggested something else entirely. Something elemental and enticing and dangerous all at once. And what should she make of his alleged knowledge of Lord Anonymous? Perhaps her theory had been right. It made more sense that he was intimate with a lady author than with a man. And the duke's reaction had been rather strong, now that she pondered it.

Fortunately she would not taste any forbidden pleasures in this garden. Chloe would intervene at any moment, and Lily would soon be relating her brush with scandal to her friends back home. She might neglect to mention it to Jonathan, however. She was supposed to be acting like his betrothed, not like a lady encouraging a dalliance with a man of Gravenhurst's notoriety.

And then suddenly she forgot she had agreed to be another gentleman's bride. She almost forgot the man escorting her. She felt him step aside so that she could enter a landscape of a literary dream, illuminated by hundreds of lights hidden in the labyrinth.

The storybook characters loomed larger than life at the end of the maze. She gazed up at the foreleg of the stallion Bucephalus, whose hooves could inflict a lethal wound and who had carried a wounded Lord Wickbury on several misadventures to safety.

Then her attention shifted to the two adversaries who had stolen her heart from the moment the author invented them. Michael, Lord Wickbury, and his archenemy, Sir Renwick Hexworthy. Mesmerizing, each in a completely different way. A lady would always choose Wickbury over Sir Renwick if she were asked. But that was the rub. Sir Renwick didn't ask. He stole whatever, whomever he wanted, and the only woman he wanted could not decide on either man.

Hero and villain waged battle across a chasm between two enormous yew hedges that had been trimmed to resemble boulders. Lord Wickbury sat astride his horse, his broadsword lifted as if to spear a star. From the evergreen dragon on the opposite side Sir Renwick Hexworthy raised his rapier-wand to intercept the call for divine intervention.

And Lily stood directly below the magnetic powers, vividly imagining how it would feel to have two magnificent characters fighting over her. A shiver rippled through her. For a moment she believed the fantasy. How foolish of her. Her emotions had not run this wild even when she had read the books.

"Look at him," she murmured.

"Wickbury?"

She made a noncommittal noise, too embarrassed to look at the duke. She could picture his mocking half smile. "Whom do you prefer?" she asked, not expecting a sincere answer. Somehow she couldn't imagine the duke losing himself in the darkly passionate tales. He appeared to be leading an enthralling life of his own.

"It depends," he said.

"On what?"

"On my mood. Or the story's flow."

That didn't make sense to her. But then, he had pleasantly muddled her thoughts from the start, and she still couldn't decide whether he was only pretending to be as devoted to *Wickbury* as were she and a legion of other readers.

"I wonder who will win in the end," she mused.

"Isn't it supposed to be Wickbury? I mean, they are his tales."

"For now, perhaps, but Sir Renwick happens to be Wickbury's half brother, and even though it isn't explained, he could be a Wickbury himself."

He looked at her. His books had started out simply enough. Wickbury was heroic and handsome. His adversary was vile and had been disfigured during an alchemical experiment by an erupting brew.

"It's happened in stories before," she said. "And Lord Wickbury could have children who might end up being little monsters."

"Don't you *like* Lord Wickbury?"

"Of course I do. Everyone does. But I suppose that's why I feel sympathy for Renwick."

"*He* is a monster. Why pity him?"

"It would be horrible to grow up in Wickbury's shadow."

Samuel was fascinated with her insight. Perhaps he should have sought out an honest reader's opinion all along. Perhaps her perception would enable him to finish the last chapter of Book Seven that was tormenting him. "I don't know what you mean, exactly." But he did, and he wanted to hear it explained in her appealing voice.

"Sir Renwick," she said. "If only he had another chance . . ."

Samuel glanced off in contemplation.

He had debated the same issue at his desk too many times to argue with her. Did a man always choose to enact evil? Did the why of it even matter in the end if he destroyed others? Should he be offered compassion or simply be stopped?

Samuel concluded that he must have some inherent capacity for evil or he would not have been able to create the fiendish characters who challenged his protagonists.

"Everyone expects Wickbury to win," she said. "Shouldn't it be a little harder this time?"

She had a point.

But who could predict what the future held?

A surprise revelation about two sons of the same sire? The black sheep could become a savior.

The two men could encounter an enemy that would force a temporary truce for a book or two.

Would it not make for an interesting twist?

Samuel's publisher would not think so.

Still, in recent months Samuel had concluded that a writer should be unpredictable. Within a liberal framework of a certain predictability, that was. He did not want to betray his readers.

But who was Lord Anonymous to determine that an unwholesome character like Sir Renwick could not repent of his sins? He could always take another dark turn in the next book.

Lovely young ladies like Lily thought it was possible.

Samuel and Lord Anonymous, who infrequently acted as one, would like to make her happy.

He glanced up, appraising the topiary figures. "We will have to leave the story up to the author. I take it that you are impressed by the garden."

"It's wonderful. Except . . . where is the woman they both want?"

"The most desirable lady in England?"

"Yes."

"She's here."

She glanced around in curiosity, wondering how she could have missed the provocative heroine. "Is she in the grotto? I don't see her."

"I do."

The low insinuation in his voice sent a sizzle of impending danger down her spine. He was going to kiss her. And she was not discouraging him. She had not made a single move to dissuade him. He wrapped one arm around her waist. His other hand caressed a path from her wrist to her throat. The garden lights that danced above them grew dim. A dark warmth enveloped her.

This was the moment to resist. Chloe would come to her rescue. Lily had been warned. Which did not explain why she raised her face and drew a breath. Or why she laid her fingers on the duke's forearm, thrilling at the latent strength that she could feel there. A nightingale sang from a nearby tree. His firmly molded mouth met hers with an intimacy that filled her with terror and wonder.

Slowly she parted her lips, the instinct undeniable. She realized what he would think—that she was inviting him to take more.

Perhaps she was.

He accepted.

There was no chance to change her mind. It happened too quickly. A rush of feelings overcame her, too intense, too tantalizing for her thoughts to follow. His tongue teased the contours of her lips before penetrating her mouth in a skillful play that demonstrated his reputation for persuasion.

She had been kissed before. But not like this.

Her mouth had never been seduced with such delicious intensity. His thumb caressed the cleft of her chin, the curls that fell against her shoulder. Shivers spun across her skin like cobwebs. Then slowly he sucked at her lower lip, his arm holding her immobile. His gaze bespoke wicked promises. She felt his intentions in the anticipation that pierced her awareness.

His slight looks had deceived her. Beneath his lithe elegance he was taut and untamed, his sinewy frame chiseled with agile strength. What else did his disguise conceal? Better that she never know. She wouldn't see him after tonight, anyway.

He gripped her harder.

She did not resist.

He was relentless. The vanquisher with the virgin.

Perhaps he sensed that his kiss had unsteadied her. Perhaps he knew that she would sink to her knees if he released her now. She wasn't the first woman he'd conquered in a dark corner.

Knight-errant.

He had meant to possess her the moment that their eyes had caught.

His hand caressed her hip. Silently she insisted that he stop. But the words never came. This gentle stroking stole her will. And still she let him kiss her, excitement flooding her veins, pulsing deep inside.

He was not forcing her. But was this surrender? His kiss awakened a part of her she had always known existed.

Why did her sense of passion demand attention now, with this man?

Could she ignore this yearning, or was it already too late? A door opened before her. Was it light inside or a portal to endless dark?

"Let us take off these masks," he said softly.

She shook her head. "Not yet."

She didn't want to be reminded it was only an illusion, the pleasure they shared. It was a fleeting dalliance he would easily forget. To see him unmasked would only strengthen his imprint on her mind. She would forbid herself to think of him after tonight.

"Whatever you want," he whispered.

A sigh escaped her. She wanted more.

He ravished her mouth with unbearable sweetness. Then he bent his head to her throat. The yearning intensified. She wondered if he guessed how hard her heart was beating. Had she affected him like that, too? She hoped she had. Her body clung to his, scandalously close, close enough that she felt how strong, how male he was. He brushed a strand of sensual kisses from the rise of one shoulder to the other. She thought she might be melting from the inside out.

He kissed a trail to the soft cleavage that rose from her golden underbodice. She drew a breath. His fingers caught her hip harder, crushing her cloak, her gown, her skin. Belatedly she pulled to free herself. Her body trembled.

He grasped her hand, gathering her back against his heat.

"You promised," she whispered.

"You are safe."

"You said you would behave."

"Take my word on it," he said. "I am stretched on a rack of self-torture. Never have I denied my deepest nature as I am at this moment."

"Deny yourself, indeed."

"I am hanging by a thread," he said softly.

"I trust it is a strong one."

"It is not the strength of the thread that worries me," he explained wryly. "It is the power of the one holding it."

"You look powerful enough to survive a broken thread," she murmured, her lips twitching in a smile.

"Perhaps it is the breastplate. It adds inches to my shoulders."

Lily started to laugh. She had noticed strength in other areas of his body that she wouldn't dare mention. "There were several ladies at the party following your every gesture. Your disguise had nothing to do with it."

"Thank you," he said politely. "But I was paying attention only to you. And now I suppose I shall prove I'm a man of my word—unless you give me permission to—"

"Enough," she said, breathless with temptation, suddenly reluctant to escape the gauntleted arm that trapped her in this delicious tension.

"Enough," he agreed reluctantly, and exhaled, relaxing his grasp but not quite letting go. "As you say." He gave a shrug of resignation.

His mouth touched hers, flint to tinder, a farewell to sin unfulfilled. His black silky hair skimmed the bare contour of her shoulder. Even that accidental touch implied intimate pleasure. The tips of her breasts tightened as he released her from his warm embrace. She sighed, bereft of his disconcerting closeness, adrift in aching wonder. So this was how the duke had earned his acclaim.

Lily would like to believe that she meant more to him than just another conquest. She had never spent an evening like this and thought she never would again.

"It has to be his spell," she said, lifting her gaze accusingly to the dark figure of Sir Renwick Hexworthy poised above them. "'Conquer the night. Embrace what is right.' Isn't that the motto?"

The duke did not respond. No doubt he thought that she was rather silly for blaming a boxwood figure for inciting what could be explained as earthly passion between two strangers who had temporarily lost control of their senses.

Still, it did seem to Lily as if the evergreen Renwick's hand was pointing straight at her heart. Had the wand in his other hand moved? Had the wizard who sinned without conscience come to life to reproach her for kissing a duke who wasn't even part of the tales? She noticed that Lord Wickbury, the Earl of Everything Perfect, had not lifted a leaf to help her.

A leaf, for heaven's sake! She had been so swept up in the duke's kiss and the enchantment of *Wickbury*'s imaginary world that she was reading her future in the foliage. Her future as another man's wife.

She glanced at the duke in hesitation. He didn't seem the slightest bit interested in the topiary figures. He was looking at the feather that had drifted into the cleft of Lily's bodice. At this rate Chloe, wherever she was, would have no trouble tracing her cousin's location by the path of fallen plumes. The duke's hand reached out to rescue the stray feather from Lily's décolletage. A flush burnished her breasts with unbearable warmth.

"You—"

"You can't go back to the party looking like a . . . plucked goose," he interrupted, his brow lifting.

She studied him in dismay. "And you've got another feather stuck in your breastplate."

His gaze dropped in amusement. In one casual gesture, he pried loose the feather and slipped it inside his sleeve alongside the others he had collected. "Now I have several bookmarks to remember our kiss by. When I finish the next *Wickbury*—"

He broke off, the wicked guilt in his grin too much for Lily to forgive. "You misled me," she said, smiling tightly. "You don't know Lord Anonymous any better than I know the prince regent."

"That isn't true," he protested.

"I don't believe you."

"May Sir Renwick strike me down if I've misguided you."

Lily waited, hoping for a branch to fall, a hint of breeze, a timely act of God to stir the wand.

"Don't you feel foolish," he asked, folding his arms, "waiting for an evergreen to answer?"

"Not as foolish as I do for believing your intentions. All you wanted to do was lure me alone into this garden."

"That isn't completely true," he retorted. "I thought your cousin would have been here to spoil the moment."

"So did I," she confessed.

His roguish grin returned. "Then you admit that it was a moment never to be forgotten."

"Never to be repeated, you mean," she said with conviction.

"I wouldn't be too sure of that."

She shook her head in regret. "I have to hand it to you—your choice of Don Quixote as a disguise was inspired. You're clearly full of dreams that won't ever come true, and I doubt you've ever read a page of *Wickbury* in your life." Of course, neither had Jonathan, but at least he was honest about it.

He lowered his voice. "I've probably read those damn books more times than any other person in England."

She snorted. "Oh, really?" If that wasn't the most outrageous statement she had ever heard in her life. "Then you consider yourself an expert?"

He shrugged cautiously. "Expert? Fine. I suppose I am."

"Then how will Juliette break free now that Sir Renwick has abducted her?"

Samuel narrowed his eyes. "Wickbury will rescue her, I assume. Isn't that what a hero is supposed to do? Isn't that what he does in every book?"

Lily paused. The rattling of the iron gate distracted her. Chloe might be finally on the way, but she was too late for chaperone duty. "What if Juliette doesn't *want* to be rescued?" she asked quickly. "What if she was waiting for Sir Renwick to take physical possession of her all along?"

He frowned up at the two figures battling in the air.

"Why is it that every woman who has read *Wickbury* fancies herself half in love with the villain? A hero has to be chivalrous."

She eyed him meaningfully. "Not every man dressed as a knight acts like one."

"Lily!" Chloe called to her from the top of the sunken parterre. "There you are! I went around the wrong way."

A cynical smile creased Samuel's cheeks. "So you're saying that you *liked* the abduction scene? You didn't think that Sir Renwick should have been hunted down for spiriting Juliette off in his carriage?"

"It was about time," she whispered. "Now she can redeem him."

"He's irredeemable."

"How do you know?" she challenged.

"Because I know his type. It's clear to me that he cares for nothing but power and won't change for anyone."

Lily edged around him. "It's clear to me that while you support the arts, you have no artistic sympathy in your soul."

He looked pleased. "Does it really show?"

"I love Sir Renwick," she said defiantly. "Next to him, Lord Wickbury looks like a twit."

The viscountess strode into view before he could respond. Which was a good thing, too. Lily had learned a lesson tonight—she wasn't as sophisticated as she thought she was. To be fair, though, she had never come up against a man as bone-deep charming as the duke.

If she had lingered in his company long enough, he might have persuaded her to do more than kiss him. He might even have persuaded her to join the league of Lord Wickbury's followers, instead of the villain she loved.

It was a good thing that she would soon be standing beside Jonathan at the altar. There were years ahead to ponder what she had escaped tonight. Or what she might have missed.

Chapter 9

*T*he viscountess studied Lily in concern. "Forgive me for taking so long. You *were* all right?"

"I was fine."

Chloe glanced back at the duke, who ambled up the path behind them, slowing to admire a yew sculpture here and there.

"We never made it to the grotto," Lily whispered.

"The grotto!" Chloe shot the duke a look of alarm over her shoulder. "Well, then I'm glad I hurried to find you. A grotto is the perfect place for a tryst."

"You took forever," Lily teased her.

"I couldn't get away," Chloe complained softly. "Besides, I didn't think there was any harm in letting the duke enchant you for a minute or so. Or are you a siren-in-waiting whose innocent looks mislead?"

"Do you know how boring it is to live in Tissington?"

"Indeed, I do. Boredom has led a lady into more than one affair she should have avoided."

They came to the gate, which Samuel made a point of locking behind them. Suddenly Lily noticed four footmen stationed above the garden wall. It was almost as if they had been told to stay out of view.

"They weren't there before," she remarked over her shoulder to the duke.

He smiled knowingly.

Chloe broke formation at the courtyard garden to take stock of Lily in the moonlight. "Well, aside from a few bedraggled feathers, you're none the worse for your walk."

The duke grinned at her, again the guileless chevalier. "And me?"

Chloe laughed. "You can take care of yourself. Now stay with me, Lily. We will enter from the direction of the cloakroom together." She curtsied as an afterthought. "Good luck with your charities, Your Grace."

His gaze followed Lily's retreating figure. "The same to you."

He lost sight of Lily when she entered the gold salon for the midnight unmasking. A gentleman wearing a papier-mâché crown had already greeted her and brought her a glass of lemonade, chatting with his head to hers as if he knew her well. Samuel suppressed a flare of resentment. Lily and the other man seemed warm toward each other, but not like a pair of lovers. Samuel could not imagine a gentleman escorting her to a party and leaving her alone for even a minute with the viscountess as guard. A brother or another cousin? Samuel debated staying for the official tour of the garden to find out. But suddenly he changed his mind.

He was a man who followed his instincts, and instinct presented a new plan that he decided couldn't wait. The gentleman hovering over Lily had risen unexpectedly, crossed the salon, and was barreling through the hall, knocking his shoulder against Samuel's lance.

"My pardon." Samuel nodded. "I trust I didn't hurt you."

The man gave an unkingly grunt. "I'm tougher than that. Mind you, you could have taken out my eyes."

"King Lear?"

"Who?"

"Your costume?"

"Yes, but please don't ask me to quote any lines."

Samuel smiled inwardly, staring past the friendly gentleman into the salon. Lily had turned to glance into the hall. When she noticed the two men talking, she hastily looked away. Maybe she was afraid Samuel would reveal her garden escapade to her relation.

"I tell you what," Samuel said in a confidential tone. "There is a lady I am suddenly enamored of, and I might lose her if I don't take action tonight to state my intentions."

The huskier man grinned. "You'll lose her if you poke her with your lance. And that shield—ye gods.

You might have cleaned it up for the party. Take my advice and hand them off to a footman. You'll never win any prizes dressed like a shabby knight."

"Aren't you competing in the midnight unmasking?" Not that Samuel gave a damn, but it never hurt to make an ally when one could.

"I have a card game going, and I might lose my throne if I can't find a friend to borrow a little cash from. I wasn't prepared to bet this heavily."

"A card game."

There was a country gullibility about this man, an innocence that evil would feed on and consume. A gentleman with any guile or romantic understanding would have never left Lily alone with the wolves of London—predators as dangerous to maidenly virtue as their fairy-tale prototypes.

He brought out Samuel's ever-present desire to protect, to enlighten before it was too late. "Do you cheat when you play?"

"Good heavens, sir, I would die before taking a crooked pence."

"But you do know that there are professional players who do?"

"Not in a house like this."

His naïveté pained Samuel. "Why not?"

"Everyone invited is well-off, or has family who is. There's no need to cheat."

Samuel stared at him, feeling his familiar obligation

to warn the uninitiated of what lay ahead. "You can't trust everyone, especially at a party like this."

"But these are the cream of the crop, educated ladies and gentlemen, refined—"

Samuel could not bear it. "Certain sensibilities are refined. Others are barbaric. And if I may I point out, most guests are in disguise."

"It's a masquerade," the man said, shaking his head as if Samuel were the person in need of instruction.

"Just remember that."

"Thank you, sir. You've a good heart to point out pitfalls that I could indeed have missed."

Samuel didn't have the patience for gambling himself, but if this genial enough fellow was related to Lily, it was to Samuel's benefit to do him a favor. "I have to leave the party earlier than expected, but since I almost ran you through with my lance, I want to make amends."

"It's all right. I wasn't watching where I was going."

"Please, allow me." Samuel held out the lance to him like a peace offering. The taller man took it, looking puzzled. "Take this to Lord Philbert. He is our host, in case you do not know him personally. Instruct him that you are to play the night away, on my account."

The gentleman broke into an appreciative grin. "I am Captain Jonathan Grace. May I have the honor of your name, sir?"

"Don Quixote, the Ingenious." Samuel nodded cordially. "Do watch your hand. There are some players in London who will do anything to win. You really have to be careful about the company you keep. As I said, not everyone is as trustworthy as you and me."

Lily had lost sight of her duke through the opened doors. It wasn't bad enough of her to have let him kiss her once or twice. Now that their little indiscretion was definitely over, she was still hoping for another look at him. And then Jonathan walked right into the duke's lance. She had giggled so openly as she watched the two men disengage that Chloe had abandoned her husband abruptly and returned to Lily's side. She was worse than wicked.

"I think someone has enjoyed herself far too much for one evening."

"Does it show?" Lily whispered, her eyes dancing in delight.

"It's a good thing you're getting married in a month," Chloe said good-naturedly. "Your Boscastle instincts for trouble are beginning to bloom."

Lily feigned an indignant laugh. "Next you'll be warning the duke about me."

"I wonder." Chloe glanced at the guests drifting into the salon. "Was your curiosity satisfied? Or merely whetted?"

"I assume you're referring to *Wickbury*."

"I assume the duke kissed you."

Lily lifted her fan to hide a guilty smile. A kiss as potent as the duke's would last her a lifetime. Of course, it would have to. She didn't imagine her future with Jonathan held the promise of that much passion. They were both so practical, but then perhaps those kinds of feelings would come for them with time. The duke had either been born with a natural talent for seduction or he had worked to perfect his skill.

Either way, she had savored every sinful moment of his company. And it was more than his kisses that had unbalanced her, she realized in surprise, now that the spell was starting to wear off.

Chloe gave her an impulsive hug. "I would be a liar if I told you that I don't understand. And, from the look on Gravenhurst's face when I found you both in the garden, I think that this attraction is more than mutual. It's a very good thing that you are going to be married to your captain soon."

Lily pursed her lips. "Do you think the duke might abduct me before then?"

Chloe sighed, pulling a face. "I suppose that we could hope. And don't you dare tell your parents I said that. Where is your captain, anyway? He's going to miss your transformation."

Lily smiled, only half listening. Footmen were discreetly snuffing out the brightest candles to dramatize the contest. The smoky glow enhanced the anticipation mounting in the salon. Lily wondered whether the winners had been chosen in advance. It didn't matter, she realized guiltily. She'd been given a private tour of *Wickbury*. And . . . was the duke escorting another lady through the garden while she stood here, her feathers wilting? It was highly likely.

"I asked you where he was," Chloe said in distress.

Lily shook off her wayward thoughts. "You saw him the last time— Oh, you mean Jonathan. He's playing cards."

"My goodness, Lily, no wonder you let the duke lure you astray. I had no idea you were marrying a gambler."

"He's no more a gambler than I am impure," Lily said defensively. "He made a few friends I do not care for—"

"And you did the same." Chloe slipped her arm around Lily's waist. "Everyone deserves at least one wicked evening in London. As long as it ends here, no one will ever be the wiser."

Chapter 10

*B*y eleven thirty that evening both the Duke of Gravenhurst and his bestselling counterpart, that corrupter of morality, had entered into a pact to join forces for one purpose: to plot out and enact the perfect courtship, marriage, and seduction of the woman who had captured their hearts.

Their merged identities had recognized the ideal match when they found her.

Of course, choosing a wife wasn't exactly like writing one of the dark books that Lily Boscastle and other astute readers like her devoured. A duke and his true-life bride could be wildly in love one day and despise each other the next. They might come to a civilized arrangement to lead separate lives, meeting amicably on holidays if there were children involved. But Samuel would never be able to resort to any literary devices that Lord Anonymous employed to end their union.

The duke would never take a vow he could not

keep. Lord Anonymous's characters broke their word as it suited their plot. But neither of them had found a happy ending when it came to any lasting romance. The duke was said to favor wellborn ladies who understood their proper place. According to what little was reported of him, the author of *The Wickbury Tales* was partial to earthy women of all classes who understood that impropriety should take place whenever both parties felt the urge.

The truth as Samuel perceived it fell somewhere in the center of these speculations. This was, in fact, the first time that nobleman and novelist had agreed on a desirable bride. A lady of wit, sensuality, and the perfect touch of wicked imperfection. The duke and Lord Anonymous wanted Lily Boscastle very much.

And while the Boscastle family was notorious for scandal, its ancient bloodlines were superior and undisputed. A duke could make a worse choice for a wife.

Was there any harm in initiating a courtship? Would Lily's parents refuse a peer as a serious suitor? Unfortunately, there *was* the matter of Samuel's alarming reputation. How the hell was he to undo the damage he had carefully inflicted on his own name? And do so before another gentleman took Lily Boscastle off the market?

She had proved she wasn't as innocent as she looked. But she wasn't as sophisticated as she thought she was, either. A flirtation in the garden did not make her a fallen woman. But with the right man, or the wrong one, which understandably her family would consider Samuel to be, her potential to play the temptress was intriguing to contemplate.

He had been enraged the first time he had come upon one of the pamphlets bearing his name that littered the streets. Really, the bedroom acts attributed to him were impossible. He was sure he had never sired a son and daughter in two counties on the same night, and all this nonsense might have been merely amusing had a particularly salubrious piece not been printed on the day he was to address the House of Lords concerning the rising cost of bread. To his astonishment that measure received more support than any of his prior efforts. Apparently, even the members of Parliament listened more attentively to a legendary scoundrel who could swive several wenches at a time than a person who gave a thoughtful speech.

Samuel could have protested his notoriety and attempted to protect his name. But he soon perceived that the false scandals he generated in London diverted attention from his private life. For some odd reason a duke who slept with dozens of women commanded the respect of his peers. And while he may not have been physically capable of pleasuring as many ladies as the papers reported, the few who had enjoyed his company had yet to utter any complaints.

So it was that he discovered the value of sensation

and began instructing his secretary to submit regular tidbits of gossip to Fleet Street, which, he let slip, came from a member of the duke's household.

He could only hope that Lily's country family did not keep up with the popular press.

He returned to his Curzon Street residence in Mayfair and sent for his solicitor, Mr. Benjamin Thurber, before bothering to remove his costume. Mr. Thurber arrived within the hour, his thick white hair ruffled as if he'd just pulled off his nightcap.

"Good evening to you, Gravenhurst," he said in obvious annoyance. "Do you have any notion what time it is?"

Samuel looked up at the clock on the mantel. "One thirty in the morning."

"That is when those of us who keep proper hours are sound asleep. I hope there is a good reason for dragging me out of bed. I am due in court in the morning. What is so blasted important that it cannot wait?"

"I met a woman."

Mr. Thurber clapped his gnarled hands to his eyes. "What have you done to her? Does she have counsel in London? Who is it?"

"I haven't done anything to her," Samuel said in irritation. "You know me better than that."

"Is she another harlot claiming a paternity case?"

"Her name is Lily Boscastle, and I want to ask permission to formally court her with marriage in mind. And you, of all people, know that my fictional indiscretions outnumber those in which I've actually indulged."

The solicitor lowered his hands. "How long have you known her?"

"It might have been years. We were at ease the instant that we—"

"You didn't share your secret with her, did you?" the solicitor broke in, business now foremost on his mind.

"I am infatuated, not insane."

"I didn't realize there was a difference." He scrubbed his stiff white whiskers. "Your Grace is incorrigible."

Samuel waited several moments for the lawyer to enact his usual ritual of pacing before the fire and sighing several times before he settled his bulk comfortably in his chair. He braced himself for the well-deserved lecture.

Didn't Samuel realize that he was acting on impulse, and that while acts of romantic aggression made for compelling fiction, not even a duke could command the world with a slash of his quill without suffering the consequences?

Did Samuel ever consider the cost of his ideals?

Did he care that booksellers and humble clerks depended on him for their bread?

Thereupon, Samuel reminded his solicitor that he retained him for legal matters, not grandfatherly advice.

Mr. Thurber threw up his hands in defeat. "What if you and this young Venus do not suit?"

"I have thought of that. Is there no way to negotiate a contract that allows either party to withdraw from the courtship in a manner that will not damage her name?" The implication being that nothing could tarnish Samuel's.

"One can negotiate anything if the price is mutually pleasing. The Boscastle family is a good strain, by the way, if prone to scandal."

"So I understand."

"It does occur to Your Grace that the young lady's family might have other plans for her future?" the solicitor ventured one last time.

Samuel glowered at him. He realized he could be hardheaded and difficult to reason with, but that was how he lived his life, and, aside from a childhood tragedy, he had done well for himself. "As of midnight the lady was accompanied by only her chaperone, and a man I assume to be a naive relation. This was her first party in London."

"One would think it was your first party, too," Mr. Thurber said tartly.

"Give me a little credit for my ability to recognize a pearl in endless miles of sand."

"A pearl, is she?" The solicitor shook his head in surrender. "Meeting the lady of your dreams was bound to happen sooner or later, but as it has waited this long, I don't see how another day could hurt."

"Absolutely not. I will not wait. That would signify indecision on my part."

"Give me until late morning to have my clerk draw up and deliver the papers for your approval."

Samuel grinned in gratitude, extending his arm to help the older man from the chair. "I would like her to receive the documents as soon as possible. Her family is staying with Viscount Stratfield. I do not know the address."

"At least you know her name." The solicitor bowed, frowning closely at Samuel as if he had just noticed his party costume. "Don Quixote, isn't it? I hope that is not prophetic. Congratulations, Your Grace."

Congratulations.

Could it be that easy? Could a man choose the course of his life and expect everything else around him would fall into place? Samuel knew better than that. Life had played with him ever since he could remember. A lady's heart was not a pawn.

But his deepest feelings had never failed him. He had written for years about love, death, loss, and betrayal. His characters were often felled by their lethal flaws and performed craven deeds. His most popular heroine, Juliette Mannering, was an unconventional lady who had escaped a convent and an arranged marriage.

I love Sir Renwick. Next to him, Lord Wickbury looks like a twit.

Samuel circled his desk, deliberately not looking at the pen and stack of blank papers that was meant to be the last chapter. He had corrected every proof he could find at least ten times before facing what needed to be done. Tonight.

The damned installment would not write itself. Perhaps he should leave the characters hanging in unresolved conflict. Lord Anonymous had not promised a perfect ending. He had a contractual obligation to Philbert, which as a gentleman he would satisfy, but was he obligated to repeat the same tiresome plot? He had a bond with his readers, a mystical connection that he did not understand but tried his utmost to keep unbroken. But neither monetary reward nor the admiration of strangers had ever motivated him to pen a single page.

He approached his desk, frowning.

He preferred working at home in Dartmoor, even if over the years he had learned that his writing skill was not limited to perfect location or circumstance. He often resisted his revisions until the last moment. Once the words started to flow, however, he drifted into another place and time. His thoughts calmed. Something inside him rose above the clamor of all else. His characters demanded that he listen.

I love Sir Renwick.

Why? Why did women adore such an unmerciful sod?

Why was Juliette Mannering attracted to a malevolent wizard who had abducted her? A murderer. A necromancer and thoroughly nasty son of a bitch who had killed his own sister to please Satan and then thought he could raise her from the grave.

Would Juliette triumph against Sir Renwick's advances?

"Excuse me . . . Your Grace?"

Samuel stared absentmindedly at the long-faced man in silver-embroidered black satin livery who appeared in the door. "Your Grace?" the man said again.

Samuel grunted as his butler glanced surreptitiously at the tidy desktop before training his features into a mask of pleasant impassivity. Why did everyone who knew Samuel sense when he was procrastinating? Bickerstaff would never say a word, but presumably he had noticed the blank pages. He was a former bank clerk whose employer had been caught embezzling funds before Samuel had rescued him from debtor's prison. He had an eye for detail that all his deference could not mask.

"Did I ring for you?" Samuel asked in a perplexed voice.

"You did not leave instructions for the carriage to be brought in for the night. Will Your Grace be returning to the masquerade?"

Samuel wavered. "I'm going to work. The book will be done by morning."

"In that case, I will have the carriage packed for Your Grace. The proofs are wrapped in oilcloth. The books you requested on raising the dead shall be shipped on the morrow."

"Excellent," Samuel said, not having heard a single word.

"We should be ready to leave at daybreak, Your Grace."

Samuel frowned. "Hang on, Bickerstaff. I think I forgot to tell you that our plans have changed. We will be staying in London indefinitely."

"But the new book—"

"Never mind that. I have to finish the last one. I can work here, can't I?"

"Your Grace can work in the middle of a military parade. But Your Grace does complain of the carts going over the cobbles, and the ladies who call at all hours."

"I will ignore the carts and the tarts."

Bickerstaff chuckled. "What about the opera singer who wished for a private audience? Shall I message her that you have changed your mind?"

"No. Her voice gives me the spleen."

"I will bring coffee then, Your Grace."

He regretted again that he hadn't stayed to view Lily revealing herself to be a princess. She was comely enough in her fairy-tale disguise without drawing more attention to her charm. Suddenly he was jealous of the other guests at the party who would watch her shed her feathers. And he was jealous of Jacob and Wilhelm Grimm, because she loved their clever writing, and here Samuel sat, his book unfinished, his thoughts chasing one another's tails like a nest of snakes.

But he could forgive the German brothers anything

for the unwitting part they had played in what he assumed would be his own storybook ending. He *would* complete the book tonight, and by this time tomorrow he hoped to be with her again. Perhaps their interlude tonight would spark the inspiration that had eluded him.

Perhaps before the next *Wickbury Tales* saw print, he would even divulge his identity to Lily. Aside from her sweet, kissable mouth and penchant for mischief, she had a delightful mind and warm honesty that he admired in a woman. And while what Philbert had said was true, that she wasn't the type that usually attracted Samuel, he had never been this attracted before. So maybe that had been Samuel's problem all along. He had been associating with the wrong kind of women.

Which, of course, brought him back to his immediate problem.

Philbert.

The final chapter of the seventh *Wickbury* book.

The chapter that Samuel had been revising for eternity. The ending that refused to be written.

Perhaps he needed to take off his costume. Being able to breathe might help his brain. He struggled out of his absurd breastplate, resisting the temptation to run upstairs and change from the tunic he wore underneath into a comfortable linen shirt and pantaloons.

But then a trio of feathers drifted to the floor from the padded sleeve of his costume. He picked them up and sat down at the desk, intrigued.

Two white. One brown.

Two innocents and a hawk. Why was a hawk considered bad? It had to eat. It raised young. Few people knew that an ordinary sparrow cannibalized other birds. What if the hawk became the hero?

He arranged the feathers in a simple pattern across the blotter.

One white. The brown in the middle. The other white at the end.

Lord Wickbury. Sir Renwick Hexworthy. Lady Juliette Mannering.

What if he changed the pattern? Would his readers forgive him? What if, during this last scene, Lord Wickbury discovered his own capacity for darkness? Would Juliette decide that he needed redemption more than his vile-hearted half brother?

Brown. White. White.

There could be only two left by the last page.

Chapter 11

$\mathcal{L}$ily stirred, opening her eyes as the carriage drew to a halt. She felt the warm shoulder she had been using as a bolster shift. "Wake up," Chloe said, gently pushing her into an upright position. "We're home."

Lily glanced in embarrassment at the handsome dark-haired viscount who sat opposite them. "London exhausts me, too, Lily," he said in sympathy.

Lily wanted to protest that she was more exhilarated than exhausted, that she hadn't been ready to leave the party. But her physical appearance argued otherwise.

Her golden gown fell in ruinous wrinkles. Her hair curled wildly from the dampness of an after-breakfast boat ride on the river. Still clutched in her palm was a twig she had stolen from the garden during the official tour and the emerald brooch she had been awarded at the masquerade for Finest Fairy-Tale Princess in the Land.

"The brooch is beautiful," Chloe commented, peering down to admire the antique setting. "I didn't see it properly last night, but look how it catches the light. It's a lovely token of your first party in London."

"Your captain seemed to have enjoyed himself as well," Dominic, Chloe's husband, said in amusement. "He and his friends were burning up the tables, from what I hear."

Chloe's smooth forehead wrinkled in a reproachful frown. "It was his first genuine party, too, and he's allowed his bit of fun. At least he covered his losses."

Lily yawned. She yearned for a hot bath and a hundred more hours or so of sleep. "His losses couldn't have been that large. He didn't have much to gamble with." Which meant that Lily would have to learn to economize as his wife. Mr. and Mrs. Grace would be well-off but never wealthy.

"Rich or poor," Chloe said, covering her own yawn behind her hand, "I've never heard anyone applaud as loudly as he did when you won your prize."

"From the door," Lily said wryly. "I think he remembered only at the last moment that he was supposed to be with me during the contest. And then he disappeared again."

"At least he remembered to announce your engagement," Dominic said, as if it were his duty to defend his own sex. "And he was very attentive to you during breakfast."

Chloe gave Lily a covert smile. "I don't think Lily lacked attention during the masquerade."

"Did I miss something at the party?" Dominic asked cautiously, glancing from one lady to the other.

Lily leaned toward the door, pretending she had no idea what either of them meant. A footman unfolded the carriage steps from the sidewalk. She gathered up her crumpled skirts, barely feeling the brooch pin pricking her palm. It was a beautiful piece, and she would treasure it, although secretly not as much as the boxwood sprig that had formed part of Sir Renwick Hexworthy's wand. The sculpture had been virtually denuded during the garden tour by the other lady guests who had wanted a tiny piece of *Wickbury* magic to remember the evening by.

Whenever Lily looked at it, of course, she would think of the duke's wicked kiss and not an evergreen clipping. Perhaps she would even follow his suggestion and use it as a bookmark. It made her smile to think of the scoundrel expecting her to believe he would keep her feathers as a sentiment. An inventive approach to seduction, she had to admit. How many ladies had succumbed to his illicit charm?

"My goodness, Lily!" Chloe's chagrined voice interrupted her thoughts. "You have grass stains on your satin slippers, and they will never come off. And those aren't leaves on your gloves, I hope. Dear me, I thought I was wayward before I married Dominic."

Dominic cast Lily a confidential look. "She hasn't

changed, that I've noticed. And I don't know why she's going on about a twig. There's a garden of the things growing right on the sidewalk."

The three of them glanced around in unison as a pair of footmen opened the carriage door. The footmen stepped back. A breathless delivery boy darted forward. A smudge of yellow pollen glistened on his chin. In his arms, looking a little bruised from an apparent jaunt through the bustling streets, lay three dozen golden hothouse lilies looped in an enormous white silk bow.

Dominic cleared his throat. "Lily's young gentleman must have come into a fortune at the tables. That is quite the gesture, considering we saw him less than an hour ago."

Chloe looked suspiciously at Lily.

Lily slipped innocently out the door.

"Did I miss something?" Dominic asked again, glancing from Lily to his wife.

Chloe raised one sleek eyebrow. "No, dear one. But it is suddenly clear that I did."

Lily took the bouquet and cradled the flowers in her arms while Dominic tipped the delivery boy. "They're gorgeous," she said, her fatigue suddenly dissipating. "But I don't see a card. Whom are they from?"

The boy straightened his shoulders. "The sender wishes to remain anonymous, miss."

She hid a smile. "Can't you even give me a little hint?"

"Viscount Stratfield will tip you extra for another tidbit," Chloe offered.

The boy wavered. "No—wait. He did say to offer his congratulations, miss."

Chloe nodded. "On her engagement?"

"Not that I recall," the boy said, backing around Dominic. "It was something about a princess taking a prize. I hope you enjoy 'em."

Chloe studied his retreating figure. "Your admirer obviously hasn't heard about your engagement."

"Or doesn't let a little thing like another man stand in seduction's way," Dominic mused.

"I should send them back, shouldn't I?" Lily asked, inhaling the elusive scent.

Dominic shrugged. "What for? They'll be no use to him wilted. Just don't tell Jonathan whom they came from."

"But we don't know *who* he is," Lily mused, brightening. "He didn't give me a name."

Chapter 12

The Wickbury Tales

BOOK SEVEN
CHAPTER LAST,
VERSION FORTY-SIX

"Are you going to untie me?" Juliette asked from the depths of the tavern bed where Sir Renwick had held her captive for the past three days. Except when a frightened maidservant darted into the chamber to tend Juliette's personal needs, she had not been allowed the freedom to move.

Sir Renwick stared at her in an agony of mistrust, longing, and self-denial. "If I untie you, my lady, it will not be so that you may warn Wickbury he is walking into a trap. It will be to make you mine."

"All the forces in the world cannot change what I feel."

"Not even if I changed for you?" He bent over her, careful to keep his disfigured face hidden in the darkness. Her wrists strained against the bindings, marking her skin. "We do not have to stay in Wickbury. I have discovered a way to visit other worlds. There is a magic portal on the moor that only I have the power to open. We will share immortality—"

"Immorality is what you mean. If you believe that you will live forever, you are not only the essence of all that is evil, but insane."

"You thought I was a brilliant man once."

"Once," she said, her voice deep with scorn.

Now her eyes revealed another reality.

Pity, determination, revulsion. Yes, once, so long ago it felt like a dream, she had claimed to love him. She had promised she would stay with him forever.

"Juliette," he said desperately. "I have killed men to impress you with my power. I can give you anything you desire."

He bent his head and pressed his mouth to hers. The wind suddenly rose up and blew open the door to the timber-galleried balcony. Juliette shivered, pushing back against the pillows. Had he finally broken her resistance? Did she understand his soul-hunger for her?

> "He's going to die unless you decide otherwise."
>
> "Then let me see him alone first."
>
> "You'll never come back to me if I do, Juliette,"
> he whispered, his body lowering to hers. "But per-
> haps if I prove to you how much I love you, you
> will not want to escape again."

Samuel blinked. The characters disappeared like ac-
tors darting into the wings to await their next scene. Sir
Renwick, he thought wryly, must be hiding in the curtains with a very erect wand. Wickbury was probably
practicing more than his lines with Juliette.

Samuel wondered what his characters got up to
when he wasn't struggling to capture his glimpses
into their lives on paper. What if Juliette actually
loved both men? The public would not forgive her. It
would seem to be a betrayal of her sex. What if she
left them both for a character whom Samuel hadn't yet
invented? Was Wickbury going to rush into that bedroom at the last minute to save her from the wizard's
ravishment?

What if Wickbury burst in and discovered that
Juliette . . .

He heard a carriage roll up outside. The wheels
splashed over wet cobbles. Rain. There hadn't been a
cloud in the sky last night. Had Lily's parents already
discussed his proposal of courtship and sent their response? That was fast. He thought it was a good sign.
Presumably one's daughter did not land a duke every

day. He had to hope that they were swayed enough by his title to ignore his scurrilous press.

A soft rap sounded at the door. "Yes. Come in. Come in."

It was his butler, escorting an erect-shouldered gentleman in a short wool cape into the room. "Coffee and breakfast, Your Grace?"

"Nothing for me," the solicitor said, removing a paper from his leather portfolio. His eyes evaded Samuel's. Right away Samuel guessed that something was wrong.

"That's a gossip sheet," he said in contempt. "Please don't tell me Lily's parents produced *that* when you explained my intentions. And if so, I trust you defended me."

"I did not meet her family, Your Grace."

Samuel's eyes blazed. *"What?"*

"I drew up the papers. They required deep thought. I had to research and contemplate—"

"Do you require my signature?"

"No, Your Grace," the solicitor said heavily. "Before we proceed, I think you ought to read the morning's edition."

"I am not interested in what some arsehole has printed about me now. Especially when I'm probably the arsehole who wrote it in the first place."

"Your Grace, please."

Samuel snorted, taking the paper to the window to read the rain-smeared print. He skipped over the description of Lord Philbert's literary masquerade, the list of famous guests, their reaction to the garden tour. He read only a few lines of "Gravenhurst's Latest Conquests." As usual it contained an inaccurate mishmash of his association with politicians and prostitutes.

But then a name mentioned in the final paragraph describing the masquerade gripped his attention.

Even the threat of rain did not dampen one couple's romantic intentions. After a chilly boat ride and sumptuous breakfast, Captain Jonathan Grace of Derbyshire announced that he and his beautiful if bedraggled princess, Miss Lily Boscastle, a country relation of the London line, would be married in a month in the private Park Lane chapel of Grayson Boscastle, the fifth Marquess of Sedgecroft.

The editors of this piece wish to congratulate the handsome couple, even if we are a little disappointed that the season will pass without another Boscastle scandal to divert us.

"What a chowderhead I was," Samuel muttered. "She eclipsed every other lady at the party. Her eyes glowed with magic, like a genie's lamp. I should have bloody well realized that she was glowing for another master."

The solicitor looked embarrassed. "A lady is hardly a lamp, Your Grace, though one could argue that they often refuse to light one moment and flare like a comet in the next."

"True enough," Samuel murmured, walking back to his desk.

"A masquerade is meant to deceive. We play a game for a few hours. We become who we wish to be or who we hope to hide during our common hours. Take Your Grace, for example. You are not Don Quixote, for all your creative powers. You lean to the whimsical, it is true, but I am thankful I've never seen you tilt at windmills."

Until now, he meant to say.

Samuel frowned. "I'm all right, sir. I will survive a rejection."

"Your Grace has his pick of more ladies than any gentleman I know. And Lord Anonymous double that. Together, well, you are a man to be envied."

"Yes." He stared down at the page he'd written, slipping on a pair of spectacles that instantly settled against the bump on his aquiline nose.

"What a load of shit," he said.

"Time will heal the small wound to Your Grace's heart. You will meet another lady. Indeed, you cannot avoid them."

"I was talking about the last chapter that is due by noon today, not your heartwarming speech."

"That's the spirit," the solicitor said. "Work will make you forget Miss . . . I can't even remember her name myself. Needless to say, I did not want to approach her family before consulting you. There would be legalities involved in breaking her engagement. The embarrassment of a breach-of-promise suit. I assume you do not wish to pursue her under these circumstances. Shall I have these contracts destroyed?"

Samuel looked up in astonishment, laughing quietly. "Why lose all that dedicated work? You never know when it might come in useful. I am, as everyone tells me, in need of a wife."

The solicitor's eyes widened in horror. "Your Grace is not contemplating stealing a bride, a *Boscastle* bride, from her family chapel? In Mayfair? These are not medieval days, when a duke has the right to—"

Samuel cut him off. "Do I seem like a man capable of abducting a bride?"

"I don't think I have ever done much study on the subject. But I am afraid to say—"

"Keep the documents with my others. And keep an eye, a close eye, on Miss Boscastle's affairs while I am away. I wish to be apprised of every detail of her life. If that means hiring an investigator, a Fleet Street informant, or a St. Giles tough, then do so. I will pay."

"You are returning to Dartmoor?"

"Of course. I need quiet to work."

"Your Grace really has finished *Wickbury* then?" the solicitor cautiously inquired, clearly eager to change the subject. And to escape. From the corner of his eye Samuel saw him rise and sidle to the door.

"Do you know what I'm going to do with the book?" he asked idly.

"Do not burn it, Your Grace. I beg you. Philbert begs you. Your creditors beg you. Talk to him first."

Samuel smiled dryly. "I am merely changing the hero into the villain, and vice versa."

The solicitor stared. "What about Lady Juliette?"

"Her fate is still in my hands."

He swallowed. "Well, let those hands be kind. She is a controversial but widely admired character. My daughter is very fond of her. We do not want to upset the little princess."

"Didn't she turn thirty last month?"

"Twenty-nine, Your Grace. And still looking for her prince."

"Ah. Well, good day, sir. I shall expect a regular report."

"I can't imagine why," the solicitor muttered, bowing before he made a hurried exit.

Neither could Samuel.

It was just one of the feelings he followed, the intuition that drove him, and he understood it no better than anyone else. Was it possible to plot a path to the altar as carefully as he did a novel? An obstacle in the beginning. Victory in the last chapter. Passion burning up the pages. Wasn't it always the middle of the story, the overcoming, that gave the author a fit?

No matter.

Samuel was going to finish his book and deliver it to Philbert before another day passed.

Lord Philbert had just settled in bed with a cigar and glass of port, as oblivious to his wife's complaints as he was to the rain slashing at the windows. A bad-tempered spaniel snuggled between them. He had locked the bedchamber door to ensure that none of his three grandchildren could burst in to ruin a heart-stopping climax.

A fictional one, that was.

Lord Philbert was reading the long-awaited last chapter of the seventh *Wickbury* book. His wife was reading the morning paper, commenting on one indiscretion or another, until he finally put down the manuscript and looked at her. Neither of them had slept since the party.

"Do you mind?" he asked in annoyance.

"Not at all," she said, peering at the manuscript on his lap. "It's very good."

His brow shot up. "How do you know?"

"I read it as soon as it arrived." She smiled knowingly at him over her paper. "It's the best ending he's written, utterly depraved and brilliantly inspired. I never saw it coming. I never dreamt that Sir Renwick would—"

Her voice droned on. He didn't listen to another word. He put out his cigar and read the final page. In fact, he read it five times over until he realized it wasn't going to change. Then he closed his eyes and clutched his head in his hands. The manuscript spilled across the bed.

"Dear God. Dear, dear God. We are ruined. What has come over him? I think he's gone mad."

"Mad or not," his wife said with a deep sigh, "he's a lovely man."

"The villain is *not* allowed to win in the end. It's against the rules. Lady Juliette cannot give herself to a wizard just because he waves his wand at her."

His wife yawned, sent him a disparaging look, and thumped onto her side. "I'd have given myself to him from the start if he had asked. They don't call him Longwand for nothing."

"Longwand," Philbert muttered in contempt. "I should never have allowed that offensive title to slip past my eye in the first place."

"You let Wickbury's Broadsword slip in, too," she reminded him.

"It's all well and good for him to hide behind anonymity. He could make me the laughingstock of the publishing world."

"He's made you rich, Aramis. Do not tell me you are ashamed of his work. I shall not stand for it."

"I never said anything of the sort." He blew out a loud breath, then took another. "The series cannot end like this—that is all. He will have to redo the entire chapter."

Lady Philbert snorted into her pillow. "Says who? I don't want to read the same story over and over."

"Lady Juliette promised to marry Wickbury, you silly—"

She sat up. He shut up.

"Unlike your wife, Gravenhurst can put all the characters he has created out of their misery," she said pleasantly. "Do remember what Lord Anonymous warns us in all his author's notes: 'Read as late into the night as you like. But snuff out the candles before you go to sleep. We would not want you to wake up dead.'"

Chapter 13

*H*er wedding day drew nearer, and Lily was swept by her female relatives into her nuptial plans. Her family arrived from Derbyshire, her mother, father, and brother sharing the strangers' suite at Dominic's town house. She was disappointed that her good-hearted German great-aunt, who shared her fondness for fairy stories, felt too rheumatic to attend the ceremony.

Lily's bridal gown had been designed by the Marchioness of Sedgecroft's French dressmaker, and she almost died when she saw the bill. Its pearl-encrusted cream brocade lace weighed Lily down like a coat of armor. The heart-shaped white silk bodice exposed much more of her bosom than the fashion plate had shown.

"You won't be able to run from your husband on your wedding night even if you want to," Chloe remarked, sitting at the dressing table while seamstresses, cousins, and two lady's maids discussed the proportion of Lily's veil to her bridal train and the height of her white silk heels.

"Two weeks," Chloe said with a delighted grin. "Everyone is coming for the wedding, Lily. Even relatives I don't know. Wait until you meet my sister Emma, though. She's the commander-in-chief of weddings. She won't let you eat a prawn without permission."

"I hope she isn't arriving tonight." Lily twisted around at the waist, eliciting cries of protest from the circle of apprentices adjusting her hem so that only an enticing wedge of heel showed. "Lord Kirkham and his stepmother are taking Jonathan and me to a play tonight."

Chloe narrowed her eyes. "Isn't his stepmother the same age as you?"

"I've never asked. Does it matter?"

"Only to a play?"

Lily suddenly noticed that the entire room had grown still. "Would you like to come?" she asked, hoping that Chloe would refuse.

Which she did.

And Lily would later wonder how different everything would have been if *she* hadn't accepted the invitation. If she had stayed home, immersed in her wedding plans, secretly reading the papers for word of the enigmatic duke whose lilies had graced her bed stand until a few days ago.

He had not contacted her again.

No love notes.

No wicked invitations that she would have to refuse.

She still pretended, of course, to have no idea who had sent the lavish bouquet.

The newspapers had reported that Gravenhurst had been spotted strolling through Vauxhall Gardens the night after the literary masquerade. A gorgeous courtesan had been clinging to one arm; a scandalous young baroness claimed the other. So Lily decided that his floral arrangement meant nothing more than that he was open to an arrangement of another sort, and it was up to her to agree. It was her own fault for appearing fast. She had engaged in a dalliance with an unabashed rogue. Did she expect him to invite her to the library to read classic literature with his grandmother?

She wished she could forget him entirely. She would eventually. He had been her first foray into the forbidden, and her last.

She lived a charmed life.

But it was a full life, so full, in fact, that she could not pay attention to the play later that same night. Lady Kirkham whispered throughout the entire first act, pointing out the guests in various boxes and recounting gossip about their personal affairs. Soon Lily caught herself looking for a familiar hollow-cheeked face and a mouth sculpted into a sinful smile.

He was not there.

He was probably in another woman's bed, the beautiful scoundrel.

How irrational to expect, to hope, that he would follow her around London when she had not been given a name to thank him for his flowers. She supposed she should be grateful for his discretion. At least their names had not been linked in the scandal rags.

What would she do if she encountered him tonight? The proper thing would be to give him passing recognition, and nothing more.

Where was he? Why did she allow him to intrude on her thoughts?

She put him out of her mind. Again.

Jonathan seemed to sense she wasn't herself. He held her hand throughout the performance, and stayed at her side as they squeezed through the vestibule afterward and waited for Lady Kirkham's outmoded coach to be brought around.

"It's too early to go home," the lady's stepson, Quentin, announced, stretching his arms over his head. In evening attire he was a pleasant-looking gentleman, but too full of himself for Lily's tastes. Still, he had carried Jonathan to safety through mud and cannon fire at Waterloo. Even Lily understood that favors incurred during the war must never be forgotten. She did wonder, though, how many times Jonathan would feel obligated to repay that debt.

As the coach rolled up, Quentin said unexpectedly, "Let's take the ladies to Vauxhall."

His young brunette stepmother made a face. "Not under my watch."

"Nor mine." Jonathan put his arm around Lily's waist. Her protector.

Quentin gave him a mocking look. "Don't you want to take a dark walk together? Or dance? This will be your last chance as lovers. In a month you'll be begging to be let off the leash."

"Someone ought to tighten yours," his stepmother said with a false smile. "We do not wish to go, Quentin. Leave it at that."

Lily restrained herself from adding that she had already walked through one pleasure garden and did not care to taint that memory by meeting the duke with another woman, or women, in his arms. To her relief, Jonathan refused to agree, and Lily decided as he helped her into the coach that he was the finest man a woman could marry.

As the coach pulled from the lane, Quentin casually suggested that the four of them drop in on a small party in Piccadilly. Lady Kirkham started to protest, then shrugged. "A half hour at most. I do not care for affairs to which I have not been properly invited."

The party turned out to be a drunken revel, attended by knaves and half-world women who so offended Lady Kirkham's sensibilities that she insisted the four of them leave the party immediately.

Lily was relieved, and so, she thought, was Jonathan. Neither of them cared for boisterous affairs. They would both rather sit by a country fire, sipping sherry and telling ghost stories with good friends, than mingle with strangers, several of whom appeared to know Quentin Kirkham well. One of them nodded almost imperceptibly at Jonathan in recognition.

"Do you know him?" she whispered.

"Who?"

"Never mind. Don't look his way."

"Go with her ladyship," Jonathan said in an odd voice. "I'll walk behind to make sure Quentin doesn't get into trouble."

Lady Kirkham hastened to the coach, not even pretending to be pleasant anymore. "Hurry up, Lily," she urged over her shoulder. "This is not a neighborhood where decent people should be seen."

Lily hesitated, glancing back. At the corner Jonathan and Quentin appeared to be having one of their frequent disagreements. Their voices rose. The street wasn't well lit, and she suddenly noticed a cloaked man emerging from the narrow alleyway to their left. Lily hadn't seen him at the party. But he moved in a quick, furtive way that sent a flash of unease through her.

"Jonathan," she implored softly, "please, let's go. It's dark and dirty."

Lady Kirkham was getting into the coach, the single footman assisting her. Lily decided to join her when she heard the cloaked man calling Jonathan by name. Jonathan glanced around, his tall frame tensing.

"*Jonathan*," she said again.

He glanced at her in concern. "Get into the coach. Now."

She shook her head, certain she'd misunderstood. Quentin had turned to the stranger to exchange words. She made out only enough to guess that it was a hostile confrontation. And that the three men knew one another somehow. From the infantry? Too much of a coincidence.

Did Jonathan lead a secret life? Impossible.

Her heart pounded. Bursts of conversation from the party drifted down the street. The coachman had parked too far away for her to attract his attention. The cloaked stranger raised his voice, addressing Jonathan now.

"You will damn well pay me tonight, Captain, or we'll meet over pistols at dawn. We made a gentlemen's agreement."

Disbelief immobilized her. It had to be a mistake. She took a step forward, her impulse to help. Jonathan turned toward her, his face unfamiliar, afraid.

"Damn you, woman," Quentin said to her between his teeth. "Do what you're told for once."

Before she could retreat the stranger moved. He reached inside his cloak. Then what happened afterward went by so fast she couldn't do anything to interrupt the sequence of events.

Something metal glistened in the moonlight. Was that a pistol in Jonathan's hand? The sight of it shocked her. She had watched him at shooting practice with his friends. A marksman. An infantry officer. But why had he felt it necessary to carry a gun to a party? He was strong enough to defend himself on the street. She knew his habits. It was the stranger's gun. Jonathan must have confiscated it.

"You owe me, gentlemen, and I will collect my due—"

The pistol shot echoed in the street. It went on endlessly, tearing through the tunnels of her present, her perfect future. A human life. A soul wailing in the night. She wanted to insert herself like a shield. Death brushed her cheek, a kiss of coldness. Had she been hit? She stared at Jonathan, willing him to be safe. He was a good man. She felt nothing, numb.

"Lily," he said in an agonized voice. "Lily, please, please. Get away from here right now. *Run*."

She saw the other man crumple to the curb. She picked up her skirts. Heavy as lead, they felt. *Hurry, hurry, Lily. Get help. It's not too late.* She reached the coach, shaking with fright. She heard her breath rasp as the footman stared at her in horror.

"Miss, miss," he said in alarm. "What happened?"

"What now? What has he done?" Lady Kirkham's voice tolled a funeral bell in her brain. "Little bastard. I told his father that boy was born evil."

Lily pulled at the footman's sleeve. "You have to help. He's shot. Tell the coachman. I can't breathe."

The coachman jumped down from his box. "Wait inside, miss. It will be all right."

Lily's voice broke. "I don't know what happened. I don't know whether he brought a gun—"

Lady Kirkham slid to the edge of her seat to reach for Lily. Lily drew away, aware that she made little sense. The coachman brushed past her with a bat under his arm. The footman gently pried her fingers from his sleeve.

"I'll show you where he is," she said. "It happened around the corner, and the man came out of the alley. I shouldn't have left home. I—"

Stronger than she appeared, Lady Kirkham caught Lily under the arms and half dragged her into the coach. She smelled of costly perfume and perspiration. "Stay here with me," she whispered fiercely. "Whatever is done is done."

Chapter 14

*H*er fiancé and his friend insisted that Lily was imagining things. There was no dead man in the gutter. Jonathan admitted that he and Quentin had gotten into a minor argument during which a drunk had rambled by and pestered them for cash. But neither gentleman had shot anyone in the street or carried a pistol to a play.

The driver and footman reassured her that they had searched the street and found nothing more suspicious than a stray dog sniffing about the sidewalk. They smiled at each other, apparently pleased to have been involved in a harmless rescue.

Quentin dismissed her story with his usual patronizing contempt concealed behind a pretense of courtesy. He was, in fact, so unconcerned that Lily began to doubt herself. His stepmother remained silent throughout the short ride back to Mayfair. If she suspected Lily was telling the truth, she could hardly confirm what she had not witnessed. Perhaps she was afraid for her own life.

Jonathan tried to calm Lily. He stroked her hair and begged her to believe him. "Haven't you known me all your life? I swear on my soul that I didn't kill anyone. Would I defile you with my hands if I had?"

She refused to meet his gaze, shrinking from his touch. "I insist that we go to the police station and give a report."

"They'll think you've gone mad," Quentin said in thinly veiled exasperation. "Your name will be ruined and mocked in the morning news. Do you think a corpse can rise from the gutter and vanish in the blink of an eye?"

"I know what I saw."

"You saw shadows in the dark."

"You are a liar," Lily said.

"You are insane."

"Please, Lily," Jonathan said in a low voice, throwing Quentin a look. "Nothing happened. Don't speak of it again until you've had some rest. You'll be yourself in a few days."

"And if any dead bodies pop up overnight in Piccadilly," Quentin said blithely, "you can turn us both in. Or you could show common sense and realize you're hysterical over nothing."

Jonathan glowered at him. "I knew it was a bad idea to go to that party."

"It was a bad idea to leave Tissington," Lily muttered, shrinking from the hand he extended to her.

"You're right," he agreed. "But we'll be going home
after the wedding. Trust me until then."

She ignored his advice. Everything she believed
about him was false.

She wouldn't ever believe a word he said.

She told her parents, Sir Leonard and Diana, Lady
Boscastle, as well as her brother, Gerald, what she had
witnessed the instant they greeted her at the door
of the viscount's town house. She even told the butler when he appeared to take her evening cloak. She
wished with all her heart that Chloe and Dominic
had not gone to Chelsea so that she could enlist their
support.

Someone brought her brandy. Her brother listened
to Jonathan repeat that he was innocent, that he loved
her, that he wanted to take her back to the country. Her
parents were bewildered, sympathetic, but torn. Their
main concern was that she not ruin her name.

"Lily, my darling girl," her mother whispered with
tears in her eyes as she sat beside her on the sofa. "I
know that you are devoted to reading romantic tales,
as am I. Is it possible that you have confused your
craving for adventure with what you think you saw? A
lady's life can be so dull at times."

Romantic tales.

She thought wistfully of a beautiful face half-
concealed behind a black domino. She remembered

that hard-lipped mouth, a kiss wicked, sweet, and wild. She had changed that night. She had glimpsed another world, darker, intriguing, decadent . . . or not? Looking back she wondered if his kiss had been an omen of ill things to come.

Had she made a secret pact with a demon? They had embraced each other under a sword crossed with Sir Renwick Hexworthy's wand. What a preposterous thought. What did Wickbury have to do with what she had witnessed tonight? She could not escape into a fictional world even if she wanted to. But why couldn't her real life be as wonderful? Yes, Wickbury held its horrors. But good always won in the end. At least there was logic to follow.

"You weren't drinking tonight, were you, Lily?" her brother asked in such a hopeful voice that she wanted to cry.

She glanced in appeal at her father, usually the first to defend her. He avoided meeting her eyes. She knew his heart well. He didn't believe her either. Everyone thought she'd popped her cork. Maybe she had.

"We will not discuss this ever again, Lily," he said decisively, standing beside Jonathan at the window. "Perhaps you ate or drank something that has disagreed with you. Perhaps you are coming down with a case of the influenza."

"We should summon a physician," her mother said, clearly relieved that there might be a physical reason for Lily's disconcerting flight of fancy.

"We should summon a Bow Street Runner," Lily retorted stubbornly.

Sir Leonard's face tightened. "You will be ruined if anyone outside the family hears of this. It is to Jonathan's credit that he is giving you his comfort."

"And his name," her mother added worriedly. "Oh, Lily, don't let this spoil your beautiful wedding."

Lily rose from the sofa. The brandy *had* gone to her head, but instead of calming her, it gave her false courage. "I can't spoil a wedding I will not attend. I'm not marrying him. I won't do it."

Jonathan strode across the room and took her firmly by the shoulders. "You are promised to me, and I to you. In a few days you will have had time to rest and reflect, and everything will go back to normal."

Lady Boscastle sighed in relief. "Wedding nerves, my love. All the excitement, the parties—"

"—the stories that stuff her head with nonsense," her father interjected. "No more of these *Wickbury Tales*, with wizards and fallen women and . . . I don't know what. I forbid you to read another page of this rubbish. It is a well-known fact that females are easily misled by literature."

Lily's brother rescued the empty brandy glass from her grasp. "That's funny, sir. I could have sworn I caught you reading one of those books after supper a week or so ago."

"I'd give everything to be in one of *those* books right now," Lily said softly.

The quartet stared at her in shock. Then her mother's eyes teared up again, and she broke into heartbroken sobs, as if she had raised a monster instead of a girl with a mind of her own.

"I think, gentlemen," Jonathan said somberly to her father and Gerald, "that we should get her into bed and dosed with a sedative. We'll want to keep the servants in the dark about this until she recovers. The embarrassment, you understand."

"She'll be standing beside you at the altar in a fortnight," Sir Leonard said in a collected voice that half convinced Lily to believe him. "And after you exchange vows, it will be your responsibility to keep this prurient reading material out of her hands."

Chapter 15

The staff gathered in the great hall of St. Aldwyn House to welcome the duke back home. He gave them a smile of appreciation and inquired about the health of their families, his neighbors, his pony, and his two pigs, Pyramus and Thisbe.

He listened politely to their replies. But he felt tired, not his usual self, and said he hoped they would understand if he went straight to his office and did not eat the vegetable pie and strawberry clotted-cream trifle the cook had prepared in his honor.

He could hear them whispering to one another after he excused himself. Unlike another man in his position, he did not bother to chastise them.

They knew something wasn't right.

He wouldn't confess what it was. But in time the head housemaid, Marie-Elaine, would find out; God only knew how. Samuel suspected his valet talked, and he would be unable to escape their infernal concern for him. He hoped to convince everyone that having to rewrite the end of the last book had made him melancholy, that he always had a hard time saying farewell to his characters for a while, because who knew when, or if, they would ever talk to him again?

He might not even care.

He might just write an epilogue revealing Lady Juliette to be a man-slaying dragoness who decided to put an end to both Michael and Renwick in one great swoop of her tail.

Marie-Elaine missed nothing.

"It's a woman," she told the cook, Mrs. Halford, while the upper staff sat grouped in the servants' hall to discuss the situation.

Mrs. Halford put a cloth over the pie sitting before her on the table. "How can you tell? He might just have gotten another stinking review."

Marie-Elaine shook her head. She and her illegitimate daughter, Josette, had been living at St. Aldwyn House longer than any of the other servants. "It's his look."

"I've never seen that look about him before," Mrs. Halford agreed. "And it's not as if he's lived like a monk."

"Yes, and he's never been in love before, either."

"His Grace and that bookseller's daughter weren't exactly acting like mortal enemies when I caught them in the pavilion last month."

"That isn't love," Marie-Elaine said bluntly. "I ought to know."

The duke's valet, Wadsworth, sat down at the table with a pack of cards. He had owned a gaming hell six years ago and had gone to prison after a knife fight on the premises had ended in a nobleman's death. "What were you doing out there anyway, Mrs. Halford, at that time of night?"

The cook rolled her eyes. "I was picking parsnips. It's the only time I can sneak out for a breather without those pigs snuffling at my heels."

"He'd have a fit if he knew," Marie-Elaine said absently. "He leads such a private life."

Mrs. Halford shook her head in worry. "Perhaps he's getting sick again."

Marie-Elaine sighed. "Shuffle the cards. Bicker-staff isn't talking, but we'll get to the root of this soon enough."

The body had not shown up in the two weeks since the murder. Lily's father leased a cottage on the outskirts of London, hoping the tranquil atmosphere would compose her thoughts. No one outside her immediate family was allowed to see her, except for a physician, who grimly revealed to her parents that he wasn't sure, but that after examining her, he thought she had tried to tell him she was turning back into a goose.

Lily heard her father shouting up from the bottom of the stairs, "It is those damned books again!"

The London Boscastles had asked their private inquiry agent to become involved. Lily knew this only because her brother had sneaked her a note from Chloe in a basket of fruit.

The boxwood sprig that Lily had saved from the literary masquerade had crumbled. So had her foolish hope that the duke would intervene on her behalf. She wasn't certain what she expected him to do. He hadn't witnessed a crime. The only thing he could confess was that he had kissed her. And that she hadn't put up a protest at all. Neither of which would boost her credibility in anyone's view.

She woke up on her wedding day and heard Jonathan's voice below. It held a familiarity that made her ache.

She slipped into a day gown, not bothering to even brush her hair, and crept to the top of the stairs.

"We are going to send her away," her brother was saying in his quiet voice.

Jonathan looked frantic. "Where? I want to take care of her. I still want us to be married."

"I don't know where she'll go or what the future holds," her brother said, apparently unmoved by this display of emotion.

Jonathan walked to the front door, then looked up

as if he had seen her behind the balustrade. "I didn't kill anyone," he said to Gerald. "Don't you believe me, either? And I want to marry her. We can go into exile, but I still love her. Tell her that for me. Tell her in those words."

Her brother was silent.

But the moment Jonathan left, Gerald turned and climbed halfway up the stairs to speak to her. "You shouldn't have come out when he was here. We'll sort this out. I'm not sure how."

She shook her head. "You don't expect me to marry him after all this?"

He glanced back at the door. "Lily, my dear. Don't you understand? It got out in the papers. Our cousin the Marquess of Sedgecroft managed to get a retraction, but the damage is done. If you don't marry Jonathan, you probably won't marry at all."

"I don't care."

He sighed, his eyes shadowed with worry. "We need to go away. Perhaps in a year or two it will be forgotten. This family has survived worse scandals."

"No. You're right. I'll never be offered another decent proposal again. I'll receive only illicit offers from now on."

And that night, when she told her parents that she would leave to spare them further embarrassment, she thought they looked relieved.

"We have plenty of relatives with young children who would welcome a hand for a year or two," Lady

Boscastle said, more animated than she had seemed since the incident. "Who knows? You might even snare an agreeable squire who doesn't care about your failed engagement or advancing age."

Lily regarded her mother with affection. "I have no intention of looking at, or for, another man as long as I draw breath."

Her mother paled. "Then what are you going to do? You cannot live alone. What will you do?"

"Apply for a position. As a housekeeper."

"To a stranger?" Lady Boscastle said, appalled. "What if he turns out to be—"

"He might be a cantankerous ogre with onions for ears for all I care," Lily said calmly. "He will assuredly not be a lout who shoots a man in cold blood two weeks before his wedding. And pretends to be utterly innocent of the crime."

Her father snorted. "What do you know about keeping a house?"

"I have lived in one all my life."

"Do you know how to plan a supper party?" her mother asked skeptically.

"No. And neither does our housekeeper, but I will buy several books on the subject and study the art."

"Books," her father said in despair. "You've never gone to the fish market early in the morning and haggled over eels."

Lily's stomach turned at the thought. "I suppose I'll have to learn."

"Who in his right mind would hire a housekeeper who is rumored to be losing her wits?"

"A gentleman who hasn't heard the gossip about me. Or better yet, one who doesn't care about gossip at all."

"You cannot blame people for speculating," her father said grimly. "You are not behaving rationally at all."

True to her word, Lily began to read the newspapers again. She ignored the social announcements and concentrated on the advertisements for domestic help. Her brother drove her to four interviews that same week, and two the following. Lily offered nothing about her personal scandal and oddly no one asked. On one interviewer's desk, however, she spotted a newspaper clipping in which she glimpsed her name. As it was not a marriage announcement, she could only conclude that she was being interviewed for prurient reasons and not for potential employment.

Sir Leonard and Lily's mother made arrangements to return to Tissington. Chloe and the viscount called once and offered to take Lily in for as long as she liked. They meant to be kind. But Lily had had her fill of society. Although the Boscastles had grown adept at shrugging off scandal, she didn't want to be stared at whenever she went out.

Gerald took her to the seventh interview and they both agreed that if this did not result in an offer, she would have to lower her expectations and move closer to the country, where her name might not be known.

"Wish me luck," she said as he parked his curricle outside the redbrick building on Bond Street. It didn't appear to be a servant registry. The bronze name plaque said it was a solicitor's office. Mr. Benjamin Thurber.

"I wish . . . Well, I wish this had never happened," her brother said. "I still can't believe it."

"Nobody can," she said with a bittersweet smile.

The agent introduced himself and escorted her through the waiting room. He studied her intently as she introduced herself and admitted her lack of experience.

He was the first interviewer who did not ask her why she wanted the position. He scribbled quite a bit in his notebook while she talked. She slid to the edge of her seat, dying to know what had struck him as important. Had she revealed too much?

"Well," he said at last, fidgeting with his pen. "I think you will be a good match. May I ask you a question or two that might seem odd?"

She braced herself. Was she willing to sell her body into the bargain? Would she mind satisfying more than her employer's domestic needs? Whatever the questions were, he seemed hesitant to ask them. She shook off a shiver of foreboding. Of course, she did not trust anyone at this low moment of her life.

Should she explain the reason for her broken engagement?

"Are you afraid of ghosts?" he asked unexpectedly.

"Of *what*?"

He glanced down at his desk, the question apparently one that embarrassed him. "Spirits, demons, haunted houses," he mumbled. "That sort of whatnot."

Lily blinked. Was she going to work for a gravedigger? "I don't believe in them, if that's what you mean. But—" She broke off with a guilty smile. "I don't mind reading stories that give me a little scare, as long as they are not too gory."

"A little scare." He nodded thoughtfully and made another annotation.

"You are not suggesting that the person who will hire me thinks he is a ghost?" she inquired in an arch voice.

He made a face. "There's no such thing, is there?"

"Not in my opinion. Does the gentleman believe in the supernatural?"

"Let us just say that he has an interest in the subject."

Lily frowned. Her previous life of privilege as she had known it was dead. That was as close to the paranormal as she had come. At least thus far. To accept employment from a gentleman she had never met surely qualified as a step into the unknown.

"Your master keeps late hours," he added as an afterthought.

"I'm not afraid of the dark, either." Lily's brows tightened in a frown. What on earth was he trying to tell her?

He dredged up a wan smile. "You must have some inquiries of your own."

"Forgive me, sir, for what might be an impolite question, but I do need to ask. *Is* there any reason why I should be afraid to accept this position?"

"You will probably never find a more protective master in the whole of England, nor—"

"Oh," she said, her body relaxing in relief. "That is—"

"—a more eccentric one."

She closed her mouth.

"In his inner circle, he is regarded to be a genius."

She brightened. "A genius?"

"Quite brilliant."

"That *does* make a difference." Although a man's intelligence was no guarantee that he would not be a philanderer or a pinch-bum.

"I would best describe him," he confided so softly that she almost missed his words, "as a trustworthy peer of literary inclinations."

Lily put her hand to her heart. "That is even better."

"However, I shall warn you that others have a lesser opinion of his character."

Lily searched his earnest face. A warning. That was fair enough. Shouldn't she return the favor? The brass knocker sounded at the front door. She guessed her brother had grown uneasy at the length of the interview.

She leaned forward. "I should warn you that I— Oh,

there is no point in hiding it. I have recently broken my engagement. The man I was to marry—"

He waved his hand in dismissal. "Yes. We know all about your unfortunate experience. We do not give any credit to gossip."

She blinked. "You . . . He . . . *knows*?"

"Your employer would not hire a housekeeper whose background I have not researched. Your family line is quite famous."

She laughed silently. Infamous, he should have said. The Boscastles had broken every rule in the book. By virtue of their unholy charm, society fondly forgave them sin after sin. And eagerly anticipated the next. Lily had never considered herself part of the clan. But if she had to play their notorious card to survive, then so she would. She recognized her brother's voice coming from the outer hall. "Does your employer have a name?" she asked.

"Well, naturally. It is St. Aldwyn. Assuming you accept the position, you will work in St. Aldwyn House."

It sounded like a sanctuary for lost souls. "I accept."

"Lily?" Gerald called quietly from behind the door. "Is everything all right?"

The solicitor closed his notebook, speaking hurriedly. "The manor house is near the town of Hexworthy, in Dartmoor."

"Hexworthy?" As in Sir Renwick? Her heart leaped. It could only be a sign, though whether good or bad had yet to be discovered.

"You'll travel by private coach to Plymouth. From there you will sail for three days. Another coach will pick you up at the port. It is three more days by land to the manor, depending on the weather."

She nodded, exhilarated and frightened in turns. The sooner she began a new life, the better. She had to hope for better.

Chapter 16

The Wickbury Tales

**BOOK SEVEN
CHAPTER LAST,
VERSION FORTY-SEVEN**

Lord Michael Wickbury climbed the stairs to the tavern's upper-story gallery. The bedchamber door of the last room stood ajar. He stared inside. He perceived a woman, bound at the wrists and swearing vociferously, on the bed beneath a long-haired man who seemed intent on ravishing his helpless victim.

The villain seemed vaguely familiar.

Michael's hand tightened on the hilt of his broadsword. The blackguard in the bedroom swung around as if sensing a threat. He motioned the woman to be silent. She subsided back against the pillows. Michael studied the man in shock. For a moment it was like looking into a mirror. One that not only distorted his reflection but that revealed the darker side of his soul.

How could this be?

Was he having a vision? He was supposed to be a gallant nobleman, favorite of the exiled king, not a debaucher of helpless maidens. Although now that Michael paid closer attention, it was not perfectly clear from where he watched whether the beautiful captive was actually fighting to escape or taking part in naughty bed sport.

Mercifully the mirror image dissolved, and Michael recognized the other man to be his nemesis, the renowned enemy of the royalist cause.

The woman on the bed lifted her free hand to her bodice. Again he wondered whether she was protecting her virtue or baring her breasts to the villain's eyes.

He shook his head in bewilderment. Was he losing his mind, his purpose? Of late he had felt more like a pawn on a chessboard than the noble hero he thought he was supposed to be. It was almost as if he and others in his world were being controlled by some unseen force, and not a particularly considerate one, either.

Why, for example, did he have to jump from one valiant deed into another? Why was it that he surmounted one obstacle only to find another immediately thrown in his path? He had escaped from more dangerous situations than he could count, each one more dramatic than the previous. He remembered little of his past.

But that woman on the bed. Suddenly, by God, he realized who she was. His beloved, Lady Juliette Mannering. Except that she seemed different. Had she played him false? Was she only pretending to please Sir Renwick to save herself? Her hair appeared a shade or so lighter than he remembered. Was she in disguise? Yes, that had to be it. Lady Juliette was cunning and resourceful. Even so, it was Michael's duty to protect her from harm.

This was no time for reflection.

It was time to act.

Lily found herself wishing for immediate death. Never had she known such misery. She was too seasick to drag herself from the yacht's cabin to the state drawing room for tea. She could not console herself with a favorite book. In fact, she had reread only a chapter of the last Wickbury book before deciding that her mother had been right.

Romantic notions had ruined her.

Her hero had turned out to be an untrustworthy liar. The only hero in her current peril was the yacht captain, who rescued her by announcing that the devil's own wind had blown the vessel into port a day earlier than planned. If she hadn't been submerged in self-pity, she might have kissed him and every one of his crew for sparing her that extra day.

She would not have cared how unladylike such gratitude seemed. All that counted was that her misery had ended. And that, as promised, a huge traveling coach and four awaited her at port. The interior was comfortable, the driver and two footmen in long black coats silent but deferential. Yet after two days of travel, broken by an overnight stay at a quiet inn, the landscape grew wild and desolate. The coach passed fewer and fewer charming thatched cottages and lumbered toward bare crags. She felt a pang of anxiety as the familiar fell away.

It might be true that a brokenhearted young lady was susceptible to rash actions. But Lily hadn't realized that in accepting a position as housekeeper to this unknown gentleman how completely she would veer from the path of her former life. She awoke from a nap on the rainy afternoon of the third day to thundering hoofbeats and decided she had also veered right off the Roman road of civilization.

What had happened while she slept?

Had the coach been captured by brigands?

She pushed aside the tasseled curtains in alarm. The creaking black coach bore her across the moor as if a demonic force had taken possession of the driver. He had seemed respectful when he had nodded at her that morning. It relieved her little to see the well-mannered footmen clinging like a pair of bats to the rear quarters. Were they being abducted, too?

She pounded upon the roof to insist the driver slow his pace. When he did not respond she grasped the leather strap for dear life, ground her teeth, and opened the window. To her disbelief the sturdy grays struggled toward a sheer wall of stacked granite that stood directly in view.

She stuck her head out the window. "Stop this conveyance immediately!"

"Put your head back inside the coach!" the driver shouted, throwing her a disgruntled look. Then his whip cracked above his head, not touching the hard-laboring horses but conducting a lightning-like charge in the air.

"We need to make the next inn before nightfall!" he bellowed.

"We also need to make it there alive!" she retorted.

He gave an incomprehensible answer. His voice was indistinct, his shoulders hunched in concentration. Lily studied what she could see of his profile. A thick woolen muffler obscured nearly all of his face. Although she had not made a prior study of his form and mannerisms, she was fairly certain that this was not the same coachman who had met her at the wharves. Whoever he was, his churlish behavior would not do.

"Sir," she shouted at the top of her voice, "if you do not slow this coach immediately, I shall report you to the master!"

The vehicle plunged forward. She thought she heard the driver give a reckless laugh. Incredulous, she real-

ized what the daredevil intended to do. Straight ahead
she perceived a narrow aperture between a pair of
towering stones. Clearly he intended to thread horses,
coach, footmen, and terrified housekeeper through the
fissure's eye.

Her breath caught.

She drew back into the coach. Every muscle in her
body tensed in preparation for what would certainly
be a lethal crash. To think she had hoped for a fresh
start, only to be annihilated by this gladiator of a
coachman.

She closed her eyes as the shadow of the stones
darkened her view. The pulsing clamor of the horses'
hooves merged into an unholy melody with her pounding heart. If she survived, she would indeed take this
Hotspur to task. After all, a housekeeper outranked a
coachman in chain of command. Unless he were one of
St. Aldwyn's relatives, in which case she would avoid
riding with him in the future.

The driver slowed his breakneck race. Lily dared
to open her eyes and peer outside. She wouldn't be
surprised to find the coach hanging cliffside in midair.
Deceptively the towering stones had overshadowed a
wider route than could be perceived from the distance.
The clatter of wheels regained a steady rhythm.

She slumped against the squabs, her nerves wrung
out.

It was raining when the coach stopped for the night
at the sign of the Man Loaded with Mischief.

By some miracle the footmen who opened the door and took her bags appeared unaffected by the hair-raising ride. The wretch of a coachman had already disappeared from his box when she stepped outside. Presumably he thought to spare himself the well-deserved scolding that Lily had prepared.

She started for the inn's entrance when an arresting figure strode up beside her from the stable yard. From the corner of her eye she saw him doff his black top hat and offer his arm. Lily resisted the impulse to accept his help. Gazing straight ahead, she edged discreetly beyond his reach.

Unfortunately she edged right into an ankle-deep puddle. She groaned at the unpleasant sensation of chilly rainwater seeping into the soles of her half boots. Almost at the same instant she realized that the gentleman at her side was the coachman responsible for her bruised posterior.

She gave him a glare that said he would answer to her later. Then she pulled up her hood to make a run for it.

"Miss Boscastle, wait."

How imperious he sounded. Or was he attempting to apologize? Wasn't it in her best interest to make a good start with her employer's staff?

She turned in hesitation.

And stared up into the most perfectly formed masculine face that she had ever had the misfortune to behold.

"Do you not know me?" he demanded softly.

Rain cooled the burning heat that had risen to her cheeks. "Yes. You are the man who apparently perfected his coaching skills in a coliseum."

He smiled. She wondered if she was imagining the sardonic intelligence in his eyes. Had she not seen that look before? Why was it so unsettling?

"Did I mistake you for a lady who sought adventure?" he asked, as if . . . as if they were sharing a private joke.

She swallowed uncomfortably. Heavens above. How had she given him *that* impression? They had not exchanged two words. He was far too familiar for a man in his position, and his veiled expression hinted at intimate knowledge. She decided that she would have to put him in his place or forever deal with his impertinence.

"I think that we should continue this conversation—" She stifled a shriek as a stable boy pounded past, splashing wet filth on her best cloak. She shook herself in dismay.

"Mind where you're going, you lout!" the coachman called after the offender, who stopped, thumbed his nose, and laughed.

The coachman straightened in an aggressive stance. "I'll show you where to stick that thumb—"

Lily grasped his wrist in grim resolve. She would

wrestle him to the ground before witnessing another act of violence. "While I appreciate the sentiment, Mr. Coachman, I would prefer you not express yourself in such a disconcerting manner. The master would not be pleased that you had fought over me in public."

He grunted. "You do not know him very well."

"I do not know him at all," Lily admitted, nonplussed at the suggestion of a ruffian employer. "I do trust, however, that he is not given to common brawls."

He slapped his hat back on and stared at her with an unsettling smile. "I'm afraid that he is."

Lily released his wrist, suddenly realizing how dangerous it was to maintain physical contact with a man who appeared to enjoy making mischief. "I do not believe you," she said. "I was assured that he was a gentleman."

"A gentleman always protects a lady," he countered.

"A good servant never causes a public disturbance," she said, looking away.

"I shall remind you of that," he said, grinning shamelessly.

A post chaise rolled into the courtyard, depositing a lone male passenger directly behind them. The traveler charged toward the inn. Lily moved off to the side to avoid his splashing boots.

Before she could manage another step, she felt a firm hand bracing the small of her back with an audacity that almost made her drop her reticule. "I can manage—"

His arm locked around her knees. She gasped. "Mr. Coachman!" And then she found herself flattened against his hard chest.

His gaze met hers. The bedevilment on his face took her breath. Indeed, he looked far too dashing for a country servant. He was an experienced rogue if ever she had encountered one. "I am a housekeeper, not a piece of luggage!" she exclaimed, blinking rain from her eyes.

"You're light as . . . a feather."

"A feather?"

She could not believe how far she had fallen. Last spring she hadn't a care in the world. Choosing a flattering style for her wedding dress had seemed to be her only problem. Her betrothed was to have protected her for the rest of her days. And now here she was, in icy gray rain, with a coachman sneaking his hand around her posterior.

It was a novel impropriety. He was an unashamed rascal whose voice might have played a chord in her memory had she not been preoccupied with keeping his misconduct to a minimum.

Lily, the light-spirited flirt, had become Miss Boscastle, the ill-humored housekeeper with a grudge in her heart. Well, the pendulum had not swung quite that far. She seemed to be caught halfway. A gentlewoman trying, literally, to stand on her own feet.

"Do *not* tell me that the master encourages you to behave in this liberal fashion!"

"I'm sorry to say that he does."

"I don't believe you."

"It's true."

"He must be . . ." She wriggled her arm up to tap a forefinger to her temple.

"Oh, he is. You should hear him go on about how beautiful the moon is when it's reflected in a moorland pool."

"I imagine that it is," Lily said impatiently. "However, being poetic is not a tragic flaw. As long as he is kind, I don't understand why you would mock him."

"He's awfully kind to animals," he confided, laughter lurking in his eyes.

She frowned. "That is a good sign."

"He doesn't eat them, either." He lowered his voice. "He follows a natural diet."

"I have no idea what you are talking about."

"Bloodless banquets."

Lily went pale. "I hope you aren't saying what I'm afraid you are saying."

"I'm afraid that I am. He will not allow animal flesh to be served in his house."

She was to plan menus for a man who ate no meat? "That *is* disturbing," she said. "A poet is one thing, but a vegetable eater. What kind of suppers am I to arrange if I cannot serve beef? Fish, I suppose, but only in season."

He shook his head. "He won't eat fish."

"Why not?"

"Because one looked him in the eye once when he was swimming in a pond. Their souls touched."

"For goodness' sake," she said before she could censor her reaction. "No wonder he had to send all the way to London for a housekeeper. I suppose the local women are wary of his peculiar ways."

His eyes danced. "It's hard to understand why, but a few of them actually pursue him. I've had to turn a dozen at least away from the door."

She arched her brow. "Of the coaching house?"

"Love can render one a resourceful suitor."

"Love can make one a sapskull. Which I think I am to listen to this nonsense."

"You are a cynic, miss. The master is a romantic, possibly even what one would call a visionary."

"You *do* give yourself airs."

He nodded, clearly amused that he'd disconcerted her again. "He's a challenge, I will confess. He's a radical, too. The Crown has declared him a subject who holds subversive beliefs against England."

Her spirits flagged. "So what you are telling me, in your indelicate manner, is that he is truly off his head."

"Am I familiar yet?" he asked softly.

"You are *too* familiar. And far too free with your hands."

"Believe it or not, I've been told that I have a welcome touch."

"By your horses and fast women?" Her breath

hitched as he carted her unceremoniously around a wide-eyed porter who had just exited the inn.

Against her will she placed her hand around his neck.

Am I familiar yet?

"Let me down!"

"It is pouring to float an ark, miss," he replied. "The master would not want you to slip and spend a week bedridden when he has need of your help around the house."

"Bedridden—you rogue."

She could only guess how much he was enjoying himself as he strode casually through the rain. She was jostled every step against his firm body. His warmth, though it pained her to admit it, was not unpleasant at all.

And those unfathomable eyes—

Am I familiar yet?

A wet gust of wind blew off his hat. "Oh, dear!" she exclaimed. "It's going to be ruined."

"Never mind that," he said with dark cheer. "There's plenty more of those where it came from. Our concern is to get you out of your damp things and into a nice bed."

"Listen to you," she said incredulously. "As if gold coins dropped from the clouds. I cannot imagine why anyone would keep such an impudent person in his employ. I vow that if you make one more reference to bedding me—"

"I never said anything of the sort."

"The devil you did not."

He feigned an injured look as one of St. Aldwyn's footmen left the shelter of the gabled roof to open the inn's oaken door.

"I will thank you not to put words in my mouth, Lily."

Lily.

Shock lanced through her.

She barely realized that he had entered the smoke-enshrouded taproom and was lowering her to the floor. She glanced around in embarrassment. Several patrons in the bar had set down their ale mugs to assess the situation. It seemed to Lily that their curiosity subsided the moment they noticed her brash companion. She assumed he had a reputation with the locals for causing trouble.

"What are you all looking at?" the coachman asked with a cocky grin. "Haven't you ever seen a villain with a lady in his arms before?"

Someone laughed.

A villain. No. *No.*

She shook her head, denying the memory of kisses shared in a moonlit garden. It could not be. Slowly she looked up at his face, the hard-chiseled cheekbones that had been half-hidden by a mask the night of the literary masquerade. The sensual mouth that had seduced her curved in a slow, penitent smile.

"I thought you would know me sooner," he said with rue.

The copper-orange flames in the inn's massive hearth leaped higher into the chimney. Her blood simmered until it blazed through her numbed awareness.

"You," she said in soft condemnation. "You . . . you have *abducted* me."

"I have not," he said quickly. "I wanted—"

Her voice interrupted him. "I know what you want." She backed away, feeling so betrayed that she hit her hip against a table, unbalancing a gentleman's glass. Ale foamed to the table's edge and dripped into the folds of her cloak.

He caught her hand. She wrenched it free. "You told me," he reminded her, "how very much you liked the abduction scene from *Wickbury*."

"Then I was a fool to confide in you and a bigger fool to believe that those stories could ever come true."

He swallowed hard. "There's only one fool in this tale. And I will make this right. I only wanted—"

She picked up her damp cloak and skirts, her voice surprisingly composed. "You have deceived me, but I am starving and too tired to even care. Furthermore, Your Grace, it is impossible to conduct a conversation in a taproom."

He released a breath. "You are not exactly as I remembered you," he said after an intense silence.

She curtsied mockingly, her response promising revenge. "I wish I could say the same of you."

Chapter 17

The Wickbury Tales

BOOK SEVEN
CHAPTER LAST,
VERSION FORTY-EIGHT

In one heroic leap Lord Wickbury slashed the bindings at Juliette's wrists and swung from the bed to confront Cromwell's men. He was out-numbered, not only fighting for the woman he worshiped, and because he had sworn to protect their rightful king, but for his life. He engaged in vigorous swordplay. Three soldiers fell at his hand.

He drove the fourth Roundhead back toward the balcony. His blade parried. Steel rang against steel in the silence. In the back of his mind he sensed the two remaining soldiers closing ranks at his back.

Fight to the death. Fight for the lady fair.

Again that sense of being manipulated, ordained to play a role he was beginning to resent. He lunged. His sword sank into the Roundhead's shoulder. He drew it free, blood dripping on his boot, and pivoted before his opponent staggered back through the door into the gallery railing. Michael heard wood splinter and the whickering of his horse in the courtyard below as the man fell.

He raised his sword.

Too late. A blade pressed into his neck. Another targeted his heart. Baffled, he wondered why in God's name he was dressed in a ruffled white linen shirt and buff trousers when he should have worn a padded vest as protection.

The shadow of his death was at hand.

What had gone wrong?

Had God abandoned him? How could it be? As far back as Michael could remember he had been considered the defender of the defenseless, noble and undefeated. He fought the chivalrous fight.

"Drop your sword, Lord Wickbury," his half brother, Sir Renwick, said from the hearth where he stood, Juliette trapped in his arms. "Do it now, or she will suffer."

Fury welled inside him as Juliette raised her face to his, except... He blinked, lowering his sword. That was *not* his lady. Had he lost his senses? Juliette did not have dark blue eyes

and hair the color of pale fire. This was another
woman, one more beautiful than his own.

Her lips curved in scorn. "You have lost, Lord
Wickbury. I will not be yours."

"Kill him," Sir Renwick said succinctly. "Let my
lovely captive witness his shame."

Lily regarded her chamber dispassionately. It was a superior room, furnished with a dining table and a spa-
cious bed that the duke had undoubtedly intended to
put to use.

What had she done? She picked at the supper tray
a maid had delivered to her room. What would she do
now?

She was too practical to take flight from a place she
could not even name. She would indeed appear to be
deluded. She finished the flagon of wine that accompanied her hot soup and bread, a Rhine wine with a
delicate flavor that masked a deceptive strength.

In the rooms below she could hear a fiddler playing in the bar, waiters bustling about. From the hall
she could hear the duke knocking persistently and
demanding she admit him until finally, her patience
frayed, she reached into her reticule for her book and
threw it across the room.

There was quiet then.

She waited.

He did not knock again.

She glanced at the book on the floor.

How dared he presume to think he could act out Sir Renwick's part?

She would never read another *Wickbury* book. She would give up yearning for courtly love and liars.

She unstrapped the trunk on the floor and found her night rail and robe and undressed for bed. She was too exhausted to think about the duke's deceit or to wonder what had possessed him to think that he could ever understand a complex character like Sir Renwick Hexworthy. Or that he could take charge of her life when she was at her most vulnerable.

So much for the gentle squire she had hoped would provide her with a haven from her woes.

It appeared, instead, that she had made a bargain with the devil, and as hideous as the situation might prove, for now, at least, she had no alternative but to calm herself and get a decent night's sleep.

Samuel pulled a chair to her bed and studied Lily's sleeping form in the firelight. She did not stir. Perhaps the miserable rain had muffled his entry into her room. He had knocked at her door for hours, to no avail. Finally he had asked for and been given the innkeeper's master key.

A duke wielded unfair advantage, it was true. And oftentimes Samuel used the advantage to further a good cause. This, however, was a personal affair, a selfish one. He had wanted her. And now she was legally bound to him.

He did not want to let her go, even if his conscience argued that it was the right thing.

She had stated an obvious truth.

He could not control her destiny as if she were one of the characters in his books. Had he really expected her to view his intervention as an adventure? Samuel had found abducting a lady in genuine fact to be an asinine humiliation to both parties involved.

Lily had not fallen rapturously into his arms. He was, as those who knew him said often in despair, a man who conceitedly believed he could take every broken creature into his care.

And something *had* happened to break her spirit. Even now he could tell by the tangled bedcovers that sleep brought her little peace.

He had devoured every tidbit of information about her that his solicitor had sent him since the week that Samuel had left London. He had even tormented himself by seeking news of her wedding. Yes, he had wished it would go wrong. He had wished that *she* would change her mind about marrying her captain. But that she had claimed to have witnessed a murder and then fallen into disgrace was a solution he had never anticipated, and not the romantic opening he sought.

The privacy of those Samuel guarded would not be violated to satisfy anyone's curiosity. And when the day came that Lily felt safe to entrust him with whatever burdened her, he would view it as an honor.

More than anything he wanted her to be the spontaneous, slightly naughty spirit he had half seduced in an enchanted garden. But something had hurt her.

Would he do the same? Had she lost faith in love? Would he find a way to restore her confidence?

What had he done?

Taken a chance, made a rash decision based on a single evening with a woman who had belonged to someone else. She was an inexperienced flirt who had enticed the wrong man. He should have known better. His solicitor had warned him. It had been arrogance on his part to pursue her. And yet it was more than arrogance now. Their lives were entangled. He had wanted her in his bed. But he did not want her as an unwilling partner, a woman who had no other choice. He would rather persuade her properly, one smile, one kiss, one confidence at a time. If he could sway the House of Lords, could he not win over the only woman he had ever truly wanted?

Even the hair that tumbled over her shoulders looked darker than he remembered. But she was lovely still. He reached down gently to raise the coverlet over the lush body that tempted his senses. His hand brushed against her breast, felt the softness and an urge to cup its weight. He could discern the peak stiffening against her muslin nightdress. Pulsing heat spread through his veins. He could not help himself. He leaned down silently.

She stirred, turning onto her side. He stared at the folds of linen that draped her back, the contours of her body.

Resolutely he stood to escape the temptation of touching her.

Her voice rose, clear and alert, before he crossed the room.

"I will not be your mistress."

He paused. *That* was more like the lady he remembered. "I don't believe I asked."

No.

He had considered asking her to be his wife.

And she, with good cause, considered him to be a conniving scoundrel.

Chapter 18

*L*ily shivered in the dawning light. She could not imagine a worse morning to travel. She had been awakened by the other guests thumping down the stairs and rain assaulting the roof. She dreaded the thought of another day in that coach. As for its owner, well, her gentle squire was a quintessential rake, and she had not decided how she would deal with him. It seemed naive to accept his apology at face value. She had no reason to trust him.

What *had* she done?

What better choice had been offered her?

Had she fled one man's deception to fall into another one's bed?

She had signed an employment contract.

Would he force her to fulfill its terms? Had she even *read* the terms? In satisfying their agreement, would he also try to fulfill his own desires? She would not make it easy on him if he did.

She took a good breakfast and dressed warmly to face whatever she would face after she left her room. The duke's two footmen introduced themselves to her as Emmett and Ernest. Ernest took charge of loading her luggage. Emmett escorted her through the bustling inn to the coach.

To her extreme relief the duke was not playing coachman today. It appeared that the customary driver had been summoned back for the rest of the journey.

And the duke . . . She should have known. He was sitting inside the coach, sorting through a sheaf of papers, and looking more vitally male in his dark coat and black trousers than her befuddled mind could ignore this early in the morning. Her throat tight, she dropped inelegantly into the opposite seat.

He glanced up. His gaze appraised her before he spoke across the uncomfortable silence. "I hope you do not object to our traveling together. I assume you would prefer it to my driving. Or to a public coach."

She searched inside her reticule for her book. As disenchanted as she had become with its improbable ideals, she would rather read it than be caught staring at him. She could not deny that he still drew her eye. *La beauté du diable.* There was nothing angelic about his allure. She would not encourage his attention.

He put aside his papers. "Is that *Wickbury*?" he asked, bending toward her.

She lowered the book. The pleasant scent of his light cologne intruded on her senses. It brought back an unwanted rush of feelings, of memory. His firm mouth upon hers. His knowing touch arousing a bittersweet wanting inside her. How dark her way had become.

"Yes." She cleared her throat. "It is the last published *Wickbury*, Book Six in the series, and the most overwrought, sentimental, romanticized pile of rubbish I have ever had the displeasure to reread. I don't know what I saw in these stories before."

He drew back, blinking as if she had slapped him. "That is a strong reaction."

She pursed her lips and lifted the book into the light. The coachman blew his bugle and gave a resounding shout of warning to the guests huddled in the rain-washed courtyard.

Lily settled against the seat to read. "Let me give you an example," she said. "Ah. Here we go. 'Beloved, is it possible that I beheld your glowing countenance from my prison cell last evening as I awoke? Was it a dream? Mayhap it does not matter. Illusion or not, the image of you has given me the courage to escape. . . .'"

A faint smile crossed his face. "I thought that you were a devoted follower of these books."

"I have outgrown fairy tales."

"Have you? Do you know that I once witnessed two elderly ladies in a library weeping as their companion read aloud the very passage that you mock?"

"Perhaps they were weeping because it was so very bad."

"My goodness. We are a sourpuss, aren't we?"

"It's all twaddle. Heroes and heroines and badly re-searched history."

"Do you honestly dislike those books?" he inquired in what, if she hadn't known better, was a genuinely concerned voice.

"Dislike them? No. I hate them," she burst out. "I despise every wonderful, horrible word. I hate them because they aren't true and that world doesn't . . . doesn't . . ."

He removed a clean folded handkerchief from his vest pocket. "Go on."

She stared at the handkerchief in annoyance. "What is that for?"

"To dry your tears."

"Do you think I would weep over a book, like your old ladies in the library?"

"There is nothing wrong with a woman having a good cry."

She nodded. "I'm more convinced than ever that a woman wrote these books. Some poor deluded spin-ster who has no idea of what she is writing about."

He tucked his handkerchief back in his pocket. "The author is not poor, from what I understand of publish-ing. Deluded is quite a possibility."

"It's indecent," she murmured, shaking her head.

"I wish," he said wryly, "that you had expressed these opinions the evening we met."

"You," she countered, "only pretended to be passionate about *Wickbury*. Why did I fall for such an obvious lure?"

"I did *not* pretend."

She subjected him to a dubious scrutiny. "What am I going to do? Where will I go?"

"We will decide that when we reach St. Aldwyn House tonight."

She turned to the window.

She felt his piercing stare. "Perhaps then," he added, "we can come to a better understanding."

They did not speak again for another three hours, until they changed horses at the next inn and the Devon countryside turned lonely in the encroaching shadows of twilight. What a perfect place for the disillusioned, Lily mused.

The horses climbed a track marked only by a stone cross. The coach wheels shook, churning up peat. An unexpected tranquillity stole over Lily. She closed her eyes in reluctant drowsiness, despite or perhaps because of the jostling rhythm. But no sooner had she begun to drift off than she felt the duke at her side, anchoring her in his arms.

"It is a perilous ride from here," he said, his breath caressing the hollow above her collarbone. "It might even be the most unsafe place on the moor."

Enveloped in his embrace, Lily could hardly disagree. His body felt like warm iron and infinitely dangerous.

"Listen carefully," he said, his voice low and lulling

as he glanced toward the window. "Do you hear anything out of the ordinary?"

"Only the wind or water rushing over a bed of
rocks. I have lived in the country, Your Grace. Nature
soothes me."

He shook his head. "But you aren't listening with
your inner ear."

"What am I doing here?" she whispered to herself.
"How did this happen to me?"

He took her chin in his hand, tilting her face back
to the window. The silhouette of a castle stood in stark
isolation on a hill. At this distance it appeared to hang
in the rising mist above the moor. The dark towers
enhanced its atmosphere of abandonment, as did the
boulder-strewn approach and its border of thorns.

It struck her as melancholy and Gothic and beautiful at once. It was a ruin for the intrepid to explore
and for the timid to avoid. The Lily of old, who'd
had influence over her fate, would have insisted that
the carriage take a detour, and she would have been
obeyed.

She gave a sudden start. "I think I just saw a figure
on the walkway. It couldn't have been, could it?"

"Who knows?" he mused, staring over her shoulder. "The castle is said to be haunted by its former
inhabitants."

Lily slowly turned to regard him. His face hovered
indecently close to hers. She slid nearer to the door. He
gave her an inscrutable smile.

"I might like to sketch that castle by day," she said to cover her discomposure. "If I stay."

"Do you sketch?" he asked, his dark eyes irresistibly warm.

"Not as well as I should after years of study. But I enjoy the art as an amateur."

"Perhaps you had better choose another subject, one nearer the manor house." Amusement deepened the seductive timbre of his voice. "*If* you stay. The castle interior is in shambles and unsafe. On misty autumn nights the gypsies take shelter and brew their potions to sell at the fair."

"That doesn't sound as off-putting to a country girl as you undoubtedly mean it to," Lily said. "Are *you* afraid to cross the drawbridge?"

He laughed. "It is not my theory that the castle is haunted and that Satan rules a court of ghosts within. The villagers believe this."

"Who owns the castle?"

"I do." He said this as if she should have guessed, and deep inside she had.

"And do you not believe in ghosts?" She recalled the question his agent had asked of her the day of her interview.

"I don't know," he said honestly. "I haven't made up my mind. I would not be scared, though, if I encountered one. Would you?"

"I'm not frightened of ghosts at all," she said firmly. "And I don't know what I would do if one appeared to me. I might chase him away. Or I might ask him for advice. But would I be scared? If I am not afraid of you, Your Grace, why should I cower from something I cannot see?"

He was relieved that she had agreed to ride with him inside the coach. It seemed absurd that as Lord Anonymous he could enact a romantic abduction and be lauded for it. When would he learn that what played out well in *Wickbury* had unfortunate consequences in reality?

Of course, as a duke, he had encountered a few women who would have relished the adventure. The problem was that none of them particularly inspired his adventurous spirit. And Lily did. Even now, his conscience stinging, he was drawn to her. It was clear that she did not return the sentiment. Had he ruined the chance to offer himself as her guardian? Could he be strong enough to deny his nature while he proved his worth?

Perhaps not. She tempted him too much. Her soft body was surely made for pleasure and a man's protection. But to earn her trust? It did not seem possible when he had not revealed his complete identity.

He had dug himself into deeper graves than this. Now the urgent questions nagged at him. Could he plot his way to the daylight? Could he merge all his identities into a man whom Lily could not resist?

Chapter 19

*A*pproaching the gatehouse from the end of the sweeping gravel drive, the uninitiated visitor would not suspect that St. Aldwyn House hid any secrets. It appeared to be a peaceful estate. The elegant gray facade presented the epitome of late Elizabethan charm, untouched by centuries of architectural trends.

Multiple rows of majestic cypresses stood like wooden soldiers on either side of the circular driveway. The manor house sat in the notch of a mossy hill upon which three or four unpastured ponies grazed on uneven clumps of grass. Granite composed the manse, stone the outer walls. A bucolic frame of broken wooden fences smothered in tea roses and sweetbriar enclosed an undetermined acreage. Picturesque, Lily thought. A proper English estate set like a multifaceted jewel against moody purple moorland and a blood-orange sky. The barn and outbuildings huddled behind the northwest wing.

And yet if one looked deeper . . .

The long mullioned windows seemed to shine a tri-fle darkly in the twilight. Perhaps she noticed this only because she had once dreamed of being a mistress of such an idyllic country manor, and not its housekeeper.

"She's here!" A gangly young girl in pigtails and a gray dress pelted across the drive. She had been hiding in the rhododendrons. Lily hoped she belonged to one of the servants and was not the duke's love child.

The duke neither discouraged nor invited the girl to approach, although one of the footmen shook his fist at her, to no effect at all.

"This is for you, miss," the girl said, sweeping up her mud-stained skirt to make a curtsy.

Lily stared at the bouquet of beheaded thistles thrust beneath her nose. "Thank you. What on earth is it supposed to be?"

"It was your wedding posy, in case the duke brought home a bride. But it took so long for you to get here, you can put them on your grave."

Lily straightened, curious to see how the duke was responding to this impertinence. He was striding up the manor's entrance steps, apparently oblivious to this dubious tribute.

"How thoughtful," Lily said dryly, taking them in her gloved hand. "I do hope, however, that you won't have to lay any flowers on my grave for a long, long time."

Naturally it was only then that she noticed the unusual triad of granite cairns cresting the hill that protected the house. The raw power of the unadorned stones appealed to Lily . . . until she recalled that such formations often marked ancient burial places.

The manor house stood beneath a graveyard.

It didn't matter.

She wasn't going back to her old life.

Miss Lily Boscastle, the disgraced bride-to-be and former gentlewoman, was as dead as one of the duke's ghosts.

Chapter 20

A sharp-eyed housemaid, the *head* housemaid, she informed Lily, was a pretty red-haired Parisienne in her late twenties. She led Lily up to her room, checked that the fire gave enough heat, that the basin of wash water felt warm to her knuckles, and that a basket of soap balls sat beneath. She inspected the bed, the desk, and dressing table before backing to the door. She was reed-thin and looked quite proper in a frilly prim cap and white apron over a plain black dress. Her green eyes sparkled with unspoken knowledge.

They stared at each other, each judging, wondering, not saying a word. Then, "My name is Marie-Elaine," she said with a proud nod. "Ring me if you need anything else. I think you shall be comfortable in here."

Lily looked around, not noticing a thing. "It's more than nice. Thank you."

"One more thing, miss."

"Yes?"

"For your own peace of mind, stay inside this room after everyone else has gone to bed. Do not explore this house late at night if you know what is good for you."

Lily stood, rendered speechless by this advice.

Before she could unfasten her cloak another maid knocked and bustled into the room bearing a tray of hot tea, scones, a bowl of tiny strawberries, and a pot of clotted cream. Lily washed and gratefully sat down at a Louis XIV table to eat. She noticed then that the room had been furnished throughout in the same lavish French style. Curious, she rose to study her surroundings.

She opened the French tulipwood desk to find it supplied with pens, writing paper, and an inkwell. To her right sat a delicate floral-upholstered armchair that seemed to call her name. Literally. She bent to stare at the cushion. Embroidered golden lilies adorned the fabric.

She straightened, looking down at her feet.

Lilies.

Woven into the carpet were naked water nymphs splashing in abandon from lily pads. She looked up.

Tiger lilies festooned the gilded frame of the rectangular mirror hanging on the wall. She turned. The crystal perfume bottle that glinted on the dressing table? It drew her. She unstopped it and sniffed the heady scent. Lily-of-the-valley.

She returned to the desk and opened the front again to examine the wax seal beside the inkwell. What a surprise. A lily. Still, the bedcover had been decorated with roses, hadn't it? Or perhaps it was embellished with the same fleur-de-lis pattern repeated on the window curtains. Irises, weren't they? Or lilies.

Lilies. Everywhere.

The duke appeared to be obsessed with the blessed flowers.

Either that or it was a coincidence. Her employer happened to have a bedchamber at his disposal with a lily motif. Perhaps he had thought it would please her.

Her skin tingled. Perhaps he had planned to bring her here for some time. Plotted, even. Schemed. The knight-errant and chivalrous dreamer who mocked everything the world believed.

She sat down on the bed, sinking back against an array of silk pillows. Was this the bed of a mistress or a housekeeper? Was he truly penitent or merely waiting for a weak moment to pounce again?

Her eyelids grew heavy. She liked this room. Irrational though it might be, she felt almost at home. And given the choice of living under the same roof with her former betrothed or a duke with a romantic nature—what should a disgraced lady do?

A pleasing place in which to do work. A pot of tea to brace the nerves. Lilies as a tribute wherever the eye wandered. A duke who had a way about him. She started to doze off, the strain of the preceding weeks slowly releasing its stranglehold on her spirit. She kicked off her half boots and stretched out across the coverlet.

Rest. For this moment, at least.

Peace.

A reprieve.

Or so she thought until she heard a distinctly female voice cry out in distress from the depths of the house. "Unhand me, you accursed grave-robbing ghoul! If I am going to lose my virtue, it will not be to a depraved creature like you!"

Chapter 21

*S*amuel threw his manuscript against the wall
and scowled over his wire-rimmed spectacles
at the woman tied by her apron strings to the arms of
an oval-backed chair. He was ready to tear out his hair.
"I did *not* write that line. Furthermore, if I had, Juliette
would not be screeching it like a rabid shrew at Sir
Renwick. God."

Marie-Elaine paused respectfully, staring down at
the pages in her lap before she erupted into an impas-
sioned disagreement. "Juliette would not be screeching or *speaking* to the Sir Renwick your audience has
come to love and loathe if this chapter made the least
bit of sense. He's going to stick a heated sword through
Lord Michael's heart. Why does Juliette think that losing her dignity will change anything?"

Samuel peeled off his spectacles. "It changes everything. Lord Michael's goals. Sir Renwick's revenge.
Juliette's . . . devotion. Perhaps as their political ele-

ments are revisited, it will change the course of English history."

"Perhaps it will change the history of this house," Emmett commented from the fireplace, where he stood with a bowl over his head, he and his twin brother, Ernest, playing two of the Roundheads waiting to kill Lord Michael.

Marie-Elaine wiggled her bound wrists in agitation. "Can you untie my apron strings? If I'm not going to give up my maidenhood, I ought to make sure that Mrs. Halford doesn't forget the broth she put on before she went to bed with her brandy bottle."

Samuel reached over his shoulder for a sword letter opener on his desk.

"Don't cut the strings," she protested. "I'll do it myself."

He lowered his arm, then froze, glancing up at the distinct sound of light footsteps running across the gallery of the west wing. "I told you that scream was unearthly," he said in a disgruntled voice. "She's going to think we are having an orgy."

"Well, it wouldn't be the first time," Emmett said from the hearth. "A fictitious one, I meant, Your Grace."

Samuel removed his broadsword from his scabbard. "That wasn't exactly the impression I wanted to give Miss Boscastle on her first night in the house."

Bickerstaff, the butler, started collecting pages of the scattered manuscript while Emmett and his brother hid props from the scene behind a towering chinoiserie cabinet. "She wouldn't have had any cause for a bad impression if Marie-Elaine hadn't shrieked to bring down the beams."

Marie-Elaine at last succeeded in tugging her apron knots loose with her teeth. "What rational woman wouldn't scream with a roomful of soldiers waiting to kill the man she loved? And being ravished at the same time by the other man she loves?"

Samuel stopped, halfway to the door, and stared at her. "So you're saying that Juliette has been in love with Sir Renwick all along?"

She pushed a crop of bright curls under her cap. "Well, that's what this chapter implies. I am only giving my interpretation."

Samuel glanced up through the door at the darkened gallery. No one was there. He was certain he'd heard a floorboard creak. "Juliette invited Renwick to her bed. She offered herself to him—in front of witnesses."

"She was haggling for Wickbury's life," the housemaid said hotly. "Of course she's going to say that she loves the other louse to keep Michael from being tortured and left to rot in another rat-infested prison."

Samuel blinked. "Well, I'm fed up with Wickbury winning every duel and vaulting over balcony railings in his ruffled shirt and satin breeches. The self-righteous bastard has to fall sooner or later."

"No, he doesn't," she said with conviction. "It would be a betrayal, Your Grace. Your readers would mob you."

"They have to find me first. I—"

Samuel looked up again. *There*. From the edge of his eye he saw Lily, darting like a wraith back to her room. "Wickbury *has* to change," he said quietly. "Otherwise he will become a cartoon of what he was meant to be."

Emmett and Ernest drew together, tall, grave faced, glancing from master to housemaid. Samuel was aware of how this conversation would sound to a stranger, to the wellborn gentlewoman upstairs who had no inkling that her employer was an anonymous writer of scandalous prose. Or that his staff of reformed varlets not only protected his secret, but contributed their personal experience to enrich the *Wickbury* world. Each of them considered Samuel as a savior of sorts. He knew their association to be the other way around.

"I have to write Michael as I perceive him," he said decisively. "I'd be lost at the first line if I did anything else."

He was almost to the staircase before he caught Marie-Elaine's mutinous retort. "You have to write Lord Wickbury as a hero. And if he loses that perfidious lady because he stands up for what is right, then I say good riddance to the little baggage."

Samuel knocked at the door of the sitting room that adjoined her bedchamber. For several moments Lily did not move from the couch. He must have seen her in the gallery. Too bad *she* had not been able to see what he was up to. Or perhaps she didn't want to know. In any event, Lily was not accustomed to receiving male visitors in her room, although it had been customary in previous centuries, when merchants displayed their wares to the lady of the house as she sipped chocolate or listened to her maid recite the day's itinerary.

But courtesans also received gentlemen in the bedrooms owned or taken on lease by their providers.

She rose in reluctance and walked to the door, not knowing what else she could do. This was not a housekeeper's bedroom. Clearly he expected more. But what? How much was she prepared to give? She opened the door, pondering this, and blinked in astonishment.

She was prepared for an indecent proposal but not for the duke in loose shirttails and an unbuckled sword belt riding low on his lean hips. At least *that* explained the disturbance she had heard from below, if not the lady's cry of distress. It appeared he had been fencing before an audience.

"Your Grace," she said awkwardly, feeling an unfair stab of resentment for having played into the hands of a man so beautifully designed that to stare upon him addled her wits.

"May I come in?"

"It is your house."

He smiled fleetingly. Lily stood unmoving as he shut the door behind him. His house. His housekeeper.

"Is the room to your liking?" he asked, studying the furniture as if he had never seen it before.

She frowned reflectively. "It isn't what I expected for my position."

"The housekeeper's parlor is downstairs." He pivoted. "Miss Boscastle—"

"You might have revealed who you were when I applied for this post, Your Grace," she said, her temper flaring. "I would have appreciated being forewarned that we had met before."

His eyes narrowed. "Do you know how many prospective housekeepers my overworked solicitor would have to interview were it known that a duke sought their services? I'd have unmarried ladies and their mothers offering two housekeepers for the price of one."

She walked him back toward the chaise. "Not to mention the number of disillusioned gentlewomen in the market for a deceitful cad."

"I deserved that."

"I am a desperate woman, Your Grace. Do not underestimate me because of it. Although I have been labeled a lunatic, I understand perfectly well what your intentions are toward me."

His face darkened. "No, you don't."

"Yes, I do."

His eyes searched hers and she felt herself dissolving. Everything she had believed in until now had proven false, and now here this blackguard stood, insisting that she put her trust in him when . . . when he was dressed like one of her Restoration ancestors.

Come to think of it, his costume seemed oddly familiar. He reminded her of someone. Yet the name eluded her. Was he on his way to another masquerade?

"I'm happy to give you the year's wage we agreed upon and have you placed in another house," he said gravely. "I have trustworthy friends who would welcome you in their employ. My coach, of course, is at your disposal—"

That was too much. "I shall not travel in that horrid vehicle again," she said, her voice rising. "Furthermore, I trusted your agent and we have a contract. If you break it, I'll challenge you in . . ."

In court? In perdition?

The rueful awareness in his eyes mocked her. They both knew she had few resources at her disposal. Yes, she could return to her family. She had chosen to leave. But for now she would have to accept that she was no longer a lady of any standing. She was a source of distress, of shame, to her parents. That did not mean, however, that she would be trundled back and forth to another house like a damaged package.

"I will see to it personally that you are returned to your family," he said in a subdued voice.

"I don't want to go home." She tried to keep the panic from her voice. He was too perceptive to trick, however.

"Why not?" he asked her softly.

"I would think that a man who went to such lengths to employ a housekeeper would have investigated her background more thoroughly. You must know about the incident."

He inclined his head, acknowledging the point. "Sit down, please."

His manner was firm.

She obeyed, wondering who he really was. The brash coachman who had embarrassed her at the inn? The profligate duke who had charmed her in a moonlit garden? She had changed roles, too.

"It is obvious," he said, seating himself at the other end of the chaise, "that I have written our characters into a corner."

Lily's brow lifted at his peculiar choice of words.

"I have embarrassed us both beyond repair," he added.

She refrained from stating that she could not have agreed more.

"But," he continued, "that doesn't mean I won't try to undo this damage."

Her throat ached as she looked up into his face. "The damage was done before I came here."

"What, exactly, happened? I won't break your confidence, but it's obvious that you did not suddenly become a housekeeper instead of a bride because it was the better choice."

She looked down. "In fact, it was."

"How so?" he prompted gently.

He could have demanded an answer. His London agent should have asked. He wouldn't believe her side of the story, as much as she was tempted to unburden herself to a person whose intellect and audacity she reluctantly admired. "You must know something of this," she said, her eyes downcast. "I saw my fiancé murder a man in Piccadilly two weeks before our wedding. It happened in the street, and he shot him with a pistol I didn't even know he was carrying. I ran for help. The footmen, our driver, and his friend searched the vicinity and found nothing but a stray dog. The entire incident was attributed to my imagination."

His expression hardened. "Indeed?"

"No one believes me." She shrugged. "Even my own family wanted me to recant what I said."

"So, for merely witnessing a crime, they cast you in exile?"

"I chose to leave." She looked up. "You must have read the papers. Your timing seemed to be providential when it came. It was hardly coincidence, however."

"I read every word," he admitted.

She narrowed her gaze in disbelief. "And you still brought me here?"

"An intelligent person doesn't believe everything that he reads."

She waited for him to say, *However* . . . followed by a covert smile and the murmured suggestion that five other persons could not have overlooked a body lying in the street. Nor could a dead man have walked away. But behind Samuel's impassive stare she sensed that he was giving her confession great consideration.

"Is it possible," he asked at length, "that he was wounded and fled into an area where he could not be found?"

She shook her head, the memory aching like an unhealed scar. "It is improbable. The man fell and didn't move again. But, you see, Jonathan and Mr. Kirkham insist he did not exist at all, that I made up the story."

His eyes held hers. "Are you prone to telling lies?"

"No," she said, smiling wryly. "But as you're aware, I am known to be a passionate reader of romantic stories."

His eyes lit up. "And for that reason alone your word cannot be trusted?"

"Well, I am a woman. That is against my favor in a gentleman's world."

"Not necessarily. Some of us are partial to women in need."

"No one believes me."

He expelled a breath. A shadow of anger crossed his face, becoming an emotion too dark, too forbidding for her to examine. "I, too, have disappointed you."

"I have walked through my vale of innocence, Your Grace," she said. "As long as you are not a murderer, then I am in a better position than as the bride of one."

"That is a dismal recommendation of my character if ever I have heard one. And, believe me, I've heard quite a few."

She lowered her gaze. The intensity of his stare reminded her of how defenseless she really was.

"I brought you here," he said quietly. "I knew what was said of you. You may stay as long as you like."

"As your housekeeper?" she challenged.

His lips curled. "That is what we have agreed. I won't deny that I want you." He took her hand in his. "But I promise you that the choice will be yours."

Defenseless, yes. But his touch warned her that he still desired her. Sensuality might be one of her strongest weapons, unless—and it was highly unlikely—she could sweep him off his feet with her housekeeping skills. He was magnetic, persuasive, a devious young duke who would be any courtesan's dream. It would be hard to resist him. Impossible to deny herself his protection, as she had nowhere else to turn.

She was bound to him for one year. She had agreed to the conditions of a contract she ought to have read. What rights had she given him?

His hand slid from hers, stealing around her waist. His scent was irresistible. It would be easy to submit. If only for a night. She tilted her face to his. She was weary. She was in his power. Her body wanted to be taken, filled, comforted by his.

"Are you in fear for your life?" he asked, his hand stilling. "If you are, then I swear that you'll find safety in my house."

A moan broke in her throat. Desire stirred darkly, a low, insistent throb. His concern penetrated her guard. No one had thought to ask her that. No one had believed her, let alone considered what risk she'd

incurred by telling the truth. Samuel's other hand
stroked the sweep of curls at her shoulder. He kissed
her with lingering attention, their pact not quite sealed,
she guessed, until she gave him sexual pleasure.

Would she succumb? Maybe so. What he was doing
now brought her unexpected bliss.

His lips burned wicked fire down her throat, then
back to her mouth. His breath became a warm entice-
ment, his tongue a brand. She knew what his kisses
would lead to. She swayed against him. This was her
fate.

It was the truth. The part of her that had grown
stronger since her failed engagement felt an inexplica-
ble affinity to this man. A rake or a romantic? A radical
or a visionary? Who better to offer refuge to a lady who
had fallen into ruin? Whom else to turn to but a man
practiced in sin? He drew his hand from her waist.

His lips brushed hers again. "A bargain is a bargain,
Lily."

His low voice enthralled her senses. A promise to
possess or to protect? She heard herself answer with
a steadiness that belied the wild beating of her heart.
She felt a surge of sexuality, a hunger to match his own.

"I will honor our contract, Your Grace."

His eyes lifted to hers. "I will accept all that you
offer and hope for more."

Chapter 22

*S*amuel sat down at his desk in utter darkness and crossed his arms behind his neck. Propped against one of the bookshelves at his back sat a dented shield and rusty lance, a reminder that dreams came at a cost. So, apparently, did employing his new house-keeper.

He smiled, reliving his interlude with Lily. She had given him a taunting look when he had gathered the control to release her. On the surface she might have been a coveted mistress who could choose any lover in the land. But Samuel knew how one could hide behind a pose.

He had lived a disguise long enough. And for all her beguiling composure, Lily had struck him as a woman lost and doing the best she could not to fall apart. The subdued emotion in her eyes brought out his protective nature.

The delightful Goose-Girl who had enchanted him

in London was gone forever. But the golden princess she was meant to become was a poignant mystery and perhaps a temptation greater than he could resist.

It was clear that his infatuation with her was one-sided, a fact that should have dampened his damnable attraction but did the opposite. She might have lost her way, but he would keep his word and take her under his wing. After all, he would have taken her as his wife.

He needed a woman like her in his life. One who would stand up for what was right.

She was forthright and resilient. She had refused to deny the truth, at the cost of her reputation. If Samuel had not fallen in love with her at the masquerade, he would have done so now. He wished he had been allowed to court her. He would have preferred to romance her until she could not resist him.

Was she less valuable because an alleged gentleman had damaged her? Samuel grunted. Whatever guilt he'd felt for luring her here was dissipating. And for the life of him he would swear that the lady had not, as the rumormongers claimed, lost her mind.

Even if she had, the same had been said of him, and she would fit in well with the other staff.

Heaven willing, in time either her appeal would diminish or she would offer him solace for his sexual needs. He had not touched another woman since the night of the masquerade. The closest he had come to a lady's bed was in Wickbury's imaginary world, where

Juliette had tendered her virtue to a villain in exchange for that dashing do-gooder's imperiled life.

He glanced down ruefully at his lap. He was as hard as a standing stone. He couldn't imagine what Lily must think of a man who hoped to seduce her without the courtesy of removing his sword belt. Which brought up a problem even bigger than that of his lingering erection: his other identity.

The Duke of Gravenhurst had vowed Lily could trust him. He meant it. He would cheerfully draw and quarter any person who gave her cause to cry.

But could Lord Anonymous trust *her*?

He uncrossed his arms and rubbed his forehead. Samuel *needed* to write, if only to harness his creative demons before they consumed him. Certainly a duke did not have to make a living by entertaining strangers with his dark imagination. Samuel had been penning lurid stories since the age of seven, when his father had sent him away from home one summer with his aunt in search of a cure for his delicate health.

A boy forbidden to play with other children for fear he would catch his death was bound to seek trouble elsewhere. Samuel had lived on to cause all the trouble he could. His family, unfortunately—with the exception of his older sister—had not survived.

He reached toward the desk for his metallic pen and the ever-present supply of blank paper. He often wrote in the dark, lines intersecting, thoughts overlapping so that the next day most of what he'd gotten down was indecipherable. In ten pages he might salvage a publishable sentence. At times he felt immersed in blessed release. At others venipuncture would have been a preferable occupation.

Sir Renwick drew Juliette into his arms and kissed her like a man drinking from a well after an eternity of drought. From the door Lord Wickbury broke free from his guard. Blood trickled down the side of his mouth. He threw himself between Juliette and his half brother, a hero betrayed. . . .

Samuel stared at his pen. Well, what was the point? He was in no mood for self-discipline, with the scent of the woman he desired still fresh in his mind. Softness. Innocence slowly unraveling. Temptation so intense it raked his nerves like hot needles.

He looked out through the window at the moor, attempting to place fragments of information into a coherent plot. Lily had fled from London to escape marrying a man she claimed was a murderer. The scandal had been quickly hushed, no doubt by the influential if infamous Boscastles. If Samuel had not personally manipulated the press so many times in the past, he would not have believed it possible.

He believed her.

And instead of crafting the first chapter in his next book or finishing the elusive last, he would write a let-

ter to Benjamin Thurber in London, empowering him
to renew all means possible to find out exactly what
Lily had witnessed and whether or not Samuel needed
to take action to protect her.

Lily woke up before dawn, wondering momentarily
where she was. And whether she had awakened from
one nightmare to find herself in one unaccountably
worse. No. It wasn't worse. Simply peculiar. She would
rather live as a duke's housekeeper than as a stranger's
wife. She could have landed in a harsher fix. She could
have ended up in an asylum, instead of a manor
house. Whatever happened at St. Aldwyn House, and
no matter what impropriety hid in the shadows, she
would at least not bear witness to another murder.

The possibility roused her from her comfortable
bed. Someone, and she assumed it had not been the
duke, had left on the sitting room chaise a freshly
starched apron, a blue muslin dress, a cap, and a circlet of brass keys, along with a map of the west wing.
This, she noted, would be her domain—the kitchen,
housekeeper's parlor, physic garden, and certain of the
outbuildings. She also noticed that from her bedroom
window she could see above the walled rose garden to
the hillside graves. She closed the curtains, shivering
a little.

She went downstairs and soon found the housekeeper's parlor, her private office. The pleasantly fur-

nished room contained a desk, armchair, small linen-covered table for meals, a clock, and a locked stillroom for the various elixirs and physics she would dispense. She could only hope to learn what she was doing before anyone fell ill.

She proceeded then to the enormous kitchen, pausing in the passageway to examine a small musty chapel. When she was not supervising suppers, she mused, she would be praying to resist temptation. The kitchen was abuzz when at length she arrived, bright with blazing firelight.

Scullions chopped juicy onions and shallots pulled from the fragrant ropes hanging from the oak-beam ceiling. The butler, Bickerstaff, gave her a distracted nod, and engaged her in brief conversation before disappearing into his pantry to spot-polish silver for a party that he said was planned for the end of the month. He explained that the twin footmen, Emmett and Ernest, shared a room off the kitchen, where they cleaned their uniforms, gossiped about guests, and played an occasional game of leapfrog.

Two scullions scrubbed ashes and vinegar in slop pails across the slab floor. The pungency made Lily's eyes water. Another maid restocked the Welsh dresser with brandy, butter crocks, and imported spices.

One scullery maid curtsied as she squeezed out the door with a bucket of slops. Another came out of a larder carrying what appeared to be a cloth-covered ham. Lily went forward to help her.

"Is this ham for our breakfast?" she asked pleasantly, setting the plate on the table.

The chitchat behind her ceased. Lily looked around and saw Marie-Elaine and Wadsworth coming down the three stone steps from the servants' hall.

The valet turned up his nose at the covered plate. "Ham? Only in our dreams, dear. The porkers who live on this estate are kept as pets."

"Pets?" Lily said in surprise.

"Pigs, sheep, chickens." Mrs. Halford made a face. "They're all our friends."

Marie-Elaine inserted herself between the cook and the table. "His Grace doesn't eat flesh. So neither do we."

Lily sighed. "I thought he was joking."

"Afraid not," Marie-Elaine said.

She watched Mrs. Halford remove the cloth from a large head of braised cabbage. "How unappetizing. I hope that isn't for breakfast."

Bickerstaff emerged from the pantry and pulled the cover back over the cabbage. "No need to stare at the thing this early in the morning. It's for lunch. His Grace will have eggs and toast, marmalade, and coffee to break his fast."

"In which room?" Lily asked, not having seen a sign of him on her way through the house.

"He isn't up yet," Marie-Elaine answered, sharing a private look of amusement with the cook. "But when he rises, he takes his meals in the east wing."

"The east wing? I studied the sketch of the house. The east wing was excluded. It seemed to be closed off."

"That is right," Marie-Elaine said. "For now you are only allowed access to the western block. This is where your bedchamber, parlor, and the kitchen are located."

"For now?" Lily wondered at this air of mystery. It made her suspect the duke had a mistress ensconced in a private suite. Her lips curled. Imagine him sneaking between wings from one bed to another.

"Is that suitable, Miss Boscastle?"

Suitable? She shook off her reverie and traced the well-modulated voice to the duke standing outside the kitchen window, a moor pony nosing over his shoulder. One of the scullery maids passed the duke a carrot. He looked remarkably well rested for a man of his indecent inclinations.

"The east wing is reserved for private use."

"It's fine with me," Lily said. "It's entirely your business if you have a collection of dead housekeepers who forgot to follow the rules, or even live ones who—"

She heard one of the maids gasp. Obviously it would take Lily a little time to remember that she was no longer a blithe country lady who could be free to tease at times. She was a servant now. She ought to stitch up her mouth.

But the duke did not look offended.

"You'll find out if you stay here long enough," he said.

And, as his laughing eyes might have implied, *if you agree to sleep with me*. Lily glanced around the kitchen in the hope that no one else had come to the same conclusion. It was obvious from Bickerstaff's rumbling chuckle that he had read plenty into the duke's meaning and that she was the only one in the dark.

Chapter 23

*A*nd so she passed her first day as housekeeper of St. Aldwyn House. And the next. Until nine days flew by, and even though she had never worked as hard in her life, she had also never fallen in so naturally with another group of company before.

She had soon realized it wasn't only the duke who kept a close eye on her. Marie-Elaine watched her like a hawk, and Samuel, for all his commanding presence, had virtually disappeared.

She began to suspect that he regretted his decision to hire her. Not only did he seem to avoid her during the day, but he spent his other waking hours in the forbidden-to-her east wing. This prohibition might have been intended to provoke her natural curiosity and thus catch her out as untrustworthy early in her employment.

But Lily wasn't the tiniest bit tempted to explore the other regions of the house. The fewer rooms under her management, the better.

She had never appreciated the amount of labor it took to maintain an estate this size. Whereas in her frivolous past she had offhandedly admired the numerous paintings, plaster busts, and cut-glass chandeliers that graced her modest Tissington house, she now regarded these objects as distasteful gatherers of dust.

The duke appeared to be an avid collector of more whimsical pieces than she had seen in any museum, a few garish and ungainly. The Irish wake table in the breakfast room gave her a jolt every time she walked past it. The knight in armor beside the staircase rattled whenever the butler closed a door.

But the illuminated Flemish manuscript on the prayer table in the screens passage was a work of art. Lily assumed he had inherited these objects until Marie-Elaine let it slip over tea that the majority had been sent from well-wishers around the globe. Strangers. Potentates. Diplomats.

"Why?" she asked as she and the housemaid restocked the cupboards with linens, soap, and candles. "I know the duke is influential."

Marie-Elaine lowered her voice. "He's different; that's all I can tell you. And there's no finer master in the world. People who've never met him send him gifts. He keeps every one. Maybe it's his politics."

"But why all these mysterious airs?" Lily asked. "Why all this dramatic nonsense about closing off the other wing? What does His Grace have to hide? I understand it's not my business to pry, but it's as if he wants me to ask. I think it's absurd."

"I didn't say he had anything to hide," Marie-Elaine replied, suddenly tight-lipped, which only heightened Lily's curiosity.

His behavior made little sense. He caroused at will in London. He was a well-known if notorious figure in society. And at home he was a man who not only isolated himself but instructed his staff to do the same. But Lily wished to hide, too. His reclusive ways suited her well. Not that she could hide from the desire that glinted in his eyes when he thought she wasn't looking.

And she had to wonder about all the lovers that he allegedly kept dangling and who had yet to appear, a situation that could hardly be helped by the daunting journey to Dartmoor.

Still, after almost a fortnight in his employ she could no longer deny that something in St. Aldwyn House was amiss, and that whatever it was did not seem to be connected to the duke's reputation.

She could not, however, pin down the nature of his clandestine activities.

Several times she had overheard the other servants laughing behind closed doors, only to encounter a deep silence when she entered the room, hoping to be included in the fun. Was it her upper-class background that ostracized her? Had they been warned she had gone off her head right before her wedding? Or did they disrespect her because the duke had not bothered to conceal his original intentions toward her?

Perhaps the duke practiced the dark arts. Lily had never forgotten his solicitor asking her if she was afraid of the supernatural. What could he have meant?

A strange instinct awakened her on the twelfth night of her stay at St. Aldwyn House. She pushed back the bedcovers and sat up attentively, wondering if the wind had blown up while she slept. Its keen gusting across the moor often carried in the stillness. But the branches of the hazel tree she could see silhouetted behind her curtain remained still.

She did not hear any cries for help.

Marie-Elaine's warning, which had sounded ridiculous during the day, now seemed fraught with meaning.

For your own peace of mind, stay inside your room after everyone has gone to bed. Do not explore the house late at night if you know what is good for you.

Lily slipped out of bed and went resolutely to the window. She could not have seen any foul play in the east wing from her proximity, even with a telescope. To her astonishment, however, she *could* make out a familiar figure dancing lithely about behind the hillside stones.

Another man—good heavens, it appeared to be Bickerstaff—was holding aloft a lantern and what looked to be a book.

The ungodly sight raised gooseflesh on her arms.

She scrubbed the heel of her hand across the pane of glass. The duke looked agitated, animated, dreamily attractive from her perspective.

She remembered that he had been engaged in a duel the morning of the masquerade. Surely a man did not challenge his own butler? Another practice swordfight? A society of spies that gathered on a remote moor for their covert enterprises? Perhaps the cries she had perceived in the dark were those of prisoners the duke kept for who knew what purpose. Perhaps she didn't want to know at all.

She drew a breath. No one would believe her now. They hadn't before. Yet the longer she watched, the more it appeared that the duke was not waving a sword in the air but rather some long instrument, as if he were enacting a ritual.

Was this man sparring or casting a spell?

She shook her head. Either way, he moved in this mist like fluid steel and engaged like a swordsman's dream. Even at a distance she had to appreciate his fencing skill—and wonder why on earth he had to practice at this hour. With a stick.

Riposte.

Retreat.

Forestall.

Lily felt a pang of longing for the times she had watched her brother fencing by the stream. Gerald's skills could not compete with the duke's ability, however. Did her brother, her family, miss her at all?

She sighed, Samuel again commanding her attention.

His long black hair absorbed glimmers of moonlight. His snug satin breeches and heavy boots molded to his perfect male form in a fashion that stirred not only her female senses but also a memory stuck deep in her mind.

She could have sworn that she had witnessed this same performance in the past. He might be an amateur thespian. This might be an act from a famous play she had studied years ago. Hadn't she wondered the night of the literary masquerade if he was an actor?

Twenty minutes or so later he and Bickerstaff vanished in the light mist that enshrouded the estate. She returned to bed, sleep impossible.

In the morning she would apply herself diligently to her job. She would remove the stubborn red-wine stain from the marble sideboard in the main drawing room. She would study her cookery books and instruct the under housemaids to carefully remove the cobwebs from the duke's Staffordshire crockery.

And she would pretend she had not noticed the duke's behavior from her window last night. She would not admit she had been spying on him, because, as irrational as it might seem to an outsider, Lily understood that she was safer here than anywhere else.

Chapter 24

"All right," Bickerstaff said, shivering in the mist, "here is the virgin's grave. Beneath lie the poor murdered bones of Sir Renwick's sister, Elizabeth Anne."

"Why do we have to enact his part?" Samuel demanded. "It was disturbing enough to write. Who would attend an opera about ghosts?"

"We are doing this as a precaution for your readers, Your Grace. You would not want to print a spell to raise a virgin bride from the dead in the unlikely event it would work."

Samuel scoffed. "You are an intelligent person. What do you estimate the chances to be of such an occurrence?"

"Having worked at St. Aldwyn House for years, I would not underestimate your abilities for one moment."

"Stop flattering me."

"One never knows, Your Grace."

Samuel leaned back against the longest cairn. "Except that in the first place, we *don't* know if there is a family buried here from the Dark Ages, or if they had a daughter, and *if* she was virtuous at all."

"That is true," Bickerstaff murmured, studying the parchment book that crumbled at the bottom corner when he turned the page. "But Lord Anonymous has a responsibility. He does not want innocents disturbed from their eternal rest because he has given away an ancient spell in his series."

"Sir Renwick is doing this," Samuel reminded him. "Not me. He's trying one last time to resurrect the sister he murdered in the hope that she can save him from the damnation he's got coming to him."

Bickerstaff sighed. "It is quite romantic, Your Grace. We all know that Lord Wickbury will renew his strength to rescue Juliette, and Renwick's forsaken sister."

"I'm not so sure. I don't know what either of us would do if some lady skeleton stuck her head through the stones and said, 'Stop trying to resurrect me. I've earned my eternal repose.' I might faint like a maiden myself."

"Should I finish reading the spell or not? It will be another month until the next full moon."

"I'll have to write around the scene if we—" Samuel caught Bickerstaff by his coattails and pulled him behind the sheltering stones. "Put out the lantern," he said in an amused voice. "We're being watched from the corner of the west wing."

Bickerstaff obediently extinguished the lantern, peering up into the mist. "Your Grace is mistaken. The— Ah, the housekeeper's window."

Samuel chuckled. "She saw us this time."

Bickerstaff closed the tome of ancient spells, his nose twitching at the moldy effluvium that arose from the fragile pages. "It is obvious that Your Grace has another maiden to worry about."

"A live one, too."

Lily was snipping flowers in the garden the next morning when she spotted the village reverend at the moor gate. He was obviously angling for her attention. She would have ignored him if he hadn't called to her until she had to look up and acknowledge his young, friendly face.

"I missed you at church last Sunday!" he shouted, his hand already unlatching the gate. "I'm the Reverend Cedric Doughty. My wife wants you to come to tea."

Lily flushed, embarrassed by her muddy boots and the pigs rooting in her wake. She had not been told to expect company. "I'm just settling in, Mr. Doughty. You'll have to excuse me. This is a large estate to manage."

"It is an estate of undefined evil," he said without preamble, and he stared Lily in the eye as if she were supposed to break down and give him reason to agree.

She straightened. "There is evil everywhere."

He dropped his voice, looking past her to the peat wagon that sat in front of the barn. Lily wasn't sure, but it seemed as if she saw a pair of feet standing in the wagon's shadow. "Have you personally been tempted to participate in any acts of sin that you would like to confess?" he asked.

Lily stared. "Are you asking me if I spy on my employer's personal activities?"

"Should the nature of these activities go against the laws of God, it is incumbent on you to bring them to salvation's light."

"It is incumbent on me to remember to take the eggs out of the sawdust for His Grace's omelet," she replied, glancing inadvertently to the hill, where last night the duke had been up to something unusual indeed.

He blinked, his face bright above his cleric's collar. "You seem too decent a lady to be led astray."

"You would be surprised. For your information, Mr. Doughty, it is my sanity that is in question. The duke took me on because no one else would hire me."

"Your sanity." He looked disappointed. "Then there is little help for that. Give the duke my regards. I shall hope to see his household—you included—at church on Sunday."

Lily watched him mount his pony and ride around

the hill. "You can come out from behind that wagon now," she said, turning distractedly and walking straight against the duke's unmoving form.

She had not guessed it was him hiding behind the wagon.

"Your Grace," she said, shivering at the long, penetrating look he gave her. "I didn't realize that you were here."

He smiled. A sudden breeze stirred the folds of his impeccably crisp neckcloth. The pure white fabric played well against his charcoal gray frock coat and fitted trousers. "I always make a point of staying out of sight when someone hopes to save my soul." His eyes searched hers. "You passed his interrogation like a—"

"Spymaster?"

"Strange analogy, but, yes."

She moistened her bottom lip. "You heard everything?"

"Yes. I thought I would intervene, but you handled him better than I ever have. I usually confess to some outrageous sin whenever he confronts me so that he'll grant me forgiveness and go away. This never works, mind you. He knows I'm lying, which is another sin by itself."

"No wonder he's convinced you're in league with the devil."

"You should not have told the pious busybody anything of your past. It is none of his affair. I give money to the parish."

Unwilling pleasure stole over her. "I did not give any of Your Grace's secrets away."

"How do you know I have anything to hide?"

His dark stare filled her with unreasonable happiness. "Whether you do or not is not *my* affair."

He glanced up at the house, his gaze musing. "It will be by tonight."

"I don't understand."

"We are having a party at eleven o'clock in the east wing."

Lily stared up at him as calmly as she could. He could have invited her to inspect the dovecote and made it seem like an adventure. "Eleven o'clock? If you have a request for a preferred menu, that is little time to prepare it properly. I . . ." She had to rein herself in. "I am still learning the rules, Your Grace."

"We don't observe many rules in this house. I suppose it is my fault for being too liberal."

"Eleven o'clock," she repeated, curbing the questions she longed to ask. "In the east wing. I shall do my best to set a proper table. How many guests does Your Grace expect?"

He gave her a smile that defied decency. "You're to be my guest of honor, Miss Boscastle. Let me turn the tables and entertain you for the night. I think it's time for the next step of your initiation into our household.

As long as you accept. Attendance, however, is an irrevocable step. You will be discouraged from leaving here after tonight if you come to my table. Do you understand?"

It was all she could do to maintain a solemn demeanor. He was quite the thespian.

"Is the entire evening to be conducted in this furtive manner?"

"Yes." He glanced at her cap. "Do you have a decent dress?"

"I have several."

She had no idea what any of it could mean. It sounded slightly depraved and entirely intriguing. "Eleven o'clock it is," she said. "As your guest of honor. I would not miss it for the world."

Chapter 25

$\mathcal{L}$ily could hardly wait for the evening. The suspense stretched her nerves. Shortly after lunch she dropped the duke's finest china bowl on the floor. Then two eggs slipped out of her basket and broke in the sink. The servants—and it was *not* her imagination—smiled and elbowed one another like secret operatives assigned to report on her every move. Marie-Elaine's daughter followed her as she gathered lavender buds in the physic garden to sweeten her bath. She could not fold a towel without the staff halting all activity to watch.

By teatime she was tempted to draw her apron over her head, pull a knife from the kitchen sink, and threaten the footmen in French to tell everything. Or else.

Another member of the staff appeared before dusk, a gentleman she had not previously met but who was introduced to her as the duke's steward. His face

looked mummified, and he wore the longest gloves
Lily had ever seen. Marie-Elaine referred to him as
"the elusive Mr. Lawton" because he visited St. Aldwyn House only twice a month. The rest of the time he
disappeared on the duke's business.

Then evening came. She bathed by candlelight and
dressed in the blush-pink gauze gown that had been
designed as part of her trousseau.

A housekeeper would never dare to wear such a
dress. Tonight Lily was a guest of honor. She swept her
hair into a prim knot upon her nape. She wore no jew-
elry. It was a relief to regard her image in the looking
glass. Her housekeeper's cap and unadorned muslin
skirt added thickness to her face and hips, two areas
that in Lily's estimation required no avoirdupois. Her
complexion had regained some color from her work in
the garden.

She realized that she had begun to recover from
her broken engagement. Her opinion mattered in this
house. True, the duke provoked her at times, but with
a tantalizing style. She provoked him, too, and yet she
sensed he did not mind. On the contrary. He seemed to
encourage her.

Would the evening live up to her expectations?

Would she discover that the duke supervised a secret society of eccentrics eager to draw another into its
fold? It was all she could do to maintain a solemn demeanor when she descended the stairs to find him, in

black evening attire, waiting to escort her to the east wing. She paused. At last.

The forbidden land.

They strolled through connecting torchlit corridors to an arcaded doorway above which a plaster frieze of biblical lions stood guard. Lily glanced back, gasping softly. The duke's reflection dwarfed hers in a gilt-framed series of Venetian glass mirrors mounted upon the walls. From the terrace outside a fountain sent glittery spumes into the air, like liquid jewels.

"You look beautiful, Lily," he said. She turned her head, unprepared for the pleasure in his eyes as he regarded her. She felt warm despite the moorland mist that crept through the open doors to curl faintly around the Ionic columns.

"Thank you," she whispered.

"Thank you for accepting my invitation. I was afraid you would change your mind."

She could see weapons mounted on the wall, statues grouped in mythological scenes, French fables depicted in the tapestries and frescoes on the soaring ceiling.

Busts of Shakespeare, Goethe, and Defoe occupied a high-arched gallery that faced the long windows. The hall appeared to be a tribute to the great storytellers of all time. At least his dedication to the arts had not been a lie.

"It is incredible," she said, shaking her head.

He smiled. "I'm relieved you think so. I was hoping that you would not be overwhelmed."

By him. Perhaps. But this wing of the house . . .

This was his domain, a world of whimsy, a secret place sculpted from dreams. And he looked as if he was its ruling prince, as if he had sprung from a fairy tale, his tailored evening wear enhancing his almost too-lean elegance. Any suggestion of slightness disappeared the instant he took her hand. Her fingers brushed a masculine torso that awakened her entire body. His hand tightened possessively over hers, steadying as well as disconcerting her. His grasp urged her to wait just a little longer for the surprise he had planned.

Wait. How much longer *could* she wait?

It didn't seem like the time to ask for him to explain the anguished moans she'd heard in the night, the pleas for mercy, the hair-raising scene she had watched him enact behind the burial cairns. Perhaps she should be frightened. If she had not been met with so much kindness in this house, she would have been tempted to turn and flee. But she was compelled by her own curiosity to discover the truth.

Would she wish afterward that she had not been told?

The least plausible explanation for this mystery was that the Duke of Gravenhurst had formed a clandestine organization of wicked ladies and gentlemen who met on his isolated estate to live out their most undisciplined desires. Their master fascinated her beyond measure.

And that Lily was to be initiated as the housekeeper of their naughty society. To judge by the monuments in this hall, its members seemed to be a well-read if lascivious bunch.

An illustration from a risqué book she had once read about the Hellfire Club and its imitators formed in her mind. A lady in a half-unhooked corset standing in a candlelit chamber with a whip in her hand, shirtless gentlemen kneeling around her. Lily quickly replaced the picture with that of a decently clad gentlewoman stirring a teaspoon. Her imagination *did* take her to strange places.

"Lily?" the duke said gently, questioning her sudden hesitation. "I think our company is ready for us."

Suddenly she decided *she* might not be ready for his company.

He smiled again.

How could she resist?

His gloved fingers squeezed hers and lent her courage. His presence infused her with a reckless excitement that overpowered her doubts. Despite her current status, she had been raised to be polite. It was too late to turn down this invitation. His eyes gleamed like smoke with underlying sparks of mayhem.

The doors opened before them.

She drew her breath.

Bickerstaff, in immaculate livery, bowed. Emmett

and Ernest stood at either end of a massive table lit with long-branched golden candelabras. Heavily scrolled silver dishes shone on the pure white damask table-cloth. The guests rose as the duke escorted her forward: Marie-Elaine, Mrs. Halford, Wadsworth, other servants, the Reverend Mr. Cedric Doughty and his young wife, another gentleman whom Samuel introduced as Baron Ardmore, a friend and poet from a neighboring village.

She stared across the table at the serving platters she had not seen prepared. Samuel walked her to her chair. The gilt figures of a lady and gentleman embraced beneath the glass dome of the ormolu clock on the mantelpiece. It was well past eleven.

"Sit down, Lily," Samuel whispered, giving her another gentle nudge. "I'm sure you guessed that I have a secret. It's past time I shared it. I know you will agree."

She glanced down again at the table. "Yes, I do wish to be told the truth." At least she thought she did.

The reverend's wife smiled at her, looking too proper to belong to any amorous club. There also weren't any whips, chains, or sacrificial altars in sight. Of course, the east wing had other rooms. Would Lily be led into another labyrinth of secrets?

Her face must have reflected her thoughts.

"Sit down," Samuel said in amusement.

His familiar manner reassured her.

She sat, her gaze narrowing on the duke. She had never known a gentleman to play such an enticing game. "A midnight confession," she said, her voice controlled, her hands trembling. "I admit it. Your Grace has intrigued me."

He lifted his wineglass to her with mordant cheer. "You're a captive audience. You belong here now."

She felt her pulse quicken. She could feel the other guests staring at her. They seemed perfectly normal, if entertaining one's own staff could be excused for a night. It was anything but the saturnalian revel she had feared, and yet she could not ignore the duke's last words, the expectancy in the air.

She lifted her chin, her voice faint but clear. "To what exactly do I belong?"

Chapter 26

*H*e could have replied, *To me.*

He wanted nothing else but to be her protector, to rekindle the spark that had ignited between them in London. Still, now that he understood why she had been forced to come to him, he would be half a man to take advantage of the refuge he had provided. Lily would have to admit she wanted him on her own. He believed that she did. Pray God he would not ruin his chance by revealing who he was tonight. And that she would not regard him as another spurious male.

He would lose everything if she betrayed him. He needed her trust perhaps even more than she needed his.

He would give anything to keep her here. Since she had come to his house, he had discovered a depth to her that beguiled him. Another woman would have considered taking a domestic position as a step down. Or a complete fall. But Lily had accepted her place with humility. She treated the other servants like friends. She had not allowed her disgrace to steal her dignity.

She was the perfect fit for Samuel, Lord Anonymous, and St. Aldwyn House. He would never find another woman like her. None of the heroines he'd created could compete with Lily for raising tension and excitement.

He smiled at her over the rim of his glass. She looked delicious in that pink gauze dress. He exhaled quietly. Her eyes reflected a good-natured confusion, a cautious willingness to play along with the game.

"Well?" she whispered with an edge of impatience, her shoulder lifting in a shrug that made him wish they were alone. "Out with it. A midnight confession. I could use a little diversion in my life."

"Welcome to Wickbury, Lily. I can't tell you how delighted I am that you have become part of our world."

She stared at him rather stupidly, the other guests erupting into a stream of chatter that went over her head. It took a moment or two for the truth to penetrate her daze. His eyes danced with sheer enjoyment, a look utterly devoid of shame.

"Wickbury," she said, hearing herself laugh, a reaction to hide her bewilderment, a rush of anxiety.

"I think she knew all along," Marie-Elaine said softly.

The reverend's wife threw Lily a sympathetic look. "I didn't believe it either, when we moved to the parish. It was two years before my husband told me, and only then because he caught me with a certain book. At that point I had to confess my infatuation with the author. I did get a scolding."

"The author." Lily rose from her chair, studying Samuel's face. "You are—"

"Lord Anonymous." He stood, smiling the beautiful smile that had riveted her the night of the masquerade.

She shook her head, disbelieving. How could she not have guessed? He had dropped more clues than she could count. "You're—"

He grimaced. "Don't make me repeat that absurd sobriquet. I didn't choose it."

"And everyone accused me of madness," she said. "I never dreamt it. *Am* I dreaming?" She sat down again, so astonished she barely noticed the other guests and staff covertly leaving the table and exiting the room. She was suddenly alone with Lord Anonymous. Part of his inner circle.

"It's as if I've walked through a mirror," she said to herself distractedly.

"What do you mean?"

"Well, this is the other side of what I saw—or what you wanted to show. Everyone appears the same on the outside, but you were only reflections before." She could not stop the note of censure that stole into her voice. "You are far deeper than I first perceived."

"And this upsets you?" he asked with concern.

She frowned at him. "Please give me a little time to decide."

The candle flames accentuated the deceptive vulnerability of his face. She gazed around him to the empty chairs that the reverend and his wife had occupied. She gasped in realization. "*Oh*," she said, her eyes lifting to Samuel's. "You put him up to testing me, tempting me to betray you. How awful of you both."

"It was his idea."

"That is no excuse."

He bowed his head, but Lily was unmoved. "You didn't betray me," he said, and looked up at her. "As I recall, you defended me."

"Yes, not knowing who you actually were. And that you weren't merely eavesdropping but hoping to entrap me."

His eyes narrowed in disagreement. "I hoped for the exact opposite."

Lily wasn't sure what to make of him. "What would you have done if I had thrown myself at his feet and pleaded for him to save me?"

"That would have been a problem," he admitted.

"I walked right into your trap," she said thoughtfully.

He leaned his head to hers. "Walk closer, I implore you."

"You're going to knock over the wine," she whispered, her voice catching. "Your housekeeper would be displeased."

"Then I shall be careful," he whispered into her ear. "I want to earn her approval above all else."

He drew his chair closer to hers and sat. His knee touched hers. She couldn't move. "What do you make of it? Is it truly a shock?"

"An understatement."

"Have some wine."

She took several sips.

"Did that help?" he asked in concern.

She nodded to be agreeable and stared across the table at his hand. She tried to picture his long, gloved fingers grasping a pen, writing the dark stories that had stolen her heart. Instead, all she could envision was his hand stealing down her back. The duke of duality. Was it a shock? She finished the rest of her wine. She didn't know if it was red or white. She was too dazed to taste the difference. Nor had she set this table.

"I have never been so wrong about anything in my life," she said without thinking.

He looked worried. "What do you mean?"

"The author of *Wickbury*. You aren't a woman."

His laughter rang pleasantly across the room. "I hope you aren't disappointed."

She glanced up at his face. "No."

She didn't know what she felt. Maybe it was elation, curiosity, most certainly relief.

He said, "You'll never know how tempted I was to prove myself to you the night of the masquerade."

She shook her head again. "I was afraid you were going to confess that you were some sort of a warlock."

"Rather like Sir Renwick Hexworthy?"

"Now that you mention him, yes."

He regarded her with an intensity that she could not escape. "I remember that you favored him over Wickbury."

She felt the wine suddenly go to her head. "Of course, neither of them is real."

His voice dropped to a confidential tone. "They are to me."

He wasn't only Lord Anonymous. He was Michael, Lord Wickbury, exiled young earl, the hero too valiant for his own good. He was Sir Renwick Hexworthy, the villain that his lady readers ached to redeem. Longwand. And Lord Wickbury—Broadsword. Of all the conceit. Or was he in fact magically endowed? The series more than hinted at the sexual prowess of both men. Why did she have to think of that now?

Lily released a sigh. So *that* was what Samuel and Bickerstaff had been doing at the cairn last night. The scene had looked familiar because Lily had seen it foreshadowed in his last published novel. How could a woman's heart not be touched by a scoundrel whose grief had led him on a ruinous path?

Betrayals. Abduction. Secret pacts. Digging up dead sisters. Trapdoors and alchemy. As if being a duke weren't enough.

Her thoughts tumbled out of control. This man—
the writer, that was—had kept her awake with his delicious intrigue for nights on end. And that was before
she had even met the rogue. Or rogues. The masked
devil in London who had unabashedly tried to seduce
her had nothing on the characters he had created. Sep-
arately, a lady might have a chance. Combined, their
magnetism simply overpowered.

Possibilities intrigued her. She was sipping wine
with Sir Renwick. Or at least with the man whose
twisted mind had invented all Renwick's thwarted
passion, power lust, and evil machinations.

Come to think of it, the duke and Sir Renwick shared
the same physical characteristics—the raven hair, penetrating eyes, the supple physique—and she stopped
that line of thought. Her lips firmed. She would *not* ask
him what had inspired the code names *Longwand* and
Broadsword.

She might have to wait until he wrote a chapter on
the subject for her alone.

A warlock. Samuel wished it were true. He understood
how she had come to that conclusion. His staff and
friends had awaited her like a coven about to wage a
metaphysical war. All this mystery and melodrama a
few minutes before the stroke of twelve. What should
she have expected? It was too late to take back his
confession. Magic in reverse. He had disenchanted his

own housekeeper. She looked as if she was still not convinced.

"I knew there was something," she murmured as he reached for the wine decanter. "But not this. I saw you and Bickerstaff on the moor, by the way."

He looked at her. "I know."

Her full lips gleamed in a smile. "Do I have to take an oath that I won't tell?"

He gallantly refilled her glass. Her company stirred more than his imagination. "Yes," he said, lowering the wine decanter to claim her hand. "Do you mind?"

"Of all the things that Chloe said were written about you . . ." Her voice trailed off. "How do you manage to keep it from society?"

"Some people have their suspicions about me," he said with a languid smile. "There is a journalist who has attempted to bribe Philbert's wife, of all people. And I'm a perfect example of why you can't believe everything you've read. For example . . . do you think I have bedded half the ladies in London?"

Lily blushed. "Well, if the gossip my cousin shared with me is true, then that estimate is going up at an appalling rate."

"It shouldn't go anywhere except in the rubbish bin," he said with certainty. "I have made up most of those unsavory rumors about myself."

"You?" She coughed delicately to cover a gasp of relief.

"Yes . . ."

His eyes radiated a playful sensuality that suggested he had enjoyed slandering himself. And that the rumors could not have been all smoke. "Was it really necessary to create your disrepute?"

He lifted his shoulder in a negligent shrug. "At first it was a bit of mischief, but it attracted notice that wasn't always detrimental to my causes."

"What causes?"

"This year it was corruption in the clergy and the war loan funds. Last winter we dealt with the low wages of rural laborers."

"You have friends in London who know?" she asked thoughtfully.

His gaze flickered over her. How arousing to talk to her like this.

"Some of them, such as Philbert and our printer, stand to lose more than I do."

She lowered her eyes demurely, murmuring, "You might be surprised. The Duke of Gravenhurst is quite an attractive catch. If he were known to be leading another life, his infamy would be irresistible."

"But then Lord Anonymous would either have to stop writing or withdraw his support for his reforming friends." He took a pause, so drawn to her unguarded warmth that he could not hide it. "What are your intentions for the morning?"

Lily glanced up, her shoulders gilded in candlelight. "It seems more appropriate to ask what your intentions are for the rest of the night."

His thumb traced across her knuckles. His hard mouth lifted at one corner. "What I want to know is whether you will pack your bags to escape me the moment we part company."

"A contract is a contract. I intend to uphold our agreement."

He felt a shudder at the base of his spine. As naturally as taking his next breath, he moved his hand to her elbow and drew her toward him. "What sort of pact would a poet seal without requesting a kiss?"

She pursed her lips and kissed him primly, her eyes heavy but not closed.

"Trust me, Lily."

"You have to trust me, too, Your Grace."

"I've promised to protect you." He forced himself to release her. "I also promised you supper, and perhaps we should have eaten before this conversation."

She drew a breath. "I think I need to be alone."

"Are you all right?"

"Yes." She nodded. "I think I am."

"Then go."

She rose, darting him an inscrutable look before she turned. It took all his control to stand and act as if the room had not suddenly become an inferno of heat and temptation. Lily would have the rest of the night to reflect on what he had told her. He would stew in his own juices.

But as she had reminded him, a contract was a contract. The law bound them to each other for one year.

And yet this illusion of power gave him little pleasure as he watched her retreat. He wanted Lily to reciprocate his attraction, to find him as irresistible as he did her.

Lily walked alone through the hall, stepping through the arrows of moonlight that pierced the tall windows. The statues above observed her flight.

Lord Anonymous.

Was it real?

I've promised to protect you.

But surely he needed protection, too.

She needed a few moments to reflect. To reconcile his identity with the man he showed himself to be. She had to admit she found Gravenhurst as wickedly alluring as she did Lord Anonymous. Imagine her accusing him of being a woman. How he must have been laughing inside.

And how completely he had won her heart. He had taken her under his wing and made her feel comfortable as part of the household. Everyone at St. Aldwyn had. He had chosen his staff well. Lily would like to think he had chosen her for her character, too. Compatible—that was the word. None of them perfect, but all fitting together.

Now he had confided his deepest secret in her. Why would she ever want to leave?

If he took a mistress or a wife, could she bear it?

She could manage his household, but she had no influence over his intimate affairs. It would grieve her to watch him fall in love with another woman. Still, he was eligible and it was bound to happen. She was the one who had sworn off romance, who had said she would never marry.

She had traveled all this way to put such complications behind her. Yet Samuel was the most tempting complication she had ever come across. She must admit it was too late to do anything about it. She was bound to him by more than her signature.

She felt his presence from the door directly behind her. She slowed, listening, waiting for him to follow. The fountain splashed from the terrace shadows outside. She did not hear Samuel's footsteps. She turned, looking around the hall. A door half-hidden behind a hanging tapestry caught her notice. She walked toward it and pushed aside the tasseled fringe, testing the knob.

Unlocked. She assumed that the small antechamber within held a private stairwell to the duke's suite. He had given her freedom of the house. Would he object if she took him at his word? She decided not.

She stared up the smooth oaken stairs that rose to her right. Did Lord Anonymous write in one of the darkened rooms that she had previously been forbidden to enter?

She grasped her skirts and took the first two steps. The wood felt different on the third. The tip of her slipper pressed a concealed device that chirped only once before a skeleton dressed like a dashing cavalier popped up from a hidey-hole on the first landing. Her heart pounded as she skirted his leering skull.

Thus assured that her quest would prove entertaining, if she could survive it, she proceeded at a slower pace up the remaining stairs.

Chapter 27

*L*ily had never done anything as brazen and in-
decorous as to invite herself to a gentleman's
bed. Samuel had hidden his identity from her, but
not his desire. Until his confession, she had not realized that she wanted to be the one to fulfill his desires,
as rudimentary as her knowledge of the carnal arts
might be. By all rights she should have been in a bridal
bed, not posed like a wanton on the duke's unmade
four-poster.

The rest of society would view her behavior as further proof that she no longer belonged. She agreed. She
was much better suited to Samuel than to the man she
had intended to marry.

She reached across the bed for the book she spotted under the pillow. She had not found his office. To
judge by the desk in the corner that overflowed with
ink-stained papers, playbills, and hand-drawn maps,
he worked here, too.

She held her breath at the sound of footfalls outside the door. An expression of shock crossed Samuel's face when he entered the room and saw her on the bed. She smiled. So did he, recovering quickly enough to drop his evening coat on a chair and close the door before she could look away.

"Reading before bed?" he asked, folding his arms with the self-possession of a man accustomed to finding an uninvited partner in his bed. "I hope it's entertaining."

She swallowed a laugh. "There are certain parts. It is Book Three of the tales."

"Not overwrought?"

"At times. But I'm finding a new meaning as I reread."

He advanced stealthily, discarding his neckcloth on the way, and pried the book from her hands. "You've strayed into my room. Into my bed. Was that a mistake?"

Her courage wavered. His vital energy charged the air. She looked up from the knees of his pantaloons to his chiseled face. His arrogant grin gave her palpitations. He glanced at the book before placing it on the Chinese chest at the foot of the bed. "Lily," he said quietly, his frame suddenly overshadowing her. "Why are you here?"

"I was looking for your office."

"Ah."

"But then I peered inside and saw the desk—"

"And decided that you would stay?"

She flushed and started to slide her feet to the floor. He sat down on the bed without hesitation, his body leaning against hers.

"Don't go," he said, cradling her chin in his hand. "Stay. You do belong here, Lily. I've been waiting for you to give me the slightest sign."

If he hadn't kissed her then, she would have further shamed herself by insisting that he did. She sank back, feeling his arm slide around her waist. He brushed his lips across hers. His kisses unraveled her senses until it felt natural when his other hand began unlacing her dress. Her swollen breasts spilled against his palms.

"Put out the lamp, Samuel," she whispered breathlessly.

He broke the kiss for only the moment it took him to reach his hand to the nightstand, an act he appeared to have done numerous times in the past. Lily felt his eyes lift to hers. He bent again. His body pressed into hers, groin to belly, his shaft against her mound. Her veins thrummed, sang in anticipation. The rustle of her skirt and petticoat, the linen sheets, mingled with his rasping breath.

She resisted the urge to shield her nakedness from his heated scrutiny. "I have a feeling that we aren't going to read."

He stroked the tips of her breasts, twisting them between his long fingers until her hips rose off the bed and it was an effort to breathe. "Not in the dark. It's bad for the eyes."

She swallowed a gasp. "I didn't come here for a bed-time tale."

He laughed quietly. "I didn't think so."

"Samuel." She brought her hand to his face. He swallowed tightly, still for several moments. "Aren't you going to undress?"

He laughed again. "Of course." He stretched back, his arms crossed. Then, pulling off his waistcoat, shirt, pantaloons, and stockings, he said, "In the words of Master Will, 'When he falls, he falls like Lucifer.'"

He was her literary devil. She was obliged to him in word and soon would be his in deed. Possession. Pleasure unbridled. She wanted to please him. She stole glimpses of his lean body from her lowered eyes. What little modesty she had left prevented her from staring.

Villain. Writer. Duke. She shivered when she felt his fingers stealing down the inside of her arm. He caressed her skin as though he were savoring the texture of silk. She wanted to hold still, but his hands would not let her. He had a master's touch in more ways than she could withstand.

"Wait," she ordered him firmly, the tempo of her breathing uneven. It was all she could do not to steal touches of her own. She should have felt vulgar, not voluptuous, ripe, restless for him to finish what she had started. "Kiss me again," she whispered.

"Where?"

She couldn't answer. It had never occurred to her

that there were places other than a woman's mouth meant to be kissed.

He leaned up on one elbow. "From the bottom up?"

Flames danced down her spine. He levered himself a little higher. Her gaze dropped from his chest. Longwand he was. Broadsword, too. That she could confirm in the dark. She closed her eyes. His impudent voice whispered above her.

"Why don't I just kiss you at random and you can tell me when I come to an especially sensitive spot?"

"So that you will stop?"

"What do you think?"

She *couldn't* think.

His seduction was so potent that her body seemed to dissolve. She held her breath as his mouth wandered downward, as he drew the peak of her breast between his teeth. "This is a nice place to kiss." Then, "This is another good spot," he whispered, releasing her tender nipple to bite playfully at her belly.

"Samuel," she moaned, "not there!"

"Then here?"

She arched, shivered at his scandalous pursuit. His tongue teased the hood of her sex. She moaned softly, tight inside. Tighter and tighter until she unwound, moving against his mouth without shame. She was slowly falling back to earth when he lowered his chiseled body to hers. She felt his thick member prodding between her thighs. She squeezed her legs together. He gently pried them back apart. In another moment he would be practically inside her, where she hurt for him the most.

"I don't—"

He raised himself up on his arms and silenced her with a deep, delicious kiss, his tongue thrusting inside her mouth. *Oh, yes.* She felt her body dampen, resist, until she surrendered to instinct and let go of all restraint. Pure reaction. He led the way. To where? Her mind did not care. A place of red mist and aching delights. Release.

"I'm lost," she whispered, panic and pleasure intermingling.

"I have found you."

"I'll never marry anyone after this, even if I wanted to."

"You'll never marry anyone else, you mean," he said.

Her eyes locked with his. "I don't think I'll make you a good mistress."

He smiled. "I am sure of it."

He had wanted her, it seemed, for an eternity. She was the elusive heroine in every story he had written. She was the woman who would redeem him by making him the man he ought to be. His deepest feelings for her had indeed become overwrought and sentimental. But right now, on the lower plane, his member pulsed as if to burst. He had waited forever, and that organ of anarchy and impulse would not behave until this pact was closed. He was desperate for fulfillment.

He spread her hair across the pillows, plucking loose her scattered pins. He wished he could see her more clearly in the dark. He studied the symmetry of her shoulders, her generous breasts, and her distended nipples, the tangle of curls above her thighs. As often as he'd pictured her nakedness, she was more beautifully made than his imagination had dreamed, lush, designed for erotic delights. Soft contours to cradle a man. Skin as tempting as fresh cream.

He knew she had bathed for the night. He'd seen the procession of hot-water buckets carried to her room. He would have preferred her natural fragrance. He was a man who indulged his every sense when he made love. Her sweet aroma made his mind swim.

"Lift your legs around my back, Lily," he said, taking an uneven breath as she complied.

He knelt over her, uninhibited, encouraging her to follow her impulses. He stroked his hand over her belly and gripped his pulsing sex to guide his entry. He ached with self-control, rubbing lightly against her. Teasing her. A little longer. The more aroused she became, the greater his own pleasure. She whimpered, a sound that tore his willpower apart. Not yet. She arched her back, pushed her breasts at him. Delectable.

He eased himself between her folds. The temptation to penetrate her became unbearable. He slid one hand under her bottom and imprisoned her in a gentle hold.

She shook helplessly and strained to lift herself against him until she had taken the tip of his sex inside. He released a soft groan as her quivering muscles closed around him. "Lily," he said in desperation. "Don't do anything like that unless you want me to—"

"I do want," she whispered. "Whatever it is, please. I want it."

He didn't have to be asked again.

His hand gripping her buttocks, he eased another inch deeper and thrust. He felt a primal thrill of domination, possession. She was his from this moment on. His body took charge. His mind emptied. He pushed deeper and ground harder, as if he would impale her to the bed. He could not help it, even as he broke through her maidenhead, and she swallowed him whole. Too soon pleasure crested, muscles uncoiled, convulsing with a force he could not hold back. On and on. *Merciful God.*

Then stillness. His blood hammered in his head, his groin, slowly receding into a lingering beat. His thoughts began to focus, fragments settling like a kaleidoscope.

Lily's legs slipped from his damp back to the bed.

He stared down at her, trying to breathe, to control the male triumph that threatened to overwhelm his concern for her.

She looked ravished, flushed, as well pleasured as he felt. And now she was where she belonged. He released the longest breath of his life.

"The deed is done," he said in unconcealed satisfaction, stretching out alongside her. "And well-done, if I say so myself." He kissed her lips, whispering, "Lily. I can't tell you how wonderful you are."

"The deed," she teased, curling against his chest, warm, heated female. "That sounds like something Renwick would say."

He combed his fingers through her hair. "He did. *Wickbury*, Book Three, Chapter Last."

"Samuel," she whispered, "you are a thoroughly entertaining man. I wish I had met you first."

"I do, too, Lily."

She closed her eyes. "It would have been so different."

"There is no doubt."

"What will it be now?" she whispered.

"Whatever you want it to be. Whatever you permit. I won't limit you in any manner."

"Storyteller," she murmured. "You cannot make up our lives as we go along."

"Why not?" he asked, his hand slipping down her nape to her shoulders.

"I don't know." She raised her head to smile at him. "Go on and try."

$\mathcal{L}$ily woke up just before light. She saw a room filled with the shadows of unfamiliar Gothic furnishings, and the duke, fully dressed, moving furtively toward the door. She was tempted to bury herself in the eiderdown bedding and pretend she was still asleep.

The enchanted night was over. What would the day after bring?

She made herself sit up. Her back ached faintly. Gooseflesh stirred her skin. Embers still glowed in the grate, but the two fire screens that guarded the hearth hindered whatever heat could warm the room. It crossed her mind that with books piled in every conceivable space, Samuel should be justifiably concerned that an errant spark would burn the place to cinders.

"Lily," he said in a low undertone, "are you awake?"

"Yes. Where are you going?"

"I have to work."

"You what? It's not even dawn."

"The seventh *Wickbury* book is overdue. I cannot ask Philbert for another extension. The series will be reprinted in a complete edition, if I finish the eighth by Christmas. But a satisfactory ending of Book Seven keeps eluding me. I think part of it is your fault."

"My fault?"

"I don't mean that the way it sounds. It is a compliment, in truth. You've forced me to look at Renwick in a different light with your attraction to the devil."

She pursed her lips. What a romantic. So much for sweet nothings whispered in her ear. Or even a pat on the head.

"You do understand?" he asked. "I shall stay if you like. I only thought to write a little while you slept."

Lily frowned up at him. His black hair framed his face in artless perfection. He still made her heart race standing across a room. "I understand," she said in a thoughtful voice.

"I'll make it up to you."

He walked back to the bed, retrieving on his way the clothing he had indecorously removed from her a few hours before. "I will not leave your bedroom wearing that dress," she said in chagrin. "In fact, I am ashamed to be seen leaving your room at all."

"No one in this house will dare say a word against you," he said with a touch of ducal arrogance.

"Well, I have my own standards, thank you," she said. "Even if last night it did not show."

He dragged a chair to the bed, propping himself on

its edge with good-humored gravity. "It's clear that you and I cannot continue to play master and servant."

"Which suggests that we are to become master and mistress."

"I suggested nothing of the kind."

"What happened last night did."

A slow grin crossed his face. Lily swallowed over the tight ache in her throat. "Say something," she whispered crossly.

"What?"

"You are the writer, Samuel! Are you at a loss for words?"

His grin deepened. "I might be."

He clasped his hands together. She noticed that there were ink smudges on his shirt. He looked once more like a warrior poet rather than a rake who assumed they could alter their arrangement on the basis of one beautiful act.

"Do you want to change the terms of our contract?" she asked, lifting the bedcover a little higher when she realized where his gaze had strayed.

He looked up, clearing his throat. "Yes. Absolutely. We'll tear the damn thing to shreds. It's unsuitable now."

"Unsuitable?"

"There is another contract that I had drawn up for us in London."

"Oh." Her lips flattened. "So, in your celebrated imagination, I was your mistress-to-be at the masquerade. You were plotting more than the next *Wickbury*. You were scheming for my seduction on paper. And you sound proud of yourself, too."

"That is *not* the kind of contract that I arranged," he said in clear annoyance. "I had a formal proposal written to submit to your father. I intended a proper courtship and, after an appropriate interval, a marriage between us. I think you realize by now that I'm a man of extreme measures."

A proper courtship.

A marriage.

And he thought he had unnerved her by revealing his identity. "Why didn't you go to my father? He has always been in awe of the aristocracy."

"Because the morning after the party, I found out that you were engaged to another man. Your first love. Who was I to snatch you from someone else? It seemed as if I had misread your reaction to me at the masquerade. You belonged to someone else, when I knew you were meant to be mine."

"It was all a lie," she said quickly. "You could have pursued me. I wish you had."

"I did." His lips thinned. "But even then I had to wait for the right moment to steal you completely. I could not give you up. But under the circumstances of your broken engagement, I was afraid I would only drag your name deeper into the mire."

She breathed out a sigh. "I believe you could have persuaded me to leave him. I thought of you often afterward. I waited for a letter to follow the beautiful flowers you sent. I searched for your face in the theater boxes. But then everything came apart."

His steady look made her shiver. "We'll never know what I would have done had you actually met Grace at the altar. I had a few plots in progress, all of which would have made me look like a complete villain."

"After your wild stint as a coachman, I don't doubt your capacity for evil. You have a diabolical mind."

"Thank you," he said, his smile wry.

"I wasn't giving you praise."

"Yes. You were."

She put her hand to her eyes. She was bared in every way possible. In body and spirit. She had lost her virtue to Lord Anonymous a short time ago, and now the duke was sitting at the bedside of that decadent scene, prying her hand from her face. This was a wonderful fate.

He dropped several delicious kisses on the inside of her wrist, stating matter-of-factly, "Lily, there is another thing that you have to know. I can't do anything properly, let alone discuss our wedding, until after I produce ten decent pages for the day. When I'm finished, I will be clearheaded enough to propose to you over champagne, and you'll have my entire attention."

She shook her head. "But I made a vow to myself that I would never marry. Nor believe in romantic endings again."

"You made those vows under duress. I shall decide such matters for you in the future."

She held back a smile. "You are completely—"

"—yours. But not until later in the day. It's turning light. I've lost the silent hours."

"How am I supposed to act in front of the other servants?" she said after she could find her voice.

"I suspect this is not going to come as a surprise."

"Who am I in the meanwhile? A housekeeper or—"

"That's up to you. My sister is visiting at the end of the month. She is important to me. A fortnight after that there is a bookseller coming, a few Cambridge fellows, and friends I see only once a year."

"Do they know who you are?" she asked.

"Two of them do. Nothing would please me more than introducing you to them as my future wife. We could be married by special license—the reverend knows how to go about obtaining one from the archbishop's office. For propriety's sake you might want to stay in your current room and keep your position until the banns are called."

"Propriety? It's a little late in the game for us to consider that. Wedding ceremony notwithstanding, how, I ask, am I supposed to sneak from this room wearing the dress everyone saw me in last night?"

He kissed her hand again, as if the gesture forgave a multitude of sins, and rose. "Rummage through my closet. There's a blue cloak inside that will cover your dress. Put it on and walk from this room as if you had every right."

She sat up, aghast at his admission. "You keep

clothes in your closet for the women you entertain in this bed?"

"Of course I don't," he said in amusement, releasing her hand to rise from the chair. "That is Juliette's cloak. I have costumes for all the characters in *Wickbury*. It enables me to see them more clearly."

She shook her head, staring speechlessly at his retreating figure.

"There is one more thing I ought to warn you about," he said as he unbolted the door.

"Good heavens. More?"

"This is *not* an ordinary manor house."

"Incredible as it may seem, Samuel, I gathered that on my own."

"The rhythm of the household revolves around my writing. There will be times when it appears that my brain has absented my body. At others what you perceive to be outlandish behavior may be my means of overcoming a stumbling stone in the story."

"Oh." Lily tried not to look utterly enraptured.

"I may ask your opinion from time to time. It is helpful that you were one of my readers before we met."

That said, he disappeared with all of Lord Wickbury's legendary aplomb, leaving Lily to wonder what would happen when she gathered her wits sufficiently to turn the next page.

Chapter 29

*H*ow had she not guessed who he was?

The question haunted her through the early hours after she had escaped the east wing and returned to her room.

Samuel had given her clues from the night of their first kiss. How shallow she must have seemed, so impressed by society's glitter that she had not glimpsed through his false armor.

The duke had deceived her again. Lily more than forgave him.

Everything about him was an illusion. He had covered himself with a shield so that nobody could see who he was underneath—the ultimate protector. How could she not love him? Why would she ever want to leave this house?

She understood everything now. If he had confided his identity to her at the literary masquerade, she would not have been able to keep it to herself. She would have confessed to Chloe that same night. And, although the thought made her ill, she would likely have told Jonathan, too.

Still, Samuel wasn't the only one in the house who had something to hide. That same morning she began to discover that nearly every member of his staff had been ruined by a scandal of one sort or another. Society had judged them all unworthy.

But how would they judge Lily?

She was neither fish nor fowl, unsure of her place. The other servants had to be aware of what had happened last night. If she was indeed to be a duchess, shouldn't she place distance between them? Or would they draw a line for her?

She would find out once she reached the kitchen.

She walked down the stairs, noting how quiet the house seemed. And then she detected whispering from the upper gallery. Her face burned. They were already talking about her. She looked up in hesitation—prepared for anything but bedsheets dropping from the sky, or rather from the railing.

"What in—"

She threw up her arms in defense and dodged the onslaught by half an inch. Marie-Elaine and two of the chambermaids admitted between hoots of laughter that they had placed bets on which of them could bomb Lily dead center.

"What if I had been a guest wandering lost through the halls?" Lily asked indignantly.

"Your reaction would have been faster," Marie-Elaine replied with uncompromising candor. "Any guest given the run of St. Aldwyn House expects to be entertained during his visit."

So much for disdain or false respect.

Lily bent to roll the bedding into a huge ball. She could only be grateful that she had stripped Samuel's bed before leaving his chamber and hidden the covers in her room. The mingled scents of her soap, his light cologne, and a rigorous bout of lovemaking combined to create a fragrance too incriminating to elude notice.

But laundry was the least of her worries. She still had to face the rest of the staff. And act as if she hadn't spent hours in the master's bed.

She had to behave with what dignity she could summon. At Bickerstaff's customary bow, she felt a wave of relief. She would carry on as she had before last night. And so, fortunately, would the staff. No airs.

"Now, Miss Boscastle," the butler said with a solemnity that made the scullery maid at the sink roll her eyes. "You are one of us."

Marie-Elaine bustled down the steps, snorting at this announcement. "No, she isn't. She never was."

"Yes, I am," Lily said in her firm housekeeper's voice.

"This should be discussed over breakfast in your parlor," Marie-Elaine said.

It was Marie-Elaine, as she already knew, who was her strongest ally in the house. Lily found out over tea and toast that Marie-Elaine had been seduced by her former master and left to raise their love child alone. The duke had employed her just after she had given birth to the impudent daughter who had greeted Lily with beheaded flowers on the day of her arrival.

Emmett and Ernest had run away from an orphanage at thirteen and had been homeless for five years before Bickerstaff had hired them. Bickerstaff had spent four years in prison, a young bank clerk who took the blame when his manager had embezzled funds. Mrs. Halford had managed a hotel in Sussex until she caught her husband in bed with a married guest. She had knocked the fool senseless with the long-handled copper griddle that held a place of honor above the kitchen fire.

Lily shook her head. "I don't think I'll ever eat one of her pancakes quite as enthusiastically after this," she admitted.

Marie-Elaine poured her another cup of tea. "He is in love with you. And soon you'll be above us all. We shall never talk this openly again."

"He might just be in love with romance," Lily said absently. "Think of his stories."

Marie-Elaine merely shrugged. "I don't have much romance left in me, but I might have a story to tell."

Lily smiled. "His head is in the clouds."

"But it is a pretty head." Marie-Elaine sighed. "Although he does the strangest things for his art."

"Such as?"

"I shouldn't be talking like this at all."

"You have to tell me now."

Marie-Elaine straightened her cap. "Once he dipped his pen in poison and pricked his thumb to study the effect."

"He didn't?" Lily asked, laughing. "How extreme."

"He isn't a man of half measures."

"Yes," Lily said. "I'm learning that. Is there anything else about him I should know?"

"Ask him yourself. I signed a contract of confidentiality."

Lily snorted insultingly. "You'd never know it to listen to you."

"Your lips are not sewn together, either."

"I *will* ask him," Lily said.

Which she might have if she had seen him that morning. During lunch Mrs. Halford confirmed that it was Samuel's habit to lock himself in the library every day and not emerge until he had completed at least ten folio pages. Lily was dying to peek in while he worked. Undaunted by the cook's warning, she prepared a tea tray as an excuse, but Bickerstaff intercepted her in the hall.

"No, Miss Boscastle. It isn't done. Interrupt him under penalty of death. When the clocks go off at four, he'll stop his work. His temper ignites like tinder if he's bothered before then."

Lily had witnessed his temper only on the rainy day he'd taken her to the inn. "*Clocks*, you say? They must be quiet. I have never heard them."

"The chimes are not quiet if one happens to be in the east wing at that unfortunate hour. The din is ear-shattering. He has to finish to escape or suffer like a cathedral bell ringer."

This revelation only piqued her curiosity. She would rather watch Samuel at work than pore over domestic guidebooks that explained how to pack a picnic for twenty, or the importance of hiring a footman with good calves.

Lily had never examined a footman's legs. But she had taken for granted the aristocratic parties she'd attended as a lady. As a housekeeper, she was only beginning to understand the invisible labor involved. She worked until midafternoon in her parlor copying menus and memorizing the dishes that Samuel preferred. For a vegetable eater, she thought distractedly, he was very virile. . . .

There was only one lady on the guest list. Alice, Lady St. Aldwyn.

She underlined it three times.

His sister. Her visit might be at the end of the month, but Lily wanted to prepare. Samuel had mentioned her importance to him.

She wondered if he would confirm their betrothal to his sibling on her arrival or keep this another secret. He was private to a peculiar degree. Had he even meant to propose to her last night or had he been shamed into it? But he *had* told her about the other contract he'd had drawn up in London. From everything she knew of him, he was an honorable man. He had no reason to lie. They had shared more than a bed now.

This was more than passion and obligation. It was trust.

Married to Lord Anonymous. She felt an unspeakable joy flood her heart. Samuel's wife.

She glanced up from the desk to the window that overlooked the garden. Late-afternoon shadows fell across the rose arbor. It was almost time for tea. Would she see him then? What would they say to each other? Would he apologize? Should she?

She was the one who had instigated their amorous encounter last evening. And if there was a proper after-protocol, she had never been taught it.

She rose and went instinctively to the east wing. She had no intention of interrupting his work. But if she was to be a duchess, she might as well learn the lay of the house.

The sudden clamor of chimes, bongs, and bells going off throughout the wing interrupted her thoughts.

"Dear God," Bickerstaff said as he appeared in the hall. "He has failed. Prepare yourself, miss. We're all in for it now."

Lily squared her shoulders. "Should I intervene?"

"Intervene? I would hide in the vaults if we had any. You've no idea the acts we have been forced to perform in the name of literature. Beheadings, stabbings, and some I cannot describe to a gentlewoman like you."

Actually, Lily *did* have an idea. And she was more enthusiastic about broadening this part of her education than she would ever admit.

Chapter 30

*H*e hadn't written one page worthy of publication the whole day. What a delusion to assume that after he had made love to Lily and sated his bodily desires, his mind would settle down. Now he could not concentrate. Her voice enticed his thoughts.

I do want it.

Overwrought.

Sentimental.

Rubbish.

Well, she was not alone in that opinion.

He had just gotten around to reading his most recent letter from his publisher. Philbert inquired about his health. God forbid Samuel should drop dead before he finished this book. Philbert also alluded to the latest critiques from Paris that showered praise on the Brothers Grimm. He then coyly apologized for an editorial in the *London Review* that blamed a rise in promiscuity on rogue writers such as Lord Anonymous.

Who, the editor added, wrote with the unbridled passion of a nasty-spirited spinster.

It was unlike Philbert to resort to a tactic like this. In fact, Samuel would have shredded the letter except for the tantalizing postscript Philbert added that said an offer had been made for a libretto on the next book.

He placed the letter in a drawer. He got up. He started to pace.

Within moments words flooded his brain. Fast. Too fast. He rushed back to his desk. He found his favorite metallic pen. It was a race to capture his thoughts before they vanished.

Images formed.

Wickbury spoke in a furious voice. But all of a sudden, the heroic earl wasn't talking for the benefit of his readers. He was addressing Samuel, character to creator, trying to make sense of the chaos into which he had been thrust. "How did this happen to me again? I demand another chance to fight for Juliette. I will be damned if an entire army could lock me in another cell with my lady left defenseless in my enemy's arms."

Fine, Samuel thought. *Then fight the battle yourself, you ludicrous jackanapes.*

"Perhaps I will."

Samuel shook his head. He must be going mad.

He glanced at the longcase clock that stood between a pair of wing chairs. Five minutes left.

Five minutes until he could search the house for Lily, the lady he had abandoned like one of his characters.

His future duchess.

His disgraced bride.

She would not regret binding herself to Samuel, and hang the bastard who had not only lost but ruined her. Samuel would make her forget she had ever known her captain. As soon as he finished the book that was suspended over his head like the sword of Damocles.

As a gentleman Samuel had to wonder why Captain Grace had not defended her and admitted what he had done. No decent man would subject the woman he loved to humiliation to save his own selfish arse.

As a scoundrel, however, Samuel sensed that the captain's connection to her had not been completely broken.

He could not understand how Grace had let her go.

There was something in the story that did not make sense. Motivation. Out of character. More than a plot thread dangling loose. An entire scene omitted. Another's perspective. The longer Samuel thought about it, the deeper his concern grew. He couldn't put his finger on it.

But the answer would come. It always did.

Lily found a message from Samuel under her door after she had gone upstairs to change her dress. He asked her if she would tour St. Aldwyn with him after he had completed his day's work. So she had wandered about the estate until supper, instructing the gardeners which roses and sprays of Queen Anne's lace should be clipped for His Grace's dinner table. Pyramus and Thisbe, the porkers that Samuel kept as pets, deigned to trot about at her heels while she walked the paths around the barns and other outbuildings. The two pigs sniffed her stockings and looked up at her as if to ask if they were going on an adventure.

Hens, turkeys, ducks. None of them destined for dinner. Lily shook her head. Samuel seemed to think he could protect all of creation. Well, she had been a goose once herself. She came to a fenced pasture and gazed over the gate to approach the moor pony inside.

"That's Bucephalus, miss," shouted Marie-Elaine's young daughter, sitting with an under groom in the straw-filled cart.

"Bucephalus," Lily said, laughing at the long-fringed pony munching at a patch of clover. "So this is Lord Wickbury's charger, the brave steed that will allow no other rider near him."

A deep voice spoke over her shoulder. "Hard to believe he's charged through execution blocks and castle gates."

She spun around, forcing herself to curtsy, if only to catch her breath. The stark emotion in Samuel's eyes pierced her composure. He didn't have to say a word to remind her of what he had done to her last night, and that he wanted her again. She would not be hard to persuade. He was temptation incarnate in an ebony-buttoned long frock coat over a cravat, linen shirt, and ecru breeches that tied at the knee.

"How are you, Lily?" he asked quietly.

She swallowed at his intimate smile. Sometimes he looked completely wicked. At others, he seemed winsome and lost. "I am well," she said. "And Your Grace's day—"

"—was an absolute waste of time. I couldn't stop thinking about you." He braced his wrists on either side of the fence rail, his cravat teasing the soft valley of her breasts. "Will you accept my formal proposal?"

Her heart pounded in the hollow of her throat. "I wasn't sure that you were serious. Women are warned not to believe promises made in the dark."

He looked offended. "Do you think I would lie to lure you into my bed?"

"Well, I was already in your bed. And you do like to tell tales."

"That isn't fair. I could not explain everything until I knew I could trust *you*. If I hadn't been trying to be-have properly for once in my life, you would have come home with me in London and that would have been it. My fault, it seems, was trying to initiate a cor-rect courtship."

"By kissing me until I nearly fainted in Philbert's garden?" she teased him.

"Lily, I couldn't help myself then. And I can't now. In most aspects of my life, I show strong self-discipline."

"But who are you? A duke with a vile reputation or

Lord Anonymous? Which one of you did I give myself to last evening?"

"I was hoping you could answer that for me. I'm both. And neither."

He was a wit, a compassionate man, uninhibited in bed. Generous. Arrogant. Beautifully formed.

He touched her shoulder. A shiver danced over her skin. His hand slid down her back. Then he bent his head and kissed her, clearly not caring who could see. She backed up against the pasture gate in breathless surprise, whispering, "The other servants are watching!"

"I suppose they shall have to get used to it. You're going to be my duchess, not one of the plaster goddesses standing in the hall. You have accepted my proposal?"

"There was never any doubt in your mind. I began to fall in love with you at the masquerade. Yes, of course I accept."

He smiled down at her. "I loved you before I knew your name."

"And I love . . . all your names."

He laughed. "Then it is perfect."

"I should be in the kitchen now," she whispered. "It's getting late."

"Don't bother with a big dinner. I'll be asking the staff for help during the evening. If you have a stout heart for fighting and a sense of stage direction, please join us. If not, lock yourself in your room and put a pillow over your head."

Chapter 31

"*L*ock myself in my room with a pillow over my head," she related to Marie-Elaine and Mrs. Halford in the kitchen fifteen minutes later. "Did he ever give either of you that advice?"

Mrs. Halford lowered her knife and began chopping up fresh mint to go in a bottle of sugared vinegar for sauce. "I can't admit that he did."

"He didn't," Marie-Elaine said from the dresser. "But I wouldn't have done it anyway. Helping the duke rehearse is better than playing whist with Bickerstaff."

"I heard that, Mrs. Halford," he said from the pantry. "I shall remember it, too, during dinner, if you ever get around to feeding us."

"You didn't hear properly, you mean old codger," Mrs. Halford said, knife flying faster. "That wasn't me talking. It was Marie-Elaine."

"Peace," Lily said, raising her hand. "Behave, the pair of you."

The duke had requested only salad and a boiled potato in mint sauce for his dinner, with strawberries in champagne cream for dessert. He asked that the food be left on a tray outside his office. Lily didn't see him again until it was time for bed.

She followed the nightly ritual that the other servants did, extinguishing all candles and coals, putting the animals outside for the night, closing drapes. By the time she finished her duties a hush had crept over St. Aldywn House. The rest of the house might have vanished into the walls.

Why should she lock herself in her room?

She wondered if everyone was playing a trick on her. She'd been initiated only last night, so it was possible that they would test her nerves by pulling a few pranks. She wandered about checking for hidden doors, but after an hour of hunting, she decided that if they meant to exclude her, then she'd go to bed.

Her bedroom.

She heard furtive whispers, glasses clinking, steel engaging steel, and Samuel's voice, husky and impatient. "Are you positive she'll figure out where we are?"

"She reads your books, Your Grace," Mrs. Halford said in a low voice. "She'll find us out."

"Especially if you give us away," Bickerstaff retorted, apparently still stung by their earlier quarrel.

Lily halted outside her door. Would this evening prove as interesting as the last? She braced herself, prepared for anything.

She turned the doorknob and entered her sitting room. Dark except for the rectangle of light that shone under her bedroom door.

She detected the rustling of papers and several soft, quiet footsteps. She wet her bottom lip. The rapscallions were lying in wait. Should she act surprised, dismayed, or—

She opened the second door and stared, laughter slowly escaping her as she recognized the assembly of scoundrels who gathered in the candlelight. "You . . . you . . ."

Marie-Elaine stood, shoulder propped to the wall, in a black periwig and the brocade costume of a page as she read a narrative to her small audience. " 'So, here, ladies and gentlemen, is our hero, Michael Francis, Lord Wickbury, heir to the earldom of Wickbury, which has been confiscated by Cromwell's forces. The old earl and his gentle wife, Lord Michael's parents, are thought to have been drowned at sea by his evil, *eeevil* half brother, Sir Renwick Hexworthy, who worships the darkness and covets everything Michael protects, including his magnificent horse Bucephalus and the lady who behaves like a lowborn tavern wench—' "

"Enough!" Samuel exclaimed, striding across the room.

Except that Samuel wasn't Samuel at all. He was the Earl of Wickbury from the gallery balcony—hero in a half-unbuttoned linen shirt, crimson satin doublet, and a pair of straight breeches that dropped into the cuffs of his leather riding boots. On his left sleeve hung a curl of hair wrapped in thick black ribbon.

Lily's eyes traveled up his bare throat to the white-plumed cavalier's hat that overshadowed his face. She had always wondered how Lord Wickbury kept it on during his adventures. But Samuel wore the dashing costume well . . . so well, in fact, that it took Marie-Elaine's discreet cough to terminate her musings.

"May I continue?" the maid asked, her eyes bright with mischief.

Samuel looked at Lily. "If Miss Boscastle doesn't mind."

Lily nodded. "By all means."

"'As our story concludes, *again*,'" Marie-Elaine continued, "'in the castle of that villainous wizard Sir Renwick Hexworthy,' who as I have stated happens to be Lord Wickbury's half brother, although his origins have never been logically explained—"

"No more editorials, please," the duke snapped, sliding his sword back into its sheath.

Lily seated herself on the stool, startled to notice Bickerstaff behind the dressing screen in a Round-head's tunic. Two similarly garbed figures peered out at her from behind the cheval glass. Emmett and Ernest? And the woman in a tavern wench's smock posed awkwardly on Lily's bed? That couldn't be Mrs. Halford playing Juliette's part? She shook her head, so intrigued she almost missed the conclusion of Marie-Elaine's narration.

"'—and even though Lord Wickbury realizes he has been led into another ruse, he is willing to sacrifice himself to save Lady Juliette's life.'" She paused. "As well as her alleged virtue."

The duke gave her a dark look. "I would prefer you read from the manuscript verbatim. I have never made any such reference."

"But one does get that impression," Lily murmured bravely.

Samuel turned to regard her in the silence that followed her observation. She forced herself to meet his stare. She had been a *Wickbury* reader before she became his lover. What was the point in all this melodrama if she couldn't voice an honest opinion? Was she supposed to sit back and merely admire?

At length Samuel ended the silence. If she had offended his artistic temperament, he was not going to comment on it. "We will answer the question of Lady Juliette's virtue, or lack thereof, in a forthcoming chapter."

Lily folded her hands in her lap, listening intently.

He said, "The problem that I, or Wickbury, rather, has is how to fight nine soldiers on a castle parapet."

"He always wins his swordfights," Lily said.

"I have written this scene a dozen times," Samuel informed her, "and Wickbury always ends up grievously injured or left to molder in the dungeon."

Marie-Elaine cleared her throat. "Or in the tavern wine cellar, depending on the author's whims."

"Didn't another prisoner help him escape in the last book?" Lily inquired with a thoughtful frown.

He smiled tersely. "This is different. Lord Wickbury is willing to give up everything for love. And so is Juliette. He might be ready to hang up his sword and settle down, even if that is the death of him."

The master and staff of St. Aldwyn House replayed the vigorous episode for five nights in a row and the duke was still displeased. He swore inside and out that with each reenactment he had made drastic changes to the manuscript. From the little Lily was allowed to read, it seemed as if he'd altered only a word or two.

At some point Bickerstaff suggested a swordfight to rouse the reader from whatever stuporous effect Samuel's tendency to wax poetic had induced. But Samuel complained that if he heeded this advice, he would either not have a living character left at the end of the book, or the survivors would all be maimed and moaning their soliloquies.

Strangely enough, though, Lily began to perceive holes in his tightly woven prose that had previously escaped her in the excitement of How Will Lord Wickbury Conquer This Obstacle? Or perhaps she would never be able to read his writing with an objective eye again.

But on the sixth night, he read Lily a page that riveted her to her chair.

"'At the last moment an unseen force intervened

and prevented Renwick from violating the woman in his bed. There was another spirit in the room. There was a power that reached beneath his spine and . . .' "

Samuel paused. His voice resonated in the silence.

"Well, don't quit now, for heaven's sake," Lily said in distress. "My fingers and toes have gone numb from the suspense. What power could stop Renwick's self-destruction? He has forsaken God. The devil has already taken him to hell and back a hundred times."

"Do you want to know?" Samuel sounded so matter-of-fact that Lily could have wrung his neck. "What I mean is—do I have the reader's attention? Would you put down the book at this point to take a nap or make a pot of tea?"

"What force is in the room?" she asked through her teeth.

"His sister," he said. "She has clawed herself from the grave for revenge."

Lily shivered. "What a twisted mind you have."

"Do you object?"

"Object? Unless it involves blood, I cannot wait for more."

Indeed, who would have imagined that Miss Lily Boscastle would engage Lord Wickbury in a fencing match? That he would chase her up his winding staircase at sword point? And that she would step into Sir Renwick's buckled shoes and fend off his advances with a magic wand? The rapt servants in the hall below became Cromwell's soldiers.

Zounds! Ye Gods!

As to be expected, Lily never won these duels. Samuel inevitably danced her up into the dark gallery with his foil and demanded that she disarm. A month ago she would not have had the stamina to keep up with him. Housekeeping, among other things, had strengthened her arm, although she doubted she would ever be the sword master that he was.

"Six nights," she said in protest, dropping the long hazel wand on the gallery carpet. "I understand that you are devoted to your craft, but this is carrying authenticity too far."

A slow smile spread across his face. "Do you fault me for trying to weave a few threads of truth into these stories?"

"The truth," she said, finally catching her breath, "is that you are an unabashed blackguard taking advantage of his housekeeper in an open gallery."

He glanced down at the small group assembled at the foot of the stairs. "I'll remind you that for the purpose of the plot, this is not a gallery, but a parapet."

"A parapet! Then perhaps that is the very problem. Have you ever considered acting this chapter out on a genuine castle walkway?"

His mouth firmed. "I do not have a castle at my convenience."

"Yes, you do. We passed it on the day you brought me here. You told me that you were the owner, in fact, unless that was another one of your stories."

He drew away, his expression strained. "It wasn't. But the interior was destroyed by a fire two decades ago that took my entire family, except for Alice and me. I'm not sure how safe it is. To be honest, I haven't had the heart to visit there in years."

"I didn't realize," she whispered.

"How could you?"

"And the rumors that the castle is haunted? Did *you* invent those, too?"

He smiled grimly. "It was a method to discourage the morbid minded. Curses, ghosts rising from the crypt to take revenge. To a certain extent it has worked. At least, I haven't been tempted to set foot in the place again. I've begun to write a story about its history but can never bring myself to finish it." He shook his head. "How did we get on this subject, Lily?"

"It was my fault. I distracted you."

"Are you certain that I have not overexerted you?"

"I will have a few aches in the morning." Although she was more liable to injure him than the other way around. Samuel was too skilled at swordplay to make a clumsy move.

"How," she asked him, "did a man who spent years at a desk become so adept at fencing?"

He answered with his typical modesty. "I spent years studying under a master swordsman."

"Angelo?"

"No. His name is Christopher Fenton."

"I've never heard of him."

"I predict he will be famous one day. He is highly regarded by society gentlemen who seek his tutelage."

Her eyes lit up. "I think my brother might have spoken of him."

He propped his arm against the gallery railing, appraising her in amusement. "Has anyone ever told you that you look comely in a black silk cloak?"

Before she could answer, she was in his arms, uncaring of their audience below, that the kisses he showered on her were more dangerous than the duel they had fought. "You," he whispered, drawing her down the hall with one hand, the other unlacing the bows of her bodice, "are the one who will force me to my knees."

She felt a rush of giddiness as they reached his bedroom door. His body pushed at hers. She recognized his heat, the hard curve of his arousal. His kisses filled her with a wicked compulsion to lift her skirts and pleasure him where they stood. The impulse shocked her. His eyes met hers in ruthless anticipation.

Infuriating. Fascinating. Epic hero or classical villain? In private, and at his best, the Duke of Gravenhurst was both.

Chapter 32

*D*uring the next few days, Lily decided that Samuel was a devil—one who followed his conscience, but a devil nonetheless. Demanding at times. Sacrificing at others. He was dedicated to what he believed and inclined to dismiss any opinions that countered his own. He felt deeply. He loved and worked with an inhuman intensity she struggled to understand. He had given her the marriage contract that his solicitor had drawn up in London. Lily found nothing to edit in this work.

She learned to interrupt him at her peril. His office was like a cave of wonders, so charmingly and untidily distracting she was shocked that he could finish a sentence.

Lyre-bound chairs occupied the four French rococo-paneled recesses. Good conquered evil in ornate marble friezes and the plasterwork that surmounted bookshelves overflowing with poetry and obscure works.

Lily would not have been surprised to find a secret passage to another realm in the stygian Gothic fireplace that was never lit.

Maybe in time she would not be shocked when she knocked at his office door with his coffee, only to hear him reply, "Not right now. I'm in the middle of a murder." Or, "If a maid were going to dismember her mistress or master, how would she go about it?"

Questions like that became commonplace. He often drew the household into his musings about the book. Fortunately for his delicate readers, few of these gruesome reflections found their way to print. Or perhaps they did and Lily had trained herself to skip over such passages.

Her concern for his health, however, overrode her fear of disturbing him. He ate little. He worked with the windows open to the mist, barefoot, in a thin shirt, and his hair often damp from holding his head under the pump to stimulate his thoughts. Sometimes she suspected he stayed up all night to work and that was what gave him his haunted look.

After days of observing his habits, she realized one morning that he had fallen asleep at his desk. She put her hand on his shoulder and shook him in hesitation. "Samuel. Your Grace. Did you even go to bed?"

He stared up at her with an indolent smile curving his mouth. "I don't remember."

At least he recognized her.

"You've moved all the chairs around," she said in

chagrin. "And your face is . . ." Dark angles. Masculine hollows. A vulnerability that she might walk through hell to heal. "What is it? It's not that scene again?"

"No. I've been forced to write past it. But I can sense another character in the wings."

"Friend or enemy?"

"Enemy," he said, frowning.

"What will Wickbury do?"

"Kill him." He smiled. "What else?"

Lily felt a shiver. She had to wonder why he enjoyed writing about murders and acts of revenge. She skimmed the most bloodthirsty parts of his books. Yet other readers relished them. She was beginning to see how his mind worked, and it frightened her.

Still, some aspects of his behavior she would never understand. While she had come to accept tidying around the maps, books, and artifacts that surrounded his desk, apple cores and animal discharges were another thing. She screamed hysterically the afternoon she discovered a trail of mouse droppings leading from his office to the adjoining library. She could not bring herself to scoop up the disgusting things in her hands. So, for a temporary solution, she kicked the tiny pellets against the wall.

When she stepped back with a shudder, she trod on a small mound she had missed, and she screamed again. Everyone in the house came running—the maids, down from ladders where they'd been cleaning the windows, the footmen steadying them below.

Samuel thundered through the melee with one of his Italian rapiers, a useless weapon against rodent leavings if Lily had ever seen one.

"What is it?" he demanded, a wild-eyed, white-lipped warrior that brought out Lily's deepest instincts to fling herself against his chest and beg his protection.

He was savage, rumpled elegance, his sword at the ready to defend her. She felt like the greatest fool in creation when she finally explained why she had gone to hysterics.

Few things terrified her.

She forced out the words, waving her fingers to depict the revolting discovery. "The nasty pieces were all over the place, I tell you, as if the king mouse were leading a march into the library. It . . . They . . . Well, I don't know what mice do, but it's possible they fight at times like human beings. They appeared to have made a formation. And some horrid mound that I stepped on."

His upper lip lifted. "The mice did not make a formation. I did. Those were the Cavaliers rallying the Roundheads. The mound was the Royalists' cannon-balls. You have succeeded in not only destroying both forces, but hours of hard work."

"You—you lined up—"

"—apple seeds. The soldiers were apple seeds, not turds. Inspiration doesn't allow me to run about the house looking for objects to capture inspiration. Sometimes I feel like . . . Scheherazade. I cannot afford to lose a thought."

Lily agreed but said nothing. Heaven forbid she should be accused of beheading a masterpiece in the making. Samuel had published successfully without her interference and he should continue to do so.

Her own education about St. Aldwyn House had only begun. What had seemed mysterious before now made sense. Samuel took long walks alone on the moor to clear his head. She had seen him talking to the moor folk from her window.

His donations funded the tiny parish, although he attended church only one Sunday a month. He had a private pew reserved for his personal use. Half the female worshipers spent the service stealing helpless looks at the back of his shapely head. Samuel appeared not to notice.

One would assume, in fact, to study his dark, kneeling figure, that he was prayerfully repenting his prior weeks of sin. It wasn't until the ride back home that Marie-Elaine revealed the truth: His Grace knelt to take notes whenever he thought of an intriguing idea. To count by the number of times he genuflected, Lily estimated a prolonged sermon might inspire another series.

Their wedding banns would be announced in the

village at the start of the month. Until that time Lily might not sit in Samuel's church pew, although she, and no other woman, shared his secrets and his bed.

She shared his bed that same night.

Her most wicked dream came true.

Sir Renwick Hexworthy seduced her.

Chapter 33

After a late supper Samuel insisted he rehearse his problematic scene from the villain's perspective. During the church sermon, he explained to Lily, he had realized that his mistake was in trying to suppress Sir Renwick's point of view.

As much as he appeared to resent criticism of his work, he confessed that he listened to all suggestions and considered any reasonable opinion.

Lily suspected he was up to no good as they climbed the staircase to her rooms. Perhaps he had already put himself in Sir Renwick's place. Her hunch proved true. Her sitting room was empty. A peat fire burned low in her bedchamber. This would be a private performance.

She watched, transfixed, as he picked up the rapier that lay across the couch. She realized then that he had not shaved since morning. He looked devilishly irresistible. When he spoke to her, his voice had a husky pitch that hinted of danger.

It was a voice she recognized from the depth of her unadmitted desires.

The rapier tip caught the ribbons at her left shoulder and crossed to the right without nicking her skin. The threads of her gown, shift, and corset yielded to this attack. "That," she whispered, lifting a hand in protest, "was not a subtle act."

"Sir Renwick isn't a subtle man," he said without a trace of apology. "And even if he were, it's too late to request his courtesy. A bargain has been made."

"What bargain?" she demanded, her fingers catching the fabric that dropped to her hips. His gaze followed the movement. "I thought we had already reached an agreement."

"Samuel and Lily did." He wrapped his arm around her waist, molding her to his hard frame. "We are different characters now. And I am not easy to please."

She trembled, entranced, pretending to draw away. He reacted, his grasp tightening until her body felt magnetized to his. The blade of his rapier rested in his hand. She could feel the cold steel through her skirts.

"Why should I please you?" she whispered.

He laughed. His hand traced down her nape to her bare back. She gasped at the sensation. He kissed her then, his mouth hard, his voice mocking as she laid her hands on his shoulders.

"That's better. You're defenseless, aren't you?"

She swallowed a moan. "Not quite."

He brought his other hand between them. His fingers stroked her naked breasts. "You don't want me to stop."

"What a wicked man you are at heart."

"You have no idea." He paused as if aware of the unspeakable urges assailing her. "But you will."

His teeth nibbled at her bottom lip. She lost her breath. She arched, offering herself, shame dissolving. He overcame her too easily.

"I'm going to put the rapier down," he whispered against her mouth. "I don't need it for what I'll do to you next." He smiled. "I have a wand for that."

She sank. He caught her before she went to her knees. Even then he kept weakening her with his kisses. He carried her to the bed. It was entirely dark in the room. He pulled off the rest of her clothes, then his. She reached for him. She ached inside. Her body knew only that he could ease her craving.

"I'll tie your hands to the bedposts," he said hoarsely. "For authenticity's sake, you understand."

She felt a tug of temptation. "It sounds more like artistic license to me. And if I am bound, I can't touch you," she whispered.

She trailed her hand down his spine, the gesture explicit. His erection thickened against her fingertips. He allowed her to stroke him for only a few moments. Then, breathing unevenly, he captured both her hands at the wrists and locked them above her head.

"If you break our pact, I shall punish you all night with pleasure."

She released her breath. "I have no choice, it seems."

"Not until I'm satisfied that you have given up your hero."

Lily looked into his eyes. "Take your satisfaction."

He bent his head, lowering himself between her thighs. His shaft branded the skin of her belly. She raised one knee, the invitation flagrant.

"Not yet." He smiled, lifting himself to taunt her, to make her beg.

She shook, her hands straining against his unbreakable hold, until, without warning, he let her go. Even then she remained captive. His hands slid under her hips. He flicked a glance at her face. Her mind darkened as he began to suckle her breasts. His tongue abraded the tender peaks until, when his mouth wandered lower, she subsided against his hands in expectation.

"You . . . I cannot breathe when you . . . How can *you* breathe in that position?"

Laughter vibrated in his voice. "Perhaps because I am breathing the sweetest perfume earth has ever known."

"Lord Wickbury will intervene." Her teeth caught her bottom lip. "He always does."

He glanced up to give her a dark smile. "Not tonight. We have to suffer a little suspense. The reader needs a reason to hate me."

"Villain," she moaned.

"'Embrace the night,'" he said with a deep laugh.

*   *   *

The familiar rituals of writing consumed him.

The pressure to send off the book took precedence over all else. His brain seethed like a cauldron. Cream rose to the surface. Unfortunately so did scum. He needed a sieve to cull it out. For three days straight he barely spoke a civil word. He walked the moor at night while the house slept.

He wrote in frantic bursts.

Always at the edge of his mind, he was aware of *her*. He knew when she would look into the room, presumably to check whether he was still alive. She made no remarks about the clutter that encrypted him. But he could feel her cringing and shaking her head as she slipped away. Sometimes the thought of her broke his concentration and he wanted to chain himself to his desk.

Pleasure would wait. Once his other obligations were met, he would marry Lily. Perhaps they would travel, but even that he could not promise. He would likely commit himself to Philbert again and the whole horrendous process of writing would repeat.

But Lily would suffer through with him.

She was safe here.

And he—

Hellfire and damnation.

He pulled off his glasses and stared in vexation at the window, open to a stimulating breeze.

Hoofbeats churned the gravel drive. It had to be an uninvited visitor. The peddlers who came across the moor once a month did not use the formal entrance. He doubted that his sister, Alice, had taken to riding on a horse. He swore roundly and waited for Bickerstaff to intervene. Except that Samuel had chased everyone out of the house, including his butler, after breakfast, and sent them to the village on various errands for the day.

He pushed back his chair, ignoring a sudden pain at his temples, and waited for the guest to go away. But the hammering at the door continued until, in disbelief, he heard heavy footsteps in the hall.

He grabbed the wand and sword that sat against his chair. He would at least scare the daylights out of the intruder. He rose from the desk, strode to the door, and announced, "I am going to kill you, whoever you are, unless you have a damned good reason for this invasion."

"I believe I do," Captain Jonathan Grace said as Samuel intercepted him in the hall.

Chapter 34

*S*amuel stared at him with undisguised contempt. "Of all the people I intend to kill before I die, you surely top the list. You dare to come to this house?"

"For Lily's sake, yes."

Samuel walked the heavier man to the bottom of the stairs. "Which weapon do you prefer?"

"I didn't come here to fight." He gripped his riding gloves uneasily in his fist. Samuel did not let the nervous movement shift his attention. Rapier and sword remained steady in his hold.

Not only had the miserable coward shot a man in front of Lily and denied the act, but he had also invaded Samuel's personal life. Blood would be spilled over this.

He prodded Grace through the hall, sword in one hand, rapier in the other. The insect deserved to be pinned to the wall hangings. "What do you want?"

Grace swallowed, but refused to lower his gaze. "I
need to speak with—"

"No."

"Whether she is your mistress or not, her life is in
jeopardy, Your Grace."

"Not as much as yours."

"Listen to me. I traveled this far not only to confess
but to warn Lily. It is true that she saw a man shot the
night we left the party. I should never have taken her
in the first place. It was Kirkham who insisted that we
go."

"Weak of character," Samuel mused in a merciless
tone. "Who would have guessed it? Did you not have
the spine to refuse?"

"I owed him a debt."

"Was it so great that you would dishonor the woman
you were supposed to protect?"

"I was in literal debt, too," Grace said, his pale eyes
studying Samuel closely. "Both Kirkham and I were.
The man who approached us demanded the repay-
ment we had promised. Kirkham pulled out his pistol
before I realized what he meant to do." He shook his
head. "I tried to stop him, but he has a violent temper,
and it was too late."

Samuel had told enough tales in his day to realize
how one person could deceive another. "Finish," he
said.

"He shot him and I helped him hide the body in the
bed of a passing cart. Later that night he paid his ser-

vants to take care of the rest. I lied to everyone, including Lily."

"Damn you," Samuel said softly. "You're all cock and no stones."

"I was frightened for my future."

"You poor thing," Samuel said. "Let us find a bucket in which to collect our tears."

"He saved my life once."

"Then you should have learned the value of sacrifice. Lily needed your protection. Give me your guns."

Captain Grace paled and reached inside his waistband. "You do not understand. Kirkham has escaped to Calais. I mean to hunt him down."

"And escape yourself into the bargain?"

Grace laid his flintlock pistols on the staircase's lowest step. "I'd have confessed to the authorities before I came to you, but Lily's name would have been brought up again."

"What a courageous soul you are." Samuel transferred the rapier to his right hand, alongside his sword, and reached down for the pair of guns. "Go, brave boy, and become a hero. If I ever see you again, I will slice you up like a blood sausage. Is that clear?"

Grace gave a stiff nod.

"You have no idea how close you are at this moment to losing more than a woman you never deserved," Samuel said. "I cannot decide whether it is a kindness to let you go and know that you will be on the run for the rest of your life, or to end your misery right now."

Grace looked resigned. "I would not blame you for demanding honor be met. And I meant no insult to Lily when I referred to her as your mistress. I—"

"My patience is depleted. I don't want Lily to see you. Ever."

"May I have your word as a gentleman that you'll tell her the truth?"

"I gave you the only promise that should concern your future. If you have one." He traced the rapier tip down Grace's arm. "Walk."

The chapter could have closed there. Samuel would have put down his pen in contentment. A confession made for a tidy ending. But the true world refused to conform to his literary ideals.

"I would give up anything to undo what happened," Grace said. "I never knew I was a gambler until I came to London. Before then it seemed to be a harmless country pastime. It sounds implausible, but I feel as if a master hand had led me into temptation and plotted my demise."

Samuel would have been delighted to take the credit for the captain's downfall. He had indeed offered Grace the carte blanche to gamble on his account. But he did not regret what he had done. If anything, he would have acted more aggressively to offer Lily his protection.

The longcase clock in the corridor along the staircase chimed four. A moment later a cacophony of timepieces went off. Ignoring the clamor, Samuel ushered Grace out the door.

Samuel climbed to his favorite cairn on the moor, his rapier in hand. It was here that Sir Renwick had sold his soul to the devil in exchange for the power to vanquish his nobly born half brother. Samuel felt a sudden and strange affection for the spot that had spawned the irredeemable character. Perhaps it was because from this vantage point he could make out the scars of the castle where his own family had lived and died. He had raged here while he mourned. It had been the darkest time he had ever known.

That was the past. The future sat in a cart that bumped along the old friar's path toward him. He had watched Captain Grace ride away on the opposite road.

Now he watched like a man possessed as Lily approached. When she finally noticed him, she gestured at Bickerstaff to slow the cart. She jumped to the ground. Samuel laid down his rapier and hastened to help her over the stone-strewn slope.

"I bought everything I saw today," she said, handing him a wicker basket before he could pull her into his arms.

But he did anyway, and the basket dropped, ribbons, tea, bread, and packets of thread falling at their feet. He ran his hands down her back, between the folds of her skirts. He caught a good hold of her bum. She made a breathless gasp into his mouth.

"You must have written at least twenty pages today," she said. "It's been days since you were this affectionate."

"I didn't write a decent word." He led her to a secure place between an outcrop of lichen-speckled rock. He turned back briefly for her basket. "We had a visitor. An unwelcome one."

Lily stared at him. "Is that why you look so careworn and . . . not well?"

"I'll tell you what happened on the way back to the house. You might recognize some of the signposts on the way."

She stared past him in dawning comprehension. She saw the ivy-covered ruins of a bridge that spanned the stream running behind the cairn. "*This* is Sir Renwick's unholy retreat?"

He managed a smile. Grace's confession had befouled his mood. "One of them. And I'm afraid if I stay here I might succumb to his influence."

The wind rose as they walked home together. Lily did not feel the cold. She felt numb after Samuel revealed what had happened while she was gone.

"Didn't he ask to see me?" she asked, staring at the bleak shadows of the moor.

The rapier tip sent several pebbles skittering into a dark pond that glistened on the path. "Yes. He did. I refused to allow it." He swung around to face her. "Did you *want* to see him?"

"No. Except . . ."

He stared at her.

"It might have been worthwhile to hear myself vindicated."

"I was not willing to take the risk," he said flatly. "If he had defied me, I would have run him through."

"Are you going to run me through, too?"

He scowled. "What?"

She motioned to the rapier he held poised in the air. "My protector," she said with a smile. "I would rather be your servant for the rest of my life than be his wife for even a day."

Chapter 35

*M*arie-Elaine shook Lily awake that same night. She had been asleep for only an hour, thinking over Jonathan's confession. She wished she had been able to confront him herself. But Samuel had been infuriated at the suggestion. Still, she wondered if this would redeem her in her family's eyes. Had Jonathan even known the victim's name? To be vindicated after her downfall. It was a hollow victory.

"His Grace has a fever," Marie-Elaine said, pulling a dress from the wardrobe.

Lily put her hand over her eyes. Moonlight shone through the curtains, the branches outside. "What? At this time of night? Tell him to wait until the morning. I don't care how many pages he'll lose. It's unreasonable to be up all hours, even for art."

"It's a real fever. It happens almost every year. He gets deathly sick."

"Why didn't you tell me before?"

"He hates anyone to think he has any weaknesses."

Lily threw off the bedcovers and dressed in her warm wool gown. "I hope you have sent for a surgeon."

"Yes." The maid's mouth turned down. "But he might not be here for two or three hours."

Lily suppressed a sharp fear. Perhaps Samuel wasn't as ill as Marie-Elaine made him out to be. Everyone in the house seemed prone to exaggeration. But he looked like a waxen effigy when she entered his bedchamber a few minutes later. Sweet herbs burned in the roaring fire in the stone hearth. The odor irritated her nose. Mrs. Halford was sponging his bare chest with a cloth soaked in camphor and aromatic oils. He regarded Lily through his heavily lidded eyes.

"Go."

She went straight to the bed. He raised himself up, dislodging Mrs. Halford's hand. "You should never have been brought here at all."

"Why not?" she asked indignantly.

He shook his head. "I'm indecent. You were forewarned. Juliette is on the balcony. A woman shouldn't lift a sword. Philbert was right."

"He's delirious," Marie-Elaine whispered. "He rambles when he's feverish."

The grooves that bracketed his mouth deepened. "The ghosts are not happy," he continued in a conversational voice, his eyes slowly closing.

"What ghosts, Your Grace?" Lily asked in panic, if only to keep him from slipping away. If he spoke of communicating with spirits when he was ill, did it mean that he was drifting into another world? "There aren't any such things as ghosts," she added. And then, without thinking, she laid her head on his chest to listen for his heartbeat.

Mrs. Halford gasped in horror. "No, no. You cannot—"

For the worst moment she had ever known, Lily thought he was gone. And it was then that she saw the scar tissue that ran from his sternum to his rib cage into his belly. She felt a firm pair of hands trying to pry her away.

"He's delirious, miss," Emmett said gently over her shoulder.

"What are those marks on his body?" Lily asked in bewilderment. She had never noticed them when they made love. But then, they had been together only in the dark. The scars looked like burns. "Why should he be ashamed?"

No one answered.

She swung around to stare at Marie-Elaine. "Why does he have to keep everything a secret? It's not right. It's—"

"He never makes much sense when he's ill like this," Mrs. Halford said, interrupting her. "I used to get the shivers every time he mentioned talking to the shades."

Lily longed to know more, but then the door opened to admit a formidable black-caped man whose frazzled red-gray hair bespoke a frantic rush to arrive. "What have I told you all before?" he asked in dismay. "It does a patient little good for you to hover around his bed like crows. Get out, all of you. Get out of here so that I may go to work."

"He needs us," Lily said blankly.

"Fetch me a basin." The surgeon withdrew a lancet from his dilapidated instrument case. "Marie-Elaine, do we still have a bottle of fresh dragon's blood in the house?"

Lily drew back against Mrs. Halford's bosomy warmth. "Dragon's blood?"

"It's only a plant, miss," Emmett said, turning at the sight of the blood pricker.

"And kindly fetch me whatever laudanum you have at hand," the surgeon added.

Samuel sat up with a glassy-eyed glare. "No opium. Never. I cannot write when my brain is numb."

"Your Grace cannot write from the grave, either," the surgeon said in a practiced tone of authority.

She did not want to leave Samuel, but the other servants swept her in a wave toward the staircase. She stumbled down the steps, Emmett and his twin reaching to steady her at the same instant. She strained her neck for a last look up at the duke's suite. Mrs. Halford's pale round face floated above the balustrade like a melancholy moon.

"I'll find the laudanum," Marie-Elaine said at Lily's back. "There's a tincture of mullein in the Welsh dresser, on the middle shelf behind the peppermint cordial."

Lily nodded, but when they reached the bottom of the stairs to go their separate ways, she whispered, "Were those scars on his torso made by a burn?"

The maid dropped her gaze. "Yes. It happened during the fire at the castle."

"But why should that be another of his secrets? He and I, well, we're . . . He never spoke of it. Does he blame himself?"

"He doesn't remember any of it," Marie-Elaine said with a deep sigh. "The whole tragedy was wiped clean from his mind. He doesn't remember how he got the scars."

Chapter 36

The Plymouth innkeeper held a glass of wine to his severely beaten customer's mouth. The chambermaid who had found the gentleman on the floor of his room had first thought he was dead. She recounted in tears to her employer that the handsome captain had tipped her generously to wake him at four o'clock that morning.

He'd had a vendetta to fulfill, whatever that was, in Calais.

"He said it was his fault that another man had stolen the lady he loved and he was going to prove to her how sorry he was." She twisted her hands, turning away as the captain released a groan.

The innkeeper shook his head in sympathy. "No one saw who attacked him, but the old gent in the next room thought he heard arguing."

"Do you think the person will come back?"

He frowned. "If he had a private grudge, I suppose it's possible. It isn't good for business. I know that."

"Well, we can't just put him on a ship and wish him bon voyage."

"He'll be better in a day or so—or he'll be dead," the innkeeper said heavily. "Until then we might go through his belongings to find mention of a relative or place of residence so that we can notify his family of his misfortune."

The chambermaid applied herself to this task, diligently searching the captain's clothes and traveling case. "There's a map of Dartmoor here, sir." She smoothed her hand across the creased folds. "It has a name written on it, too. A duke, no less. Have a look for yourself. Do you think he could possibly be the person responsible for beating this gentleman?"

"Anything is possible in the aristocracy," he answered with a bitter shrug. "But I am not sure we want to tangle with a duke. The peerage is above the law."

The duke's fever broke on the third night.

His illness had depleted the emotional reserves of his staff. Lily dozed off and on the entire day after she realized he would get better. The cook burned a kettle of soup, and it was Bickerstaff who, sniffing the scorched air, flew into the kitchen and smothered the flames with his best broadcloth coat.

"God have mercy on us, woman!" he cried. "Can

you imagine what the master would think were he to awaken and smell smoke?"

Mrs. Halford burst into tears. "I was halfway out of my chair before you knocked me back down with your theatrics."

"That is a lie, Mrs. Halford." He stared at his ruined coat. "It was your snoring I heard from the pantry."

"Where you were sneaking a nip," one of the scullery girls interjected, because she could afford to snap at the butler, but not the cook who generously fed her. "You all but pushed her from the hearth. I saw it. And I will testify in court if I have to."

"Is that so?" he asked. "Then why didn't you tend the kettle, you lazy slattern?"

"Mr. Bickerstaff," the cook said, throwing her arms around the girl's shoulders. "What a devilish thing to say!"

"Speaking of which," a droll voice remarked from the arched doorway, "I daresay it is quieter in Dante's Inferno than in this house. How, I ask, is a man supposed to work in this commotion?"

Lily's eyes filled. What a dramatist. And yet she loved him all the more dearly for his sense of tragedy.

She hung back as the staff crowded around. Mrs. Halford blinked away tears and offered to make the duke a meal. Bickerstaff heaved a sigh, motioning for Emmett to bring His Grace a chair. The scullery girl picked up a broom and swept the ashes from the hearth.

And Samuel merely smiled, looking more embarrassed by the fuss than anything, staring into Lily's eyes with an intimate gratitude that pierced her heart.

Lily plunged from one panic to another.

She wanted to make a good impression on Samuel's sister. Lady Alice was his only surviving relative. She and Mrs. Halford pored over such gastronomical delights as mushroom soufflé, fried apples in custard, and cream-of-carrot soup. The Gobelin carpets were beaten again to within an inch of their weave. The housemaids, under Marie-Elaine's command, even dared to infiltrate the library to dislodge the cobwebs strung between the vellum-bound volumes that were arranged from Abelard to the life of Zarathustra. Any apple seeds discovered were cautiously moved and reassembled in exact formation on the windowsills of the duke's office.

None of this pleased Samuel, who, having regained his strength, came to Lily's bed when she was too exhausted and preoccupied to put up a protest. He had regained his vigor with unearthly speed.

"You can't continue to take these liberties when your sister is under the same roof."

"Why not?" he inquired lazily, her nightdress discarded, both of them naked as sin, his fingers caressing her in an undisturbed, determined rhythm.

Lily's hands moved down his back to his lean buttocks. He did not tense when she touched his scars. "Because I want to make a good—"

He entered her slowly, flexing his spine. "Go on," he said, his attention clearly superficial, his penetration so welcome that Lily soon lost her own thread of thought.

"I'll stop if you insist," he acceded in a whisper, withdrawing from her as if it were a courtesy and not intentional torment.

She locked her ankle around his. "I have to rise before daylight—"

"As do I."

"—to attend my housekeeping duties."

He whispered the words that her unconventional heart most wished to hear. "To hell with housekeeping, Lily. It was not mentioned in the terms of our original contract. Do you think I worry about the cobwebs in the corners?"

"I—" She arched off the mattress and parted her legs to draw him back inside her, whispering, "I don't care much about cobwebs myself at the moment."

His tongue swirled around the rim of her ear. Blood stirred in the hidden reaches of her body. "What do you care about?" he asked, his hand encircling her waist.

She shifted, aware that his voice had deepened, that his body felt tense. "Only you," she said before his eyes locked with hers and he drove so deeply inside her that she cried out in surprise.

"Let me know if this is too rough."

"It isn't," she said breathlessly.

He bent his head and kissed the swollen tips of her breasts. Her heart quickened at the relentless strokes that impaled her. She wanted to feel him embedded all the way. She twisted up, into him, seeking more, until she felt a tightness in her womb. The unbearable tension of impending relief.

Elusive. She was in knots. Soon. She whimpered as he kissed her with a deep and devastating tenderness that left her trembling. "Samuel," she said in desperation. "I can't take any more of your teasing. I thought you were kind."

"But I am."

She knew then what he meant to do, that he was prolonging, heightening her pleasure. "Cruel," she whispered, and let him lure her closer and closer until she felt herself uncoil and break into pieces.

He reared up before she recovered. The lines of his face deepened in concentration. His body demanded the same bliss he had given her. She cushioned his every determined thrust, encouraging him by obeying her own instincts.

He moved like seduction unleashed at her urging. She wondered if *she* would be able to move at all the next morning, if she would even try. For an electrifying moment she met his gaze. She saw past his sensuality to the intense emotions he struggled to hide from the world. He beckoned her into their dark vortex, revealing his vulnerability to her without a word.

She realized then how much he needed her—he wasn't a man who easily shared his nature.

"I care about you," he said in a husky voice that pierced her heart. "I care so much I would do anything to keep you."

He gave a deep moan and thrust a final time, the impact forcing the breath from her body. Even then she thrilled at the feel of him pulsing inside her. When he withdrew from her, she felt as if she were slowly falling to earth.

He stretched out beside her, stroking his hand along her shoulder, down her arm to her wrist. She could not summon the will to stir. She was content to absorb the heat of his hard-boned body.

"We are not hiding the truth from my sister," he said as her heart began to resume its usual rhythm.

"Does she know everything about you?" she asked curiously.

"She did until I met you. Now we will tell her together that I have found happiness."

Chapter 37

$\mathcal{L}$ily warmed to Samuel's sister the moment that the duke introduced them in the great hall. Lady Alice was infinitely softer and more understated than her charismatic brother. She had a refined beauty that was more subtle than his. With her aristocratic bearing and easy grace, she made Lily recall the status she had once taken for granted. She felt a poignant stab of longing for her own family. Would she ever see them again? Would Samuel's rank impress them?

"I understand now," Alice said very quietly as Lily rose from a curtsy, "why Samuel is so late to return my letters. It is not only his work that claims his time. And do not make a knee to me again. You will be my sister-in-law, and you were not meant for subservience."

"You can say that again," Samuel murmured before he left their company with some excuse about proof sheets he had received in the mail.

"Let us walk in the garden, Lily," Lady Alice suggested, lifting her brow as she spotted the sword Samuel had forgotten on the stairs. "My bones ache from the coach travel here."

"*That* I understand," Lily said, laughing. After all the work she and the staff had undertaken, it would be a delight to relax for a few hours. And it was soon clear that Lady Alice refused to acknowledge her as a housekeeper. She treated Lily not only like an equal but like a friend.

Soon Lily fell under her spell, too, slipping back into the position of gentlewoman before she knew it.

"I am glad that my brother found you," Lady Alice said when they reached the rose arbor. "I was engaged once to the only man I will ever love. Stephen was wounded defending his troops at Ligny. His last request was that he come home to marry me in the probable event that he would die. Samuel and the staff helped me care for him for three months before his merciful release." She turned toward a rose trellis. "We never did get married."

"The war was wretched," Lily said, shaking her head. "I hated it."

"But it had to be," Alice said with a sigh.

"Don't you get lonely?" Lily asked.

"Honestly? Not really. My friends insist I will find another wonderful gentleman, a widower perhaps. But what for? Samuel pays my bills. The pair of you will give me nieces and nephews to spoil—besides, at twenty-seven, I've grown too fond of my independence to play the game of love."

"I wouldn't have understood that before I left home," Lily admitted. "I was convinced I would never love anyone again."

Alice laughed, biting her lip. "Didn't you know how persuasive Samuel can be?"

Lily thought fondly of Chloe's warning on the night of the masquerade. "I suppose I had to find out for myself."

Later on the night of her arrival, Alice came to Samuel's office. She had never been afraid of him. They had been conspirators against the elderly aunt who had raised them after the fire.

Samuel made himself put aside his pages and beckoned her from the door. "Come inside—if you can find a spot to sit. Lily despairs of the mess. I've no idea why."

A stack of golden sovereigns spilled across his desk, collapsing against his inkwell. He and Alice held their breath. The inkwell held.

"Lily was never meant to be a housekeeper," Alice said. She carefully moved the folio pages arranged on the couch to make room for herself. She had a black jeweler's box with a gold clasp in her hand. "How exactly did it happen?"

"I met her at a masquerade."

"Romantic."

He sighed. "From my point of view. I had a marriage contract drawn the same night."

"Well, why aren't you married?"

"There was an obstacle I had overlooked. Another man had claimed her first."

"I'm surprised you let that stop you."

His eyes glinted. "It didn't."

He went on to explain the chain of events that had brought Lily back into his life. He emphasized Grace's part in her fall and downplayed certain nuances of his own role. Alice would have to fill in these holes by herself. She would. She had grown up with Samuel and knew what a devious scoundrel her younger brother had been. They had fought bitterly as children.

"I have something for you." She rose to hand him the box. "Or rather, for you to give Lily on your wedding day. It belonged to our mother."

He unhooked the box's hinge. "Her diamond-and-pearl necklace?" he said in surprise. "I know how much it means to you."

"I have never worn it, and pearls are meant to be worn or they lose their luster. It's as if they come alive when they're put on. They are believed to take on the wearer's vibrancy. You're the artist, Samuel. I don't have to describe how warm they will look on Lily's skin."

"Thank you," he said, moved by the gift. "You're right. These pearls are one of the bright memories."

"You will make others, Samuel."

He sat back in his chair. "So will you."

"It took years before I stopped having nightmares about the fire," she said. "I don't know how or when it happened, but now at least it has become a bearable ache."

He nodded. "For years afterward I would think it was coming back to me. I'd hear screaming or I would smell smoke. But I'm not sure it wasn't my imagination." He smiled at her. "Don't fret over me. I feel their presence often, and I take comfort from them."

"Yes," she said softly. "I understand."

Lily brought Lady Alice the whiskey toddy she had requested in the drawing room before bed. She smiled up at Lily from her chair, still wearing her plum silk evening dress. She had removed her shoes and crossed her bare ankles on the footstool. "You should have one of these, too," she said, taking her drink.

"I have to keep my wits about me in this house."

Alice laughed. "I can imagine you do. Samuel was a veritable demon during our childhood." She closed her delicate fingers around the mug. "Well, at least until the fire. You know about that, I assume?"

Lily hesitated. She was torn between her instinct to protect Samuel's privacy and her need to know everything about him. Who better understood him than his sister? "He's talked of it a little. But when he got that frightening fever, I saw . . ." She shook her head.

"The scars from his burns?" Alice said, putting her whiskey on the table between the two chairs.

"Yes."

"You have a right to know," Alice said.

"Then how did it happen?" Lily asked.

"Father was painting a portrait of our mother, and our other aunt was watching my two younger sisters. Nobody knows exactly *how* it happened. It was a month before Christmas. A fire always burned in the solar, and we had beautiful old tapestries that hung opposite the windows." She exhaled softly. "Oil paints, turpentine, and a spark, I've been told."

"But you and Samuel weren't there?"

"We were too restless and sick with coughs to sit for a painting," Alice said. "He and I had gotten into the guardroom downstairs. We heard Aunt Leona screaming from the top of the private staircase. We thought she wanted us to come upstairs to sit, and at first we ignored her. And then Samuel said he heard pounding."

Lily said nothing.

"Samuel doesn't remember running up the stairs. We only got halfway. The flames had spread through the upper hall and the smoke beat us back. Lawton had to save us."

Lily's brow furrowed. "The steward who is usually off on business?"

"Our devoted Lawton."

"The quiet gentleman in the long gloves?"

"To hide his burns," Alice said. "He smothered the flames from my dress sleeves and Samuel's jacket with his bare hands. Then he carried us both outside and instructed the castle cook to dress our wounds and take us to St. Aldwyn House, where our other grandmother lived."

"I thought Lawton was unfriendly." When would Lily learn not to judge? "I almost asked him once to remove his gloves."

"He's the only servant still living from the old house," Alice mused. "He stays at Gravenhurst to guard the place, because that has been his duty since time immemorial. He's even made friends with a band of gypsies who put curses on the occasional journalist or ghost hunter caught sneaking past the gates."

"I'm sorrier than you'll ever know," Lily said. "And grateful that the three of you survived."

"For a long time I wished I'd been the one who couldn't remember. Now . . . I have doubts. It doesn't matter how many times I have told Samuel what happened. He cannot seem to recall for himself. But then he was burned and I was not. Considering his temperament, a blank memory might be for the best."

Samuel's demanding shout resounded profanely in the pensive lull: "Come out! Come out, wherever you are! I need volunteers to put me in a pair of manacles and lock me in the pantry. Ladies are not excluded from participation."

Alice reached for her whiskey. "He's been like this from the day he was born," she whispered. "He's never going to change."

"I hope not," Lily said, coming to her feet. "I've gotten used to being entertained at all hours."

Chapter 38

$\mathscr{A}$lice complained over breakfast the next day that Lily could not continue to act as St. Aldwyn's housekeeper. She would soon become the Duchess of Gravenhurst. Samuel openly agreed. At this point, however, he would have agreed to practically any- thing either woman asked of him, because he wasn't really paying attention to their requests.

He planned to complete his revisions in the next few days and send a partial of the current book off to Phil- bert, along with the last chapter that still did not feel right but would have to do. He swore he wasn't going to commit himself to another *Wickbury* until well after the wedding. Perhaps not even until after his honeymoon.

But with Lily and Alice amusing each other for a while, he could sneak off for a good stretch of work. They wouldn't even notice he was gone. Then, over their second pot of coffee, Alice said, "You've always known how I feel about the castle, Samuel."

"You like to visit once every so often," he said absently, wondering if his paper and pens had arrived. He always started the week with a fresh crow quill and new paper. It was a ritual he had observed for years.

"I want to live there," Alice said. "In the castle."

He lowered his cup. "*Live* there?"

"Yes," she said, not shrinking at his tone.

"It's uninhabitable," he said with a frown.

Lily broke in. "Alice said that Lawton has restored much of what the fire damaged."

He stared at her. "But what about all the ghosts? *We* know they aren't real, but other people don't. She'll become known as an eccentric."

"Well, she has to live somewhere, Samuel," Lily said, "and the castle is ever so much closer than Lynton. She and I will be close to each other."

He grunted. "I suppose I will have to look it over, to make sure it is safe."

"May I come?" Lily asked. "I do have some experience as a housekeeper."

Samuel realized he'd been caught in a clever female snare. Lily knew he wasn't about to leave her alone after Grace's confession. If he did, it would only be to hunt Kirkham down and bring him to justice.

Alice also had to know he would not refuse her a home. He did, however, wish to make sure the castle was sound and not the mausoleum that it had become in his imagination.

"So it is all right if we leave tomorrow?" Alice asked, unsuccessfully holding back a grin.

"That soon?" he said. "It will take longer than a day to load the coach and collect my writing supplies."

"We've already packed a few necessities," Lily admitted, biting her lip. "Just in case you agreed. The staff can bring whatever else you need."

"Wicked women," he said in resignation. "What would my life be without them?"

The duke's coach could follow the ancient track only so far. A menhir said by the locals to be one of the devil's first teeth marked the road that climbed to the castle. Only the moor folk, the gypsies, and the occasional rider used it now. Every so often the coachman stopped so that he, Samuel, and the footmen could join forces to roll a rock that obstructed the way.

By sunset the coach started to descend the steep incline. Lily stared out the window at the castle so that she would not stare at Samuel. The last time she'd traveled in this coach she had been hoping to forget her past. And she had been wickedly tempted to throttle him.

Now they were traveling together to meet his past, and she was tempted to do things to him, *with* him, that she hadn't dreamed possible during her initial journey.

The glint in Samuel's eye, when inevitably she did meet his gaze, promised he had plenty of other dreams in mind. The look she gave him in return said she was more than game.

"I can see Lawton on the west barbican flying the Gravenhurst standard!" Lady Alice exclaimed. She swung away from the window, lifting her folded gloves to fan her face. "It's awfully warm in here all of a sudden, isn't it? I shall be glad to get out in the cool air."

From the approach Castle Gravenhurst presented a forbidding countenance to discourage the uninvited. A pack of wolfhounds prowled the inner bailey. Their unholy howls raised the fine hairs on Lily's neck. She glanced up slowly. Evening mist enshrouded the darkened towers. The teeth of the raised portcullis grinned as if preparing to snap the invaders in one fell bite.

"Good heavens," she said to Lady Alice as the duke led the way across the groaning drawbridge. "I think His Grace has a good point. Are you certain you could live here? It does have a certain atmosphere."

Alice glanced back across the moor and took a deep, bracing breath. The servants of St. Aldwyn's straggled up the incline in the cart, lanterns flickering like fairy lights. "There is nowhere like Castle Gravenhurst in the world."

Lily stared straight ahead, disinclined to argue. She glimpsed Samuel striding ahead in his cloak. Suddenly seven or so hounds materialized from the mist to encircle him. He pulled his small traveling case from their slobbering welcome and laughed, motioning over his shoulder for Lily and Alice to follow.

"I'm going in ahead," he said as Lawton darted out from the northwest barbican to call back the hounds.

"Should we let him go alone?" Lily whispered to Alice.

"Why would we stop him?" Alice asked softly.

Lily didn't answer for several moments. She could barely make out Samuel's figure in the shadows, although he appeared to know where he was going. She felt a sudden chill, an awareness of something malignant in the air.

She looked up. An ominous shadow moved on the walkway that connected the two gatehouse towers. She blinked. How silly of her. It was only the Gravenhurst standard.

Samuel was the one who had made up all the stories about ghosts haunting the castle. There was nothing more menacing at Gravenhurst than unhealed memories, and those were unsettling enough. Lost in her thoughts, she suddenly noticed him looming in front of her.

"What is the matter?" he asked, taking her hand.

Warmth returned to her veins in a welcome rush. "Nothing. I don't know my way around, that's all."

"It looks different in the day."

She shook off her trepidation. It was hard to be afraid of anything with Samuel beside her.

Chapter 39

The castle interior was not as dreadful as Lily had anticipated. The wall torches threw warm shadows toward the oak beams of the great hall and across the heraldic panels below. Whatever Samuel felt as he and Lily trailed Alice from one room to another, he did not reveal. Alice avoided the spiral staircase, which Lily assumed led to the solar.

She glanced at it once. Any damage the old fire had inflicted either was not visible from where she stood or had been repaired. She looked up to see Samuel staring past her with a resigned expression. "I remember playing up there," he said, pulling her by the arm as if protecting her from some unseen menace. "And not much else."

Alice took Lily's other arm. "We had a family of jackdaws that set up residence in the fireplace after everyone left," she said. "Lawton said it was almost impossible to move them out."

"That is because jackdaws mate for life," Samuel

said. He lowered his head, his mouth grazing Lily's ear. "And so, by the way, do St. Aldwyns."

Two hours later the servants' cart rumbled over the drawbridge and deposited the staff in the bailey, providing the disruption that Samuel needed to explore by himself. He climbed the spiral staircase and walked straight to the solar. Bittersweet memories of his life before the fire rose up in his mind. The old dogs lying in front of the hearth, muscles twitching. His father begging him to pay attention to the chessboard while his mother read quietly to Alice and his two younger sisters from Perrault's fairy tales.

He closed the door and walked slowly down the stairs. When he reached the last step, he turned and looked up again. He had made peace with his elusive memories of the fire. He could not bear to think of his family having suffered. But as he told Alice, he knew somehow that they were safe.

One day, when he was old and tired, he would ascend the stairs a final time and find everyone he thought he had lost waiting for him to come up and rest.

Until then the lower world, with its work and play, its problems and joys, took precedence. He could not leave Lily unprotected. He had their story to watch unfold. With grace, it would be a fabulous tale to pass down to their children.

*   *   *

Samuel managed to sneak off after supper to the east gatehouse turret to work. It grieved him that he had lost time traveling to the castle, and lost the comfort of his office at St. Aldwyn House. Still, family came first. At least the watchtower provided seclusion. It also had a walkway on which he could take air and swashbuckle with his characters when he needed exercise.

At last he had found the perfect quiet.

He lit a lamp and sat on an uncomfortable oak settle. No chance of dozing off here. He leafed through the last chapter of his overdue manuscript. *Quiet*, he thought absently.

Too quiet.

Several minutes later the castle wolfhounds began howling at heaven only knew what. Samuel got up, papers in hand, and descended the spiral staircase to the walkway. A light glowed in the window of the opposite watchtower. Lily, Alice, and Marie-Elaine had offered to set up a temporary library within to appease his complaints.

Strains of feminine laughter drifted in the stillness. He fought the temptation to join in their coterie. But then he would lose what was left of the night's work.

Temptation.

Would it ever end?

Probably not, now that Lily was part of his life. His entire life, in truth.

*   *   *

Lily sent Alice and Marie-Elaine off to bed, promising she would not remain in the west watchtower much longer herself. She suspected they knew her true motive was to be close to Samuel. She would not have denied it had she been accused. She needed to be near him. She also enjoyed dipping into the books he had brought from St. Aldwyn House.

How could she resist peeking through the pages of a book entitled *Satan's Invisible Principles*? Could she discover which, if any, of these works had inspired Lord Anonymous? It would be fun to try. A challenge.

And the west watchtower required a thorough cleaning. Lawton, the yellowed steward, and his gypsy staff of three had maintained the castle as best they could. The keep, where Alice would live, was more than habitable. In time Alice would hire more servants and invite friends to visit.

For now until her wedding, Lily would not relinquish her role as housekeeper. Perhaps, if Samuel continued to create clutter, she would always be tempted to tidy up after him.

She swept a bit. She unpacked most of the books he had brought. After organizing them in what seemed to her a logical fashion, she realized she had wasted her energy. He would have them disordered before breakfast the next morning. There were no shelves in the tower, in any event. She had to make do with a pair of trestle tables and an old trunk.

She sorted through a box of old papers. For a heady moment she thought she'd come across the original draft of the first *Wickbury Tales*. But it was only a collection of letters from his avid readers, most of whom appeared to be female and who confessed their undying affection. At length she sat on a stool to read a well-worn copy of *Don Quixote*.

The opening made her smile and forget the sad ending. Soon she was so caught up in the story that when she detected footsteps on the tower staircase, her heart gave an instinctive leap of fright.

How awful. Would she suffer from nerves forever? When would she forget what she had seen in London? Lady Alice and Samuel had recovered from misfortune. But both of them had been changed.

It could only be Samuel coming to check on her. She sprang to her feet, setting the book on the stool. "Are you ready to turn in for the night?" she called down into the stairwell's void of echoing dark. "It's getting late. And cold. We ought to go to bed soon."

He didn't answer. Lost in thought again, she supposed.

"Samuel?"

She hoped it was Samuel she had heard. In this part of the castle it could have been a rat or a badger. But a heavy-footed one to have drawn her from *Don Quixote*.

She descended the tower staircase one cautious step at a time. It was so dark. She should have brought the lamp. She would have to climb back to fetch it. Her skirts dragged against the old stone. "Samuel?" she said again, aggravated now. "Do you mind not hiding in the shadows?"

The wolfhounds in the bailey broke into a howling racket. She'd have been alarmed if she hadn't known their ferocity disguised a friendly temperament.

Perhaps she had read too many of Samuel's earlier books about feudal Scotland and midnight raids. She fancied that her bones ached in foreboding. Or, more likely, from sitting on an uneven-legged stool for too long.

Her nerves eased as she clambered down the stairs and reached the walkway. She peered out at the vaporous crags of the moor.

Anything could be hiding behind the menhirs or in the hollows on the horizon. An army could be waiting to attack behind the moorland hills. It was too misty to see past the track. Still, for now she seemed safe from claymore-wielding clansmen or even nocturnal creatures skulking about, unless one counted Samuel.

A light shone from the tower where he was still working. She knew he wasn't wearing his warm coat. She knew he hadn't drunk the pot of chocolate that Emmett had carried up, silver pot, cup, and spoon clanking like a ball and chain.

She would not have minded a footman or two to accompany her. She assumed Samuel had forbidden any further disturbances.

She shouldn't disturb him. She should wait for him to come to bed. Wasn't she resigned to spending the rest of her life waiting, feeling loved but ignored? She sighed as she noticed his slender figure in the tower window. Back. Forth. Another fencing match. She leaned her elbow against one of the merlons to watch.

Sir Renwick's rapier-wand danced a magical display that enthralled her. Indeed, it looked as if her villain was going to win this match. What that meant for the future of *Wickbury* provided delicious fodder for her mind. She decided she *would* disturb him. Art was all well and good. But she had no intention of being neglected *every* night of their lives.

Besides, a chill had crept into the air. Samuel was lightly dressed, as usual. He would overheat himself, only to come out in the cold. She had a duty to protect his health. And a desire for his presence.

She knew her way around St. Aldwyn House. Castle Gravenhurst presented a mystery she did not care to solve by herself. She had a morbid enough imagination without fending off a wolfhound wanting to make friends at this hour.

In truth, she was gripped again by the implausible notion that a phantom danger awaited her in the dark. It was such a strong feeling that it overpowered her fascination with Samuel's performance. She slowed.

Surely the shadow that fell beside her was another of her fancies. She turned. The cruel face of the man advancing on her confirmed what her logic had struggled to deny.

Chapter 40

No sooner had Samuel cut a fresh nib and dipped his quill in the inkwell than his thoughts took wing. It was too late to work. He needed his other pen. Would it hurt to sneak across the walkway and lose a few minutes helping Lily? He cringed to think of the disarray the woman would wreak upon his library. He also knew that a few minutes would lengthen into the rest of the night.

Work, you besotted fool. Write just one more sentence. If it wasn't done right the loose threads would tighten into a noose. Strung by the tongue.

Brilliance. *Scrape it out of your marrow. Do not force a word.* Intuition trumped intellect. He could go into hiding. Philbert would hunt him down. They would sue each other into perpetuity. Good. Better his publisher finish him off than his readers.

A blessing he was anonymous, although that did not stop Lily from pointing out every mistake Lord

A had ever made. He swore she took pleasure in unearthing the tiniest errors. Perhaps he should ask her to transcribe his pages to keep her occupied. But then she would only change his punctuation.

It was enough to inhibit his creative impulses. But not for long. He often thought that if he did not hover on the brink, he would die of boredom.

And as for dying, he had left poor Wickbury languishing in the dungeon, a priest summoned to administer the last rites. Sir Renwick claimed victory. His rival's prison cell was impenetrable. Wickbury's communion chalice contained enough poison to foil an unlikely escape. He would die a martyr to the Royalist cause, like the beheaded King Charles I.

Wickbury's ragged band of retainers had been captured or killed. No man could deliver him from this snare.

A woman of unconventional courage could, however.

A writer *had* to leave a reader with hope.

Lady Juliette Mannering had always been more than a heaving bosom in a black velvet bodice. Or in a priest's vestments, as described her current attire. She had shorn her hair for her role as Wickbury's rescuer. The details of his liberation would be refined in the upcoming tale. Samuel hoped that by then he would be able to put Lily from his mind long enough for Juliette to be herself again. And that these odd visions of Wickbury talking to him would end.

All in all, however, Samuel thought it a fitting irony that Juliette don a religious disguise to save the one who had enabled *her* to escape the veil. Of course, there were critics who would accuse Anonymous of depicting another immoral act.

Maybe they were right.

Kirkham locked his left arm around her waist. She thought her ribs would crack from the pressure. The instinct to scream died as the steel blade of his sword settled across her throat.

His voice rasped against her cheek. "I'm going to quiet you, Lily. And Jonathan can't do a thing about it. No one can. Look how low you have fallen. A duke's whore. A servant. No one will miss you."

She lifted her head to swallow. The blade pricked her windpipe. She felt drops of stinging warmth pool in the hollow of her throat. Kirkham brought his left hand to the wound, slowly smearing her blood. Lily became less aware of the pain than of her anger. She struggled free for only a moment before he caught her again.

"Ladies," he said in a mocking whisper, "are supposed to be silent."

"Death to Wickbury," Sir Renwick had proclaimed, raising his rapier to the night. Or tower roof, as it were.

Samuel was surprised that the prospect made him feel maudlin. Had it been that long ago that he'd been tempted himself to finish off the popular hero? Killing him would end the series. Was it possible to reinstate himself as one of Michael's supporters? To admit he believed in the prig? Good grief. It was true. He couldn't say farewell to the hero. When and why had he lost faith in Michael?

He laid his rapier against the wall. He wanted to weep and ask Wickbury's forgiveness. Preposterous. It was as if Wickbury were talking to him again. *Had* Samuel come unscrewed? His thoughts had gone delusional. He wasn't on the brink. He was falling off the cliff. *Oh, God.* He couldn't be getting another fever.

He pressed his fingers to his forehead. As cool to the touch as castle stone. It was damned perishing in the tower, in fact. He needed exercise to get his blood going. Or he could visit Lily, whose blue eyes managed the same effect. She shouldn't be up here this late.

He stood up and stretched his arms.

Should he go?

"Go."

He swung around, shaking his head. The tower was empty.

"Go," Wickbury said in a voice that Samuel had never heard before.

"And take my sword."

*   *   *

Samuel had thought of the tower stairs as snail shells when he was a boy. Curving, to slow an enemy on the attack. Difficult for anyone to maneuver in the dark unless one knew to seek the handholds and avoid the broken stones that could cause a fall.

His world fell the instant he sighted a man on the walkway with a cavalry sword laid across Lily's beautiful throat. Her eyes flew to his. The horror in them raised a bloodlust that obliterated every gentle impulse that composed him.

His hand tightened around the broadsword's hilt. "Let her go."

Kirkham pulled her closer. "Why should I?"

Samuel stepped forward, staring at the blood on Lily's skin. Dark like the ink that signed Kirkham's death warrant. Fury consumed him.

He heard footsteps echoing from beneath both watchtowers. Emmett and Ernest rarely disobeyed his orders to stay away. What instinct had alerted them tonight?

"I said, let her— To hell with it."

He lunged toward the wall, swinging his weapon low, and pivoted in a half crouch. By the time he straightened, a bright line of crimson appeared from Kirkham's right thigh to his shoulders and he'd dropped the blade from Lily's throat.

"Well-done," Lily whispered, closing her eyes. "But—"

He could have done better. He regretted that he

wasn't carrying Renwick's rapier. The broadsword was heavier to wield. Still, when the blade sank a blow, it tended to be deadly.

Kirkham looked down at his shirtsleeve, then shoved Lily to her knees. Without waiting for a signal from his master, Emmett darted across the walkway to lift her away from harm. His twin brother stood at the opposite stairwell, watching Samuel's back.

Samuel watched Kirkham. "Take her downstairs, Emmett. Lock her up in the keep with the others. Warn Lawton—"

Kirkham hefted his sword and flew at Samuel before he could finish.

Lily gave a cry. "We can't leave him." She broke away from Emmett as he dragged her to the arched entrance of the lower stairs.

"Ernest is standing on the opposite side," the footman said, positioning himself to block her return. "You ought to know we always travel together."

"You ought to know *I* won't leave him. And that we always stand in the background to direct his duels."

"Not this time, miss," he said, his mouth set. "He'll have my head, and I've known him longer than you."

Panic quickened her pulse. She could not lose Samuel. How could she help? Would she only distract him? She stared down into the spiraling blackness of the stairs. "I'd rather stay up here and die myself than flee like a . . . a frightened old duchess."

She saw Emmett hesitate. Her advantage. She took it, jerked from his hold, and pummeled his shoulder with a strength she had never suspected she could summon. For an instant he froze, so stunned by her attack that she almost could not move for the guilt she felt.

He blinked, recovering before she did. "No, miss," he said, and recaptured her arm as she stole another frantic look in Samuel's direction.

He danced with a fatal beauty that deceived the beholder. Had he woven that cloak of mist to enchant Kirkham into making a careless move?

"Emmett, I'm begging you. No. I *order* you."

"He orders me first."

"Then what are you doing here now?" she cried. "He wanted privacy. You disobeyed him by coming back."

"Yes, but we heard the dogs barking and thought something might be wrong."

She shook her head in desperation. "He doesn't order anyone. We do what he wants without being asked because we cannot help ourselves."

"I have an obligation to him," he said, doubt in his voice.

She was going to bubble over like a cauldron. "And I have an obligation not to witness another murder while I do nothing but wring my hands in horror."

He didn't budge.

She added, "He would do the same for us."

"No." His voice caught. "No. He's got his honor."

"And you are willing to lose him for that?"

He looked across the walkway.

Lily looked past him.

Above, rising higher than the eye could perceive, was Lily's heaven, and her heart.

Shards of light lanced the mist.

It irradiated the terrible smile on Samuel's face. She gave a gasp.

The broadsword lifted. Emmett released his grip on her arm, transfixed. She started to turn away and stopped. She didn't want to watch but something compelled her. Samuel had a talent for commanding an audience.

She would forever be his most devoted follower.

His broadsword flew up as if to spear a star. Power coursed through his veins, from whom or what he would ponder afterward, if he survived. Rapid. Cross blades. Lunge. Did he see lightning? Parry his rival's amateur thrusts. The cool air invigorated him.

He heard Kirkham panting between movements. The bugger showed a rudimentary skill. Point to the breast.

Play with him awhile.

He half wished that Lily would see what he could

do in an earnest duel. That was selfish. Vanity. Better that she not witness the end of this.

He didn't know how it would end. Not knowing, defending Lily, gave him the edge.

Kirkham might have gotten away with murder in London. He might have killed others, disposed of them with the same callous disregard as he had the man whose death Lily had witnessed. He was a bully who mistreated women and took advantage of his friends. A desperate adversary who fought for what was wrong.

He had never fought the combined forces of a duke, an exiled earl, and a charismatic necromancer who wielded a magic wand.

"*Who* are you?" Kirkham asked in a hollow voice. Sweat trailed down his temples. "No bloody nobleman fences like this. It is . . . ungodly."

"You drew Lily's blood."

He grunted. "She's only a woman."

"Horrible choice of words."

"Words?" Kirkham echoed in disbelief. "You talk of words when I mean to kill you? You're mad."

"I know." Samuel nodded. "I know. It can't be helped."

"There are rumors that question your manhood," Kirkham taunted, staggering as he swung his sword in an arc.

"Are there?" Samuel laughed. Had he invented them? Damned if he could recall at the moment. But then, Lily had repeated the same slander about Lord Anonymous.

Kirkham's eyes mirrored contempt. "You . . ."

He had run out of breath. He needed whatever energy he could gather now for defense. His shoulders hunched; his stare became unfocused.

Samuel felt his own strength challenged. He had lost awareness of Lily. There was only the other sword that sought an opening in his chest.

He beat again and again until Kirkham fell back, barely sidestepping a lunge. Kirkham retreated until his heel caught in a murder hole. Timing. Samuel forced him against the crenellated wall.

> *Conquer the night.*
> *Embrace what is right.*

I've never killed a man except with a pen, he thought. *Could* he do it? Blood. The man had drawn Lily's blood.

He hooked his sword under Kirkham's left knee, notching the blade to the joint. "This is going to be painful," he said with a grimace. It would not kill him, but it might make Kirkham wish it had.

He set his teeth. But as he jerked the blade, anticipating the pop of broadcloth, flesh, and fibrous cartilage, Kirkham pulled a pistol from the back of his waistband. His bloodstained hands shook as he leveled the gun at Samuel's chin.

Samuel, knowing how much Kirkham liked to play

with guns, was not entirely surprised. He twisted the sword through Kirkham's knee, wrenching it out and up so that the blade hit the pistol from the man's wrist. Samuel caught it in his left hand before it fell. Renwick's hand.

He braced himself and squeezed the trigger. He detested loud noises. They reminded him of missed deadlines and the clocks that went off daily at home.

The shot echoed between the towers and the merlons and across the moor.

Death made a mess he would not forget.

He averted his face.

He noticed Lily from the corner of his eye. Emmett was shielding her at the top of the stairs. Samuel could feel both of them staring. He planted his legs apart and stepped over the body, the broadsword resting across his hips.

He was sure he looked like a predator over his kill. All he cared about was keeping Lily and Emmett from seeing what was left of Kirkham's face.

Disgusting.

He swallowed back a surge of bile and brushed the gristly parts from his shirtfront. He hoped never to enact a death scene in such accurate detail again. He preferred romance, adventure, a political editorial, anything to this.

He understood now what Wickbury had been trying to remind him all along. Or what Samuel had been trying to remind himself. A hero had to come through in the end. There existed villains in the world who could not be saved by humankind. And some, like Kirkham, had to be stopped.

The crisis that had been building between Wickbury and Renwick had been only a manifestation of the conflict inside Samuel. He wanted to believe the best of everyone. Sadly not everyone wanted to be redeemed.

But all that could be pondered at another time.

Samuel intended to change and hold Lily for the rest of the night.

Chapter 41

$\mathcal{S}$amuel paid for Captain Jonathan Grace's funeral in London. He paid for the hearse and
six black horses, the mourning coaches, the cloaks for
those in the procession. At first, when he was notified
by the Plymouth innkeeper of Grace's death, he was
uncertain what the captain's family would think of
him. After all, Samuel would soon stand in their son's
place and marry the woman Jonathan had lost.

He was relieved—moved, in fact—when the elder
Lord Grace asked him to serve as pallbearer, along with
Lily's brother. She was upset and Samuel understood
her sorrow. Jonathan Grace had made a mistake and
paid the ultimate price in attempting to redeem himself.

Lily's father, Sir Leonard Boscastle, also attended the
funeral. Afterward, he invited Samuel to a private dinner
at the Park Lane mansion that belonged to Chloe's eldest
brother, Grayson Boscastle, the Marquess of Sedgecroft.
It was one of the finest homes in Mayfair. Samuel and Sir

Leonard sat alone at the table. Lily had been taken off by the other ladies in the family, many of whom she had not met until now. Samuel's sister had decided to stay at the castle, daunted by the long journey to London.

"I despised you when I learned of your repute and that Lily was working in your home," Sir Leonard said. Neither man had eaten much of the sumptuous meal. Samuel's stomach had curdled when the marquess's senior footman brought a tureen of turtle soup to the table for the first course. He ate a sprig of parsley and drank innumerable glasses of white wine.

It would not help his cause to drop drunk at Sir Leonard's feet. Nor would it disprove his reputation. Then, at some time during dessert, he realized that Lily's father was outdrinking him two glasses to one.

It was likely that neither of them would remember much of this conversation in the morning. They would wake up with hammering skulls. Samuel would not write a word, blaming the wine, the intensity of making a good impression, the relief that Lily's family had forgiven him for taking her away. By far the deepest relief he felt was when her father asked Lily's forgiveness at the end of the evening and admitted how miserable it had been since she had left home.

The wedding party overflowed the Park Lane mansion. A procession of carriages blocked the streets of Mayfair for hours. Lily would have been at her wits' end had she not learned a few things recently about what mattered in life, and why it was the small moments and not the grand gestures one tended to treasure most.

She stood, her father giving her away, her mother dabbing her cheeks as the ceremony began. Lily loved her dress, another of Chloe's inspired creations— glimmering gold silk with a flowing down-the-back veil of white lace. She wore the diamond-and-pearl necklace that Samuel had given her the night before. A cap of small white feathers had been attached to the bridal cape, a poignant reminder of the costume she had been wearing when she met Samuel.

"The only thing you will shed this time," Chloe assured her, "will be tears of happiness."

Lily's eyes did grow misty as she exchanged vows with the Duke of Gravenhurst. Samuel looked divine in well-tailored trousers and a long-tailed dark blue coat. For now she held his total attention. There were no pens, books, or unfinished manuscripts in the chapel to lure him away. She realized that she would lose him again from time to time when they returned to St. Aldwyn House. But she entered this marriage with full knowledge of who her husband was and the happiness she could expect in their life together.

Samuel had wavered between wanting a private wedding at home and a traditional ceremony that included Lily's relatives. Tradition won out. There were so many Boscastles in the banqueting hall that Lily's family filled most of the chapel. Samuel had invited a few friends himself. It satisfied his principles to know that a member of Parliament was sitting between a pair of milkmaids. He laughed when, during the wedding breakfast, Lord Philbert asked if Samuel had sold tickets to his own nuptials.

"I might have if I'd thought of it," Samuel said. "But you remember what I told you before. That young lady in the white dress and feathered cap has swept me off my feet. I have difficulty thinking properly when she is in the room."

Lord Philbert sighed. "Lily is very lovely. I shall take credit for introducing you to her. Not that I'm convinced I did her any great favor. Does she understand what it means to be married to a writer?"

Samuel looked at his wife, who looked right back at him from the bride's table, where she presided with not only her parents and brother, but also with her cousin Chloe and Viscount Stratfield.

"Lily knows me better than anyone."

"Good. Then I shall approach her when your next book is late."

"Take my word on it, Philbert. The duchess considers it her duty to keep me on task."

"Congratulations, Samuel," Philbert said with uncharacteristic warmth. "I should have trusted your instincts from the start."

*   *   *

Lily had sent Samuel so many inviting looks that even her father noticed. He clasped her hand in his. "He is the right man, Lily."

She felt tears sting her eyes. "You have no idea."

"Forgive us?"

Lily lifted her other hand to his face. He had aged since their estrangement. Although his disbelief had hurt her, she had become the stronger for standing her ground. Admittedly she'd had help from Samuel and his staff of characters. "None of us knew the entire truth," she said, thinking of how she had misjudged Jonathan, convinced that he had committed murder. She would have testified against him.

Her brother lifted his champagne flute in a blatant bid to dispel the somber mood. "This is a wedding. All is well and forgiven."

Lily's mother started to cry. "I can't help myself. I missed you so much. And I worried about you. . . ." She glanced up briefly, watching Samuel approach the table. "If only I had met him before you left, Lily," she said in a quieter voice, "I would have known in my mother's heart that you would be safe. Who do you suppose is wicked enough to spawn all the gossip about him?"

Lily looked up at Samuel, her eyes kindling in delight. "Whoever it was has quite an imagination."

And everyone in the wedding party seemed content to leave it at that.

Epilogue

Early Summer
St. Aldwyn House

"*W*hat is the only true religion?'" Samuel read from the manuscript, pacing before the dramatis personae gathered in the gallery.

"Compassion," a voice answered.

He halted, his gaze seeking out the respondent. "I did *not* write that line. Who," he demanded, stopping in front of Lily, "did?"

Bickerstaff flushed. "I confess, Your Grace."

Samuel shook his head. "It is—"

"—quite brilliant," Mrs. Halford said, "and I do not give my praise to just anyone."

"Isn't that the truth?" Bickerstaff said, then turned to acknowledge her. "But thank you, Mrs. Halford. It is a high compliment, coming from you."

"It *is* a lovely line, Mr. Bickerstaff," Lily said, sneaking a look at Samuel.

He drew a long breath. "May we continue? And the line . . . will stand. For now."

Lily cleared her throat. "I have a question about this new character you have introduced. This Baroness de Beaucoup."

"De *Beauville*."

"Unless I am misreading, it says toward the end of the scene that the baroness invites Sir Renwick to her bed in exchange for a potion of eternal youth."

Samuel nodded. "That is precisely what it says."

"But . . ." Lily looked down at her pages. "The stage directions also indicate that they disappear into a tavern room together and do not come out until the next morning. Two lines later you refer to a castle."

"What of it?" Samuel shrugged dismissively. "Scenery can be changed. This is for a libretto, not only a library."

"And Wickbury has thrown his broadsword in the air."

"It's a dramatic gesture," Samuel said. "You do not understand the nature of creativity."

Lily frowned. "You do not understand the law of gravity. Bucephalus is standing in the courtyard below. As is your mounted groom."

"Change the directions, Wadsworth," Samuel instructed the valet, who was wearing a pearl earring in his left ear and a rapier at his side. "Does that sit well with you now, Lily?"

She pursed her mouth. "It's fine. Sir Renwick may

sleep with any strumpet he chooses. I do have to wonder, though, why you gave Marie-Elaine the baroness's part. I would like to wear a high French wig and diamond heels instead of a priest's cumbersome clothing or a revealing bodice."

Samuel gave a weary sigh. "She is of French descent and carries herself with a certain Gallic arrogance that suits the part. I believe she also has more experience in—"

"—everything," Marie-Elaine said. "Do not fret, Your Grace," she whispered to Lily. "The baroness is going to come to a bad end. She doesn't last through the next act."

Lily expelled a sigh. "I should have known."

"No," Samuel said crisply. "You shouldn't. Not if I am doing a decent job. How do *you* know, Marie-Elaine?"

"I saw Your Grace's notes on the carpet yesterday," Marie-Elaine said, "and I picked them up. Naturally, I put them right down when I realized what they were."

"Naturally," Samuel said in a droll voice, resting his head on the railing.

"The baroness is a fraud, an assassin paid by one of Renwick's metaphysical rivals," Marie-Elaine added.

"All the better," Lily said with enthusiasm.

Marie-Elaine shrugged. "If you would prefer the part, I don't mind exchanging it for yours."

They stared at Samuel's down-bent head.

"No," Lily said, her mouth lifting in a smile. "I shall remain Juliette. Our characters should be consistent."

"Thank goodness." Samuel straightened, full of his usual energy. "Let's start at the top of the page."

Marie-Elaine cleared her throat. " 'It was a stormy night. The moat waters crashed against the castle walls.' "

"Why," Lily asked, lowering her pages again, "does it always have to be a stormy night? Why, this reader wonders, shouldn't it be clear and starlit for once?"

Samuel walked up to her. "I like stormy nights, and I am the author. Stormy nights lend themselves to drama and to gentlemen called upon as guardians."

"Yes," Lily said after a short hesitation, "but he's going to put her in the turret again, and it's obvious what will happen next."

Samuel raised his brow. "One more editorial and I shall have to deal with you in private."

He turned, motioning with his manuscript to continue.

"In that event," Lily said quickly, "let me just slip in a few tiny corrections, lest I forget to mention them later. Your referral to the Battle of Worcester is off by a mere thirteen years. A minor error. And it is a trifling mistake, to be sure, but the sun rises in the east. It does not set there."

His eyes darkened.

"Furthermore, Your Grace," she said, "there is a place on page—" She broke off to sniff the air. "I smell something. Are Renwick and the baroness burning herbs in a mystical incantation to weaken Lord Wickbury?"

"There are no fires in this scene," Samuel said, alarmed.

The assembly broke apart, Wadsworth checking the fireplace at the gallery's end, Marie-Elaine behind closed doors, and Mrs. Halford pounding down the stairs to the kitchen. Nothing was found except a scullery maid scraping the black off the bottom of the pot.

Samuel stood alone with Lily in the gallery, shaking his head in resignation. "What you smelled was probably the foul miasma of this manuscript. Obviously I am not holding anyone's interest, or we would not be so easily scattered."

Lily clasped his hand. "We are going to hold a private editorial. The scene will be all the better for another revision."

She lay beside Samuel on their bed, sifting her fingers through his hair. It was still light outside. The moor seemed to be swathed in magic. "I've had a change of heart," she said from out of the blue.

Samuel stirred. "Tell me."

"I've decided that I prefer a hero to a villain."

He lifted up on his elbow. "Does this mean you're no longer in love with Sir Renwick?"

"He will always have some of my sympathy," she said with a wistful shrug. "But it is one thing to enjoy reading about an evil character and quite another to encounter him in actual life."

He reflected for a long time. "I am neither good nor bad. What kind of man does that make me?"

"An exceptional one."

He turned over and lightly kissed her on the mouth. She closed her eyes and waited. She waited to be surprised, seduced, swept into another world. But when she finally roused herself, she saw her husband had left her side and was sitting at his desk.

"I shall be right back, I swear it, Lily. I have this idea—the ending for the next book."

She scooted against the pillows. "Shouldn't you worry about writing the rest of the story first?"

He didn't even pretend to look back at her.

"I am trying a different approach. It is my hope that once I envision the end, everything else will fall in place. Do you understand what I mean?"

"Half the time."

"And the others?"

"The other times don't matter. I'm happy enough to wander about in the dark. And—"

He bent over his desk, pen in one hand, the other raised at his shoulder to forestall her. "Wait just another moment, my love."

"As I was going to say, Samuel, we will have a little Lord or Lady Anonymous after Christmas."

"I know," he murmured, nodding faintly. "Yes. Tell me again later. Catch me up on all the news."

Later—seven hours later, in fact—he got into bed

beside her and gently shook her awake. "Repeat what you just told me."

"That was yesterday!" she exclaimed. "You've a mind like a colander. It needs to be refilled every few minutes."

"It was a few minutes ago that we spoke."

She turned her head, only to find him lying beside her. His dark eyes searched hers. "I am a dunce, Lily. Is it true?"

"Your dragon's-blood doctor seems to think so."

He caught her face in his hands. "What shall we name this little progeny?" he asked.

"We shall have to sleep on it. Or maybe when you're not working, it will come to you. Go on. Finish your writing. It's where your heart is."

"You have never been more wrong," Samuel said. "I can write a book when I am eighty. I won't be able to make a child then."

"You might," she said in a reflective voice. "Some men are capable."

"At that age?"

"You are probably one of them."

"I can't see it. I would never get a page done."

When Lily awakened the next morning, she knew by the light on the floor that she had overslept. And that Samuel had gotten up at his usual time to go to work. She wrapped a sheet around her like a toga and slipped out of bed.

At his desk she saw the freshly inked paper he had left her.

Lily,
You are my wife.
My heart is yours.
But do stop editing my work.
I love you,

Samuel

P.S. The last sentence of the next book reads:
Temptation does not have to end in tragedy.
Thank you for inspiring me.

The Bridal Pleasures Series

*D*on't miss the next captivating romance in Jillian Hunter's new series—a story about the strength of a love that begins in friendship, a secret bond that is bound to be challenged, and the lengths a man will go to guard the woman he desires, even if he has to walk away from her to keep the first promise he ever made.

Coming from Signet Select in
October 2011.

Penguin Group (USA) Inc. is proud to join
the fight against breast cancer by encouraging
our readers to "Read Pink™."

read pink™

Penguin Group (USA) Inc. is proud to join the fight against breast cancer

This October, in support of **Breast Cancer Awareness** month,
we are proud to offer 8 of our bestselling mass-market titles
by some of our most beloved female authors.
Participating authors are Nora Roberts, Amanda Quick,
Bertrice Small, Lynn Kurland, Christina Dodd, Catherine Anderson,
Lauren Willig, and Jillian Hunter.

These special editions feature **Read Pink** seals on their covers conveying our support
of this cause and urging our readers to become actively involved in supporting
The Breast Cancer Research Foundation®.

Penguin Group (USA) Inc. is proud to grant a $25,000 donation
to the following nonprofit organization in support of its
extraordinary progress in breast cancer research and awareness:

The Breast Cancer Research Foundation®

Join us in the fight against this deadly disease by making your own donation to this organization today.

How to support breast cancer research:

To make a tax-deductible donation online to **The Breast Cancer Research Foundation**
you can visit: www.bcrfcure.org

You can also call their toll-free number, **1-866-FIND-A-CURE (346-3228)**, anytime between 9 A.M. and
5 P.M. EST, Monday through Friday. To donate by check or a U.S. money order, make payable and mail to:

The Breast Cancer Research Foundation, 60 East 56th Street, 8th floor, New York, NY 10022

About The Breast Cancer Research Foundation®
www.bcrfcure.org

The Breast Cancer Research Foundation
is an independent 501(c)(3) not-for-profit
organization whose mission is to achieve
prevention and a cure for breast cancer in our
lifetime by providing critical funding for innovative
clinical and translational research at leading
medical centers worldwide, and increasing public
awareness about good breast health.

Since its inception, the Foundation has raised over
$285 million to support clinical and translational
research at medical institutions across the globe
conducting the most advanced and promising
breast cancer research that will help lead to
prevention and a cure in our lifetime. BCRF
support for promising yet untried ideas is a crucial
component of this research.

The Foundation welcomes and depends on contributions from all those concerned with women's health.
Working together, we know we can find a cure in our lifetime.

Go to www.penguin.com/readpink for more details.
Read Pink™ today and help save lives!
Read Pink is a trademark of Penguin Group (USA) Inc.